The Rebel Princess

Katie Clark

The Rebel Princess
COPYRIGHT 2020 by Katie Clark

All scripture quotations, unless otherwise indicated, are taken from the Holy Bible, New International Version(R), NIV(R), Copyright 1973, 1978, 1984, 2011 by Biblica, Inc.™ Used by permission of Zondervan. All rights reserved worldwide. www.zondervan.com
Scripture quotations, marked KJV are taken from the King James translation, public domain. Scripture quotations marked DR, are taken from the Douay Rheims translation, public domain.
Scripture texts marked NAB are taken from the *New American Bible, revised edition* Copyright 2010, 1991, 1986, 1970 Confraternity of Christian Doctrine, Washington, D.C. and are used by permission of the copyright owner. All Rights Reserved. No part of the New American Bible may be reproduced in any form without permission in writing from the copyright owner.

Cover Art by *Nicola Martinez*

Watershed Books, a division of Pelican Ventures, LLC
www.pelicanbookgroup.com PO Box 1738 *Aztec, NM * 87410
Watershed Books praise and splash logo is a trademark of Pelican Ventures, LLC

Publishing History
First Watershed Edition, 2020
Paperback Edition ISBN 978-1-5223-0292-6
Electronic Edition ISBN 978-1-5223-0291-9
Published in the United States of America

Dedication

To my loves, always.

Also by Katie Clark

The Rejected Princess

Enslaved Series

Vanquished
Redeemer
Deliverance

Beguiled Series

Shadowed Eden
Whispering Tower

What People are Saying

The *Beguiled Series* ~

"*Shadowed Eden* is a unique and intriguing tale that will keep the reader guessing and turning pages to find out the secrets of this mysterious story, and the suspense doesn't stop until its surprising end! I highly recommend it." ~ Melanie Dickerson

"A truly original premise, *Shadowed Eden*, is an exciting supernatural adventure filled with danger, redemption, and a cast of teenage characters that I grew to love. I enjoyed Clark's story and look forward to seeing what she comes up with next." ~ Jill Williamson

The *Enslaved Series* ~

"An emotional and unique take on a world of haves vs. have-nots that will pull you in from the author of Touch of Death

"Hana's journey continues in the page-turning sequel to *Vanquished*. Greater City is not what Hana hoped or expected and now she must choose between a privileged life of silence and lies or the dangerous road to truth and deliverance."
~ Donna Marie West

Kingdoms

Chester's Wake, the northern kingdom, ruled by the Hamiltons

Dawson's Edge, the southern kingdom, ruled by the Dawsons

Lox, the western kingdom, ruled by the Bellevues

Jakbar, a kingdom from across the ocean

Characters

Prince Benjamin of Lox, engaged to Princess Roanna of Dawson's Edge (formerly the princess of Chester's Wake)

Prince Gregory of Chester's Wake

Prince Stefan of Dawson's Edge, married to Princess Isabella de St. Paul of Jakbar

Ambassador Roland Dawson, fifth brother of the King of Dawson's Edge

Merry Stern, former Dawson's Edge nobility, whose family was outcast after being exposed in the national rebellion

Wesley and Gideon, royal guardsmen in Chester's Wake, and friends to Prince Gregory

Royal Histories

Four hundred years after the Great Wars, the kingdoms of Chester's Wake, Dawson's Edge, and Lox find themselves on the brink of peace at last. Aided by advancements in chemistry and alchemy, their use of steam-powered air ships, genetic testing, and robotic technologies are helping to foster good relations between them and bring them to their long-awaited goals.

However, not all want peace. Dawson's Edge has long refrained from using the baser technology of Termination, which the other kingdoms see as an advancement. The rebels within Dawson's Edge wish to embrace Termination in order to stomp out the anomalies which give their rulers unknowable powers.

Can this world of fairy tales and steam-powered engines ever be truly whole?

1

A thick, red blood droplet hit Roanna's hand. Then another. And another. A moment later, a warm trickle reached her upper lip. She blew out a frustrated breath and reached for a handkerchief. "I can't do anymore today." She turned to Roland Dawson, her uncle and the brother of the king of Dawson's Edge. She moved the conversation to her mind. *It's too much. I'm not strong enough yet.* She wiped the blood from her face, thankful she had pinned back her dark locks that now reached well past her shoulders. She wore simple clothes when training with Roland in the palace gardens—a full, knee-length, cotton skirt with a blouse and a vest. She had learned that, at times, she wasn't quick enough to stop the nose bleeds, and she had ruined more than one gown. Today, Roland was trying to teach her to search out others with her mind and identify those with whom she could speak—namely, those who also had the power to communicate via thought.

While she had adjusted to the idea of having powers, or anomalies as they were called back home in Chester's Wake, she had not yet mastered her skills.

Roland sighed. "The ability is there. You simply haven't unlocked it yet."

Easy for him to say. His ability was small, at least compared to hers. He didn't understand the pressure that built in her head when she concentrated so hard, when so much power rushed through her.

Not that the Dawsons were aware of the full extent of her powers. She didn't trust them enough to show them. At least, not yet. Perhaps when she had known them longer. Been through more with them. Maybe when she could stake not only her own life but also the lives of everyone she loved on their actions.

When she didn't answer, Roland sighed again. He reached for his top hat then slipped into his waistcoat. "Very well. We can resume training later this week." He paused as if he didn't want to say what he would reveal next. "I am leaving for Santa Rio for a few days to return by the end of the week. Has my brother mentioned that Prince Benjamin is arriving any day?"

Roanna pressed the handkerchief against her nose. She stretched her eyebrows upward, and her heart sped up. "Ben is coming?" She had barely seen him since revealing she was a Dawson nearly a month ago. He had accepted her new reality with all the grace and love she had hoped but had not expected. Her family hadn't reacted so mildly.

Mother and Father, the king and queen of Chester's Wake, had flown into a rage when she told them she was the presumed-dead princess from Dawson's Edge. She explained how she and Ben had uncovered clues that led to the proof of her claims. Father had nearly attacked King Dawson—Roanna's real father. It had taken hours of talking, explaining, and showing her parents the genetic test results to calm them enough to even consider the possibility. Then, Father had insisted on his own genetic tests. The independent testing yielded the same results—Roanna was, indeed, the lost princess of Dawson's Edge. Her olive-toned skin matched that of the Dawson family, and she was even of similar height and build, slightly taller than most women, and thin. How had she never noticed the lack of similarities with the Hamiltons before now?

The Dawsons had praised the advancements of the alchemists and scientists that had developed such advanced genetic testing. Her family from Chester's Wake had bemoaned them.

Now Roanna split her time between Dawson's Edge and Chester's Wake, with the majority of her time being spent at the Dawsonian palace. Chester's Wake was in turmoil. She had expected her parents' shock and dismay but hadn't considered how the people of her kingdom would feel. They had spent decades terminating anomalies—yet the princess had been allowed to live. Some saw her as an injustice while others saw her as a threat.

Her parents had not changed their stance on termination, yet they loved her. Their personal struggle was seen as weakness and hypocrisy by many within their country.

Roanna did not enjoy the moments her mind drifted to these thoughts. Her own people no longer loved her family. Perhaps they would have their own rebellion, one to rival Dawson's Edge.

"Roanna?" Roland's voice brought her back to the present conversation.

"Is he coming to interrogate the Sterns again?"

Ben had visited twice in the last four weeks, both for short jaunts to question the Sterns, the leaders of the rebel band who wished to rid the Dawsonian kingdom of the royal family.

Roland frowned, still seeming to hold back. "No, I don't think that's the plan."

Roanna's pulse quickened even more. "Why is he coming?"

"Perhaps you can speak to Queen Katherine about it." His gaze danced away, and his frown deepened.

Uncomfortable, perhaps? He still didn't like Ben. It didn't matter that Ben had never stolen her from Roland—she was his niece, and they would not have married regardless of Roanna's relationship with the Prince of Lox.

Nor did it matter that Ben had played a vital role in bringing the Dawsonian rebels to justice. Roland, and King Dawson for that matter, distrusted her betrothed.

Roanna didn't care what they thought of him. She couldn't wipe the smile from her lips. "Thank you, Roland. You leave tomorrow?"

He nodded.

"Have a safe trip." She bolted from the garden and hurried toward Katherine's offices. Katherine would explain what was happening. She often indulged her long-lost daughter, much to King Dawson's dismay.

Roanna went to the queen's personal rooms. Soft voices came from inside, so Roanna knocked. A moment later the door swung open. Julietta, Katherine's maid, stood in the doorway. Her long blonde hair was twisted into a thick bun at the base of her neck, and she wore a lacey white cap on her head.

"Miss?"

"Hello, Julietta. I'm looking for Queen Katherine."

Julietta curtsied. "One moment, my lady." She disappeared into the room. A moment later, she returned, beckoning Roanna to enter.

Katherine sat at a small desk in her relaxation area. She was bent over a paper, pen in her hand. She smiled when Roanna entered. "Hello, darling. How did your training go?"

"As well as could be expected. Things are coming along." Her parents knew that Roland was helping her develop her powers—the anomalies she had been born with. The anomalies that might have gotten her killed if she had truly been born in Chester's Wake. While Dawson's Edge did not practice termination, not everyone in the kingdom felt entirely comfortable with the royal family's powers. "Roland mentioned that Ben is coming. What are his plans?"

Katherine smiled. "He is coming to speak with the king regarding the marriage agreement."

Another grin erupted across Roanna's face. What was wrong with her today? She wasn't some silly, love struck child. Ben was her best friend, and better yet, now he was her betrothed. While the rest of her new life often felt like a nightmare, Ben's role felt like a dream come true.

Katherine patted her hands. "Don't get your hopes up just yet. Now that we have Lox's alliance without the marriage treaty, your father is much less willing to let you go so quickly."

But he wouldn't stop the marriage, not if Lox was still willing. Would he? A month ago, King Dawson couldn't get the marriage underway soon enough. But since Dawson's Edge had cooperated fully in catching and prosecuting Lox's attackers, the two kingdoms had become better allies than ever. And then there was the alliance with Chester's Wake. It was both stronger and more unstable all at once, but they would certainly come to Dawson's aid when needed. Perhaps Dawson's Edge no longer required the marriage, after all.

"You look so gloomy. You needn't." She turned back to the paper and continued writing. "We are throwing an engagement ball for you. I'm finishing some of the details now. Prince Benjamin will be staying for two weeks at the least, and we expect to throw the party just before he returns home."

An engagement ball? Roanna forced herself to remain poised this time around. "Thank you, Katherine." Her birth mother must have had something to do with the whole arrangement since Ben irritated the king so incessantly.

Katherine's face lit with a quiet joy. "You're quite welcome. Now, go get rested for supper tonight. Many nobles will be joining us."

Roanna nodded her consent. Ben's arrival was a bright spot in her dim world. She tried to stay positive, but in her truthful moments she missed being home in Chester's Wake. And then, when she was home, she felt like an outsider. Her parents treated her differently now. Were they disgusted because they knew the truth? They'd spent their rule terminating children with physical or powerful anomalies. Have cancer in vitro? Terminated. Have the ability to read minds? Terminated. Only to learn after eighteen years that the daughter they had raised had an anomaly herself—and wasn't their true daughter.

Besides, now they were dedicating their resources to learning what had become of their real daughter, the true princess of Chester's Wake. Lox was graciously aiding in this effort. The Loxian rulers hadn't reached out to Roanna at all since Ben had explained to them the truth. The thought brought pain.

Pushing gloomy feelings away, Roanna focused on Ben's arrival. And he'd be around for weeks! The idea was like a soothing balm. She would relish it.

"I can't wait to hear every detail." She hugged Katherine one last time then turned to leave the room.

A knock sounded at the door. Julietta moved to answer the knock, and this time, she returned with a frown. She curtsied to Katherine. "My Lady, a guard at the door."

Katherine rose and hurried to the door, and Roanna followed directly behind her. The guard stood ramrod straight, and stern, in the hall. He nodded to Katherine. "Your Highness, the king has sent for you." His gaze flickered toward Roanna then back to the queen. "Both of you." His tone bespoke urgency.

Katherine took Roanna's hand. "Come along, then."

They walked hand in hand toward King Dawson's office, Roanna matching Katherine's long strides. The dark hallways seemed to close in on her, and not for the first time she wished she was back home in Chester's Wake.

The king's offices bustled as usual. Inside, Roland stood beside the king at a desk, both bent toward a letter.

The king glanced up. His gaze locked onto Roanna, and his shoulders relaxed some. He waved the letter. His nostrils flared and he looked to Katherine. "Another one." His ominous words sparked fear in Roanna.

Katherine frowned and stepped forward, her eyes wide and wary. "What is it, Bartholomew?"

The king looked back to Roanna. His own face

blanched. "More threats against Roanna. The rebel band is not dead."

2

Merry Stern...

Merry Stern gripped the envelope as the auto approached the palace in Chester's Wake. Fog filled the air—fog or smog, she wasn't sure which. It was nothing like the clean, open air in the Dawson's Edge countryside. She recognized the landmarks throughout the city as she passed—a large fountain outside the city's huge cathedral, the palace on the riverfront, and most notable the various Rejected homes. She'd never seen such homes before her first visit to Chester's Wake a few months ago.

That visit seemed so far away now, like a dream.

Unease crept into her stomach as the auto drew closer to the palace gates. Her stomach twisted and fluttered, and she took a calming breath to steady herself. Laying the envelope aside for a moment, she pulled a handkerchief from her bag and wiped her sweaty hands on it. She touched her blonde hair, which had been coiled into an elegant knot at the nape of her neck, and she smoothed her plain brown skirt and white blouse. Everything was in place.

She shouldn't be so nervous. Chester's Wake had approached her, not the other way around. They'd offered her asylum in exchange for information. Wanted to use her to infiltrate the rest of the rebels within Dawson's Edge. Make her a spy against her own people. Against Papa.

She had never been a spy before, but she had been deceptive plenty of times.

She bit her bottom lip and stared straight ahead. A moment passed and her teeth released the delicate skin insider her lip. She straightened her shoulders. She could do this. Would do this.

Must do this.

Papa would not rot in prison because she'd foolishly trusted Roanna Hamilton, the exuberant and charming princess from Chester's Wake. Or rather, Roanna Dawson, the lost princess from Dawson's Edge.

The thought gave her another moment's pause, and she almost returned to gnawing her lip, but she refrained.

The auto pulled to the front of the palace and an armed guard met them. The sight of the weapon at his hip made her heart skip a beat. Asylum or not, she was barely more than a prisoner here. She was a Dawsonian rebel. It seemed fitting that the one to greet her should be an armed guard.

A moment passed and another figure stepped from the castle—Queen Charlotte Hamilton. They'd been friendly when Merry visited months ago. Of course, that was before anyone had known she was a rebel.

Queen Charlotte smiled as Merry climbed from the auto. She took Merry's hand and pulled her close. "So nice to see you again, Lady Merry." She kissed Merry's cheek.

Heat burned under Merry's skin. Why was Queen Charlotte being so friendly? She wasn't sure what to feel or expect at this point. She'd been wrong enough lately, hadn't she?

"It's nice to see you again as well, Your Highness. Thank you for hosting me."

Hosting me. As if she were a legitimate guest.

But Queen Charlotte only smiled sweetly. "You are most welcome. Please, come in and I'll show you to your rooms."

Rooms?

Merry had half expected to be forced to bunk with the servants, or to have a room in the dungeon. But the queen led her up the grand central staircase and to the right, toward the guest wing.

Merry marveled once again as they maneuvered through the palace, much as she had marveled on her first visit. The royal residence was so open and light, not like the dimly lit halls of the Dawsonian palace in Dawson's Edge. Here in Chester's Wake, windows lined the walls, and electric lighting illuminated every nook and cranny.

They climbed a smaller staircase, and a moment later, Queen Charlotte led her through a doorway.

Not only did Merry have her own room, she had a suite of rooms. Odd, considering not six weeks ago she'd been arrested for treason in her own country, caught by Queen Charlotte's own daughter. Or the girl Queen Charlotte thought was her daughter.

Merry sighed inwardly. The whole situation was too bizarre and confusing.

"You'll be comfortable here?"

"Quite." Merry took in the sitting room, dressing room, and bedroom. "In fact, I worry this is much too grand for me."

"Nonsense. You are our guest here. You may rest for the remainder of the day, and tomorrow, you will begin working with me in my offices."

"Your offices?" This was quite a surprise. She'd imagined hours of interrogation in the king's office, under lock and key. Perhaps even while in shackles. "I look forward to it, Your Highness."

"Supper will be at seven. Someone will come for you."

Merry smiled her thanks, and the queen left her alone in the suite as she awaited the servants bringing her luggage. She took in the room again, and tears sprang to her eyes. This was so much more than she could have ever hoped. So much more than she'd expected after weeks of house arrest in Dawson's Edge.

Perhaps Chester's Wake didn't intend to use and break her so much as work with her. It could be they truly forgave her for her crimes. For working toward an end that would have resulted in their princess's death—albeit, Merry hadn't known Roanna possessed an anomaly at the time.

Papa had worked with the Maynes as the heads of the rebel forces in Dawson's Edge—forces that aimed to remove the Dawson family from the throne. The rebels had one goal, and that was the advancement of the kingdom. Too long had the Dawson family's backward practices held back the success of their people.

But Merry had trusted Princess Roanna, and the rebel band had been caught. Papa was thrown in prison along with the Maynes and several others. Merry had been separated from her sister, Rachel, who was innocent in the whole affair. Her shy nature had never lent itself to rebel work. Now Rachel lived with a different noble family within the kingdom. Merry hadn't heard from her in many weeks.

The unpleasant memories filled her mind, and her resolved wavered. What about Papa? She couldn't implicate him, no matter what the Chester's Wake royalty said. She couldn't sentence him to life in a dungeon, no matter if Queen Charlotte treated her as an equal instead of a criminal. It didn't matter if she was given her own suite of rooms in the palace. Her main objective was not helping the Hamiltons trap rebels. It was helping exonerate Papa, at any cost. She must free him from the dungeons in Dawson's Edge.

She remembered the envelope she still held in her hands. It contained her legal papers. Her freedom. But she had another envelope hidden deep in her suitcase. Papa had pressed it into her hands moments before the guards had arrested him weeks ago. Instructed her to hide it and keep it safe.

She would use it only if necessary.

She trembled.

Merry took another deep breath to steady herself. Time to gather her thoughts.

Supper. Her next mission was getting through supper.

Would Prince Gregory be there?

They hadn't spoken since she was named a rebel. What did he think of her now?

Her stomach tightened again, and she ground her teeth. It didn't matter if she had to stare him in the eye and lie to him outright. She couldn't betray Papa. Her family.

A servant stepped through the doorway with the first of the luggage. Merry snapped out of her indecision and began moving as she always had. With purpose and confidence. She would make time for her ghosts later.

3

Merry stared into the mirror as Fraja finished curling the last blonde ringlet of Merry's hair. Fraja stepped back and smiled. "It looks nice, yes?" Her strange accent was music to Merry's ears. She'd missed her maid terribly during the short time their servants had been taken away for questioning. Most of them had not returned, choosing to find employment elsewhere. But not Fraja. She was an old woman with thinning silver hair and shaky, wrinkled hands. She had been tending to Merry since her early childhood.

"Very nice. Thank you, Fraja." She stood and wrung her hands together.

Fraja stepped close and covered Merry's hands with her own, stilling them. "Do not be filled with nerves. All will be well."

Merry gave her a tight smile. She hoped all would be well, but she didn't know how. "Queen Charlotte said someone would come for me." As she finished speaking, a knock sounded.

Fraja shuffled to the door and opened it. A young girl stood in the hall. She was dressed in the immaculate dark green of the palace servants.

Merry stepped forward, giving Fraja one last

smile. "Wish me luck." She stepped into the hall and followed the girl down the corridor and to the winding staircase. It wasn't as if she needed an escort, as she'd spent a little over a week in the palace during her visit a couple of months ago. She and her family had come with Ambassador Roland Dawson when he had journeyed to negotiate the peace treaty.

Despite the queen's warm welcome, the Hamiltons must not trust her entirely.

They're right to be wary.

The thought shamed her, however truthful.

Noise filled the hall as they neared the dining room. Cheerful, boisterous noise. A party? Merry frowned. What had she gotten herself into? The servant girl stopped her at the doorway to the dining room, curtsied, and hurried away. Merry stood at the door only a moment. She sucked in a breath for courage and glided into the room, quickly surveying for a place to sit. If it truly was a party, she likely had an assigned seat. Why had no one told her?

The dining room was full, with few empty chairs at the enormous table. Nearly fifty diners sat mingling. Queen Charlotte caught her eye and smiled. She gestured toward the middle of the table, and Merry's eyes followed the motion. An empty seat near a group of other ladies. Merry returned the queen's smile then moved to the empty place.

Her palms were sweating again. Who were these ladies? No one she recognized. If they were from Chester's Wake it was unlikely they'd heard of Merry Stern the criminal of Dawson's Edge.

The thought gave her at least a modicum of relief. She smiled and introduced herself into the conversation. The lady to her left was older, closer to the queen's age. She was a duchess along the eastern coast of Chester's Wake in a province called Higgins. She smiled and asked about Merry's life in Dawson's Edge.

Merry watched the duchess closely as she spoke. The woman smiled and nodded, *oh'ed* and *ah'ed*. If she was aware of Merry's crimes, she didn't let on.

"Do you visit the capital often?" Merry asked. She'd gained the attention of a few of the others near her with her tales of life in Dawson's Edge.

"Not often, no." Her eyes lit up. "My daughter is here as a prospective bride for Prince Gregory. Have you met him?"

The others nearby listened to the duchess's answer.

"On occasion." The words came out so smoothly. How did she manage that? She sucked in another breath and went on before the sting of the truth could settle. "I would love to meet your daughter. Is she here tonight?" She'd asked only to be polite. And maybe to have something to say.

"Actually, the prince took her out for a private supper. Isn't it exciting?" Her eyes were clear and her smile genuine.

Still, Merry couldn't help but smile back. "Very exciting. Your daughter must be giddy."

Somehow, the duchess's smile grew. "Positively giddy."

Some of the other ladies cut in, and Merry took a steely breath. She hadn't had the courage to look around for Gregory yet. Now she knew she didn't have to. He wasn't at this supper.

What must he think of her, the girl who'd smiled with him? Laughed with him? Let him kiss her, not once but twice?

Did he think it'd been a ruse? That she'd tricked him? Fooled him?

It definitely hadn't been a ruse. When she had visited all those months ago, she'd thought Chester's Wake would be on the rebellion's side. She'd had no idea the disaster brewing in secret with Princess Roanna. She'd had no idea she would be pitted against Gregory's family, and Gregory.

She forced thoughts of the absent prince away and went back to the conversations at hand. The ladies spoke of the weather, the palace, the scandals going on in Chester's Wake. The duchess mentioned a parcel of land with a manor her husband had recently acquired. He'd obtained it from a family called the DeWalts, and how she couldn't wait to vacation there.

The others offered their words of admiration over the duchess's news, but it didn't take long before the conversation turned to Princess Roanna. Their voices lowered.

"She spends most of her time in Dawson's Edge," the lady on her right said. She had blazing red hair piled on top of her head, and she was a young baron's wife who lived full time in the capital city. "They say she has powers, yet the Hamiltons didn't terminate"

Tsk'ing pursued.

"They're growing soft on the issue," one woman said.

The duchess lifted her chin. "Prince Gregory holds fast to his beliefs, though. He is faithful to the values of Chester's Wake."

A few others agreed, and the subject around the table shifted. But Merry tucked that information away. If Gregory held fast to his beliefs, did that mean he might still be on the rebellion's side? It was something to consider.

The duchess continued. "I heard the other Dawsons have powers as well." Her voice had taken on a sharp edge, but then she froze. She turned to Merry. "Begging your pardon, my lady. You probably know more than us all."

Friendships. She needed to make friendships in Chester's Wake. Especially if she was going to figure out a way to get Papa released. "I know a little, though not much," she admitted. "As you know, Dawson's Edge does not practice Termination. It's been long known among our people that the royal family is," she paused, thinking, before settling on a word, "different. I can neither confirm nor deny the existence of anomalies, although others throughout the country do possess certain unique traits and abilities."

Mostly true. She knew the family possessed anomalies, but she'd never experienced them firsthand. She'd been told the royal family was evil, but after spending time with Roanna she had found nothing more devious in her than in anyone else. She didn't divulge that opinion, however.

The women chattered on, moving to the betrothal of Princess Roanna and Prince Benjamin. Finally, they settled on the impossibility of a lost princess. Merry listened intently. She hadn't honestly considered what had happened to the real princess of Chester's Wake, Gregory's real sister, but she knew she could learn the truth easily enough.

There were those who knew what had happened all those years ago, she was sure of it. When the time presented itself, she could use that information to free Papa.

Regardless of her knowledge of royal anomalies or lost princesses, she did know that Princess Roanna had become betrothed to Benjamin of Lox. She'd even heard rumors that it wouldn't have mattered if Roanna had married Prince Roland or if Benjamin had chosen a Dawsonian bride—Roanna and Benjamin would have been together anyway. They were madly in love and meant to be.

She stopped herself just before biting her lip in public. What must a love like that feel like? It was no surprise, considering the time she'd spent in Chester's Wake previously. Prince Benjamin and Princess Roanna had been practically inseparable. In fact, if she remembered correctly, the Loxians had stolen away in the night after an incident where neither Benjamin nor Roanna could be found.

Merry smiled secretly to herself. That night she had danced with Gregory most of the evening. It was the first night she'd realized the prince fancied her as much as she fancied him. When he'd asked her to walk with him along the lower banks of the river, he'd even kissed her. It'd been a brief kiss. An innocent kiss. But she'd remembered it specifically because later she'd heard Prince Benjamin had been praying along the lower banks—and she'd known it was a lie because she'd been there herself.

Had Gregory told? Unlikely, as it would have meant he'd have to admit how he knew.

Gregory, the prince who had fancied her. And now he courted another lady. Someone more fitting to be a king's wife. Someone not a criminal, not tried for treason against her own country.

4

Merry awoke long before the sunshine filtered into the windows in her suite. Nerves again. They had kept sleep at bay for most of the night.

She took a deep breath and pressed her hand firmly against her belly, begging it to calm down. She'd be working with the queen today. What did that mean? Would the queen interrogate her, then? Or something else? Was she to be some type of lady-in-waiting for Queen Charlotte?

Moving to the window, she peeked out at the estate. Her room faced the river rather than the bustling capital city. The river flowed steadily. It was stable, offering a little respite from her busy mind.

Fraja came in just as the sun rose and just as Merry finished showering. "You have awakened."

"It's hard to sleep when I'm so nervous."

Fraja smiled. "I tell you there is no need for the nerves. Come. I'll ready you."

Merry sat at a large vanity and allowed Fraja to brush through her long, blonde tangles. Once her hair had been wrapped in a loose bun, Fraja dressed Merry in an ankle length brown skirt, white blouse, and brown corset.

"What do you suppose I'll be doing all day with the queen?"

Fraja shrugged. "You do whatever she says, and things will work out, yes?"

Merry took a deep breath and nodded. "Yes." Things would work out. They had to.

Soon after Merry finished readying for the day, a knock sounded on the door. Fraja opened it to a different servant girl.

"I've come to escort you to breakfast." She eyed Merry nervously, as if she were afraid Merry would chide her.

If anyone had something to be afraid about, it was Merry. She didn't want the girl to feel nervous because of her. She smiled. "Thank you so much. I'm ready."

The girl's tense shoulders relaxed, and she nodded. "Right this way."

The servants were probably unused to escorting guests anywhere. They probably wondered who Merry Stern was, that she should need escort.

The dining room was much quieter this morning, with less than half the number of guests. The duchess was nowhere to be seen. Merry glanced around casually, but again, Gregory was absent. Her lip went to her teeth before she could stop it. Did Gregory know she was here? Could he be avoiding her on purpose?

Ridiculous. She was reading too much into it. They had spent little time together in the grand scheme of things. She was being vain.

At the table, she sat between an elderly gentleman and a small, meek looking woman. The man was on the king's council. Did he know who Merry was then? The woman was a member of the queen's visiting Loxian family. "How do you do?" Merry asked them each. They held an easy conversation about their favorite breakfast foods. If Merry was good at anything, it was talking to people. Putting them at ease. Guiding them in the direction she was going.

Being with other nobility at a king's breakfast table was no hard feat for her. But as the meal ended, her stomach began to churn once more. Working one on one with the queen was a whole different matter. One she hoped she was up for. The meal ended, and Queen Charlotte approached. She smiled. "Did you sleep well, Merry?"

"Yes, thank you. The room is lovely."

The queen nodded and took Merry's elbow. "I hope you'll make yourself at home. If you need anything at all, please let someone know."

"Thank you, Your Highness." She paused. The queen seemed genuine. "If I may ask, why do I need an escort for meals, Your Highness? I remember my way around from my last visit. I mean no disrespect, of course. If you'd prefer me to be escorted, I understand."

Queen Charlotte took in her plea and nodded. "I wanted to be sure you were comfortable, but if you are confident you know your way around, then I'll let you be."

"Thank you, Your Highness. I remember my way to the dining room, as well as the gardens and banquet rooms. Once I see your offices today, I'm sure I'll be comfortable making my way there as well."

Gregory had previously shown her around various parts of the palace—the observatory, the library, the gardens. But she didn't go on. Didn't want to bring up the prince who may or may not be avoiding her.

Queen Charlotte nodded again. "Very well. I want you to be at home as you'll be with us for quite some time."

"Oh!" Merry reached into the large fold of a pocket in her long, brown skirt. She retrieved the envelope with her legal documents. "I forgot to give these to you last night."

The queen took the envelope with another gracious smile. "Thank you, my darling. You must have lots of questions."

Merry bit her lip but quickly stopped herself. "Many, yes. I'm not entirely sure what to expect during my time here."

Queen Charlotte nodded. "I will try to explain." They turned a corner and a small reception area was situated in front of them. Two women and a man sat at desks in the area. Beyond them was a door. The queen led them through it, and Merry found herself in the queen's private office. Merry sat, and the queen took her seat across the desk after closing the door.

The office was small, but it seemed efficient with a large Messenger in the middle of the desk as well as several shelves of books. There were two windows that looked out over the garden.

"We know there must be others in the rebel forces in Dawson's Edge. My daughter, Roanna, provided a list she was given by your father. However, the list was short and vague. You indicated during your interrogations that you aren't aware of any other names. This is correct?" She spoke it in such a friendly manner that it put Merry at ease immediately. During her interrogation she'd been uptight. Nervous. All of that fled in the face of Queen Charlotte's calm kindness.

"Correct. I realize there must be others who were involved. I heard rumors of Bella de St. Paul's family being privy to information. But I don't know any other names."

Queen Charlotte frowned slightly, and her eyes grew distant. The reminder that a princess from across the ocean might be involved in the rebellion surely wasn't a pleasant one. Bella de St. Paul had married the crown price of Dawson's Edge, but her family was made up of the wealthiest rulers in all the second continent.

"Well, that is where we believe you will be helpful," the queen finally went on. "I have noticed how you excel at making friends." The smile in her eyes revealed how honestly she meant the compliment. "You are congenial, genuine, and outgoing. Given the right circumstances and contacts, I don't believe it would take you any time at all to uncover the names of other rebels within Dawson's Edge."

Merry kept her face neutral, but her mind buzzed. Why should the king and queen of Chester's Wake care about the rebellion in Dawson's Edge? But then she remembered Princess Roanna. If the rebels had their way, the princess would certainly be in danger.

Merry nodded. "I understand, Your Highness." But truly, confusion pooled inside of her. How could she mingle with the rebels when they knew she was a war criminal? No one would trust her, least of all the Dawsons.

Queen Charlotte reached across the desk and squeezed Merry's hand. "I'm glad you're willing to help. You won't regret it. There is, however, the matter of loyalty." She paused and held Merry's gaze, her look imploring. Serious.

"I need you to understand that your loyalty is of utmost importance. If there is any whim of you working against us, it cannot end well. I do not say these things to intimidate you, only to make you understand."

"Of course, Your Highness. I am loyal to Chester's Wake." Merry gave her another smile, hoping she came across as genuinely as the queen believed her to be. But inside, she writhed with indecision. Learning of the other rebels could help Papa, as well as the cause. Whether the anomalies were dangerous or not, the Dawsons were not exactly trustworthy. They were superstitious and distrustful. Overthrowing their dynasty would help move the country ahead.

Besides, the rebels would set Papa free. That mattered more than even the cause.

She could use the information to save herself here in Chester's Wake, or she could use it to further her family's mission. Eventually, she would have to choose.

5

Merry spent the afternoon reviewing names of the noble families in Dawson's Edge. Queen Charlotte was impressed with Merry's knowledge of her country and people. Merry had always been skilled with a detailed and easy memory—she remembered the entire family trees of the majority of the Dawsonian nobility. She knew where they lived. She also had a decent idea of which families preferred which types of activities and outings.

"You have a blessedly organized mind, my darling," Queen Charlotte said as they finished up a paper list. It was the end of their workday, and Merry would be allowed to wander at her own leisure until supper that night.

Merry smiled and shrugged. "I enjoy organization and taking care of the details."

One of the queen's aids entered and handed a few papers to the queen. "These need signatures by tomorrow afternoon."

Queen Charlotte took the papers and began signing. "Don't wait for me, Merry. You go ahead."

"Thank you, Your Highness." Merry turned to go but paused. She looked back at Queen Charlotte. "Your

Highness, may I ask you a question?"

Queen Charlotte's eyebrows rose. "Of course."

"Why am I working on this project with you? I assumed I would be held as a prisoner." She stumbled on the word prisoner but forced herself to go on. "I thought I'd be working with investigators or military personnel."

This time the queen didn't smile or try to reassure Merry. "This project is important to me, as I'm sure you can understand. We have considered extensively the best way to go about it, and this was the way we determined would be most successful. Would you rather work with someone else?"

"No!" It came out too quickly, and Merry smiled nervously. "I've had a lovely day with you." It was true. Queen Charlotte was a joy to be around.

The queen smiled again. "I have enjoyed it as well. I'll see you at supper."

Merry nodded and backed from the room. Her memory allowed her to easily make her way back to the main entry of the palace and then to the grand staircase leading to the guest wing. As she reached the bottom of the stairs, a small group of soldiers marched from the direction of the state offices.

"Did the prince give any indication of their numbers?" a soldier in front asked.

"Negative," another soldier replied. "He said he would have more information for us by morning. He was finishing up for the afternoon."

The soldiers rounded the corner, leaving Merry staring after them. She glanced around, wondering if she'd be caught gawking at the men. But no one seemed to pay her any attention at all.

It was silly the way she was paralyzed at even the

mention of Gregory. They'd spent such little time together—one week here in Chester's Wake and later an evening at a ball in Dawson's Edge. They'd kept in touch briefly via post, and yes, he'd kissed her. Not only in Chester's Wake but also at the ball. But it was hardly a solid relationship. He'd probably moved on quite easily once he learned of her crimes.

Taking a deep breath, she turned away from the direction the soldiers had left. As she spun, two men came around the corner from the state offices. Their heads were bent over a mutual report, but one of them glanced up briefly.

Their eyes met, and Merry's heart stilled. She immediately recognized his tall frame as well as the regal and confident way with which he held himself. His light brown hair fell across his forehead, and his dress clothes seemed slightly rumpled after a long day.

Gregory stumbled. He quickly muttered an apology to the man he consulted with. He shoved the report to his companion, growled some type of excuse, and stomped back the way he'd come without another look Merry's way.

She turned quickly, her cheeks burning, before the companion could spot her. She climbed casually toward the guest wing so as not to draw attention to herself.

But what did it mean, the way he'd seen her then hurried away? Perhaps he truly was avoiding her, as absurd as the idea had seemed.

Merry found her room easily.

Fraja hummed a happy melody as she worked at unpacking the remainder of Merry's things, making sure she laid everything out to avoid wrinkles. "How was it?" Fraja asked. "Did you perform well?"

Being back with her beloved nurse and maid brought quiet relief to Merry. "I did. I think I met and even exceeded all of the queen's expectations."

Fraja smiled. "Very good."

Merry slipped off her shoes and laid on the bed. Her mind bounced between various subjects. How were Papa and the others? What would happen to her family's estate? Would she ever see her childhood home again?

What of the other noble families? Which of them might secretly be part of the rebel cause? Queen Charlotte seemed certain that some of them were involved. But was it well known that Merry had come to Chester's Wake? Surely, none of the nobility would welcome her with open arms if they knew. But Queen Charlotte seemed to have a good understanding of the plan they had in place. She had likely thought of everything, including a way to endear Merry to her own countrymen.

Could she do it? Betray Papa's cause? Dawson's Edge would never advance on the world's stage if the rest of the planet saw them as backward and superstitious. She agreed with that much, most definitely.

So, what she needed was to figure out how to do enough to save herself and still be true to her beliefs. First, though, she would need more information. More time.

Those thoughts were all fleeting, however. Mostly she thought of the startled look in Gregory's blue eyes when his gaze had met hers.

She fingered the soft blankets on her bed as she stared at the ceiling. He was quite obviously very involved in military matters in Chester's Wake. In fact, he'd mentioned it before during their short time together. He enjoyed military tactics, and he preferred it over economic matters. He would need a queen who excelled at this other side of ruling, to balance out his rule. He'd said it with stars in his eyes and a smile on his lips. He'd said it after Merry expressed her interest in and talent for making plans and enacting them to fix specific problems.

Of course, that was before. Now, he needed a queen who wasn't a traitor. She could never be that queen, and she needed to stop focusing on him. He would forget about her in time. Until then, he would continue ignoring her.

6

True to her word, Queen Charlotte had cancelled the escort, thus Merry made her own way to supper that night. The noise from the dining room sounded long before Merry reached the doorway.

So perhaps it wasn't a party at all. Perhaps most nights in Chester's Wake were this boisterous.

She took stock of the long, mahogany table as she entered. The king and queen each sat at opposite heads of the table, surrounded by nobles and state dignitaries. One or two empty seats scattered throughout the middle, and the crowd tapered off as her gaze reached the end of the table. She made her way to the far end, but someone called her name and stopped her.

"Lady Merry, do come sit with us!" It was Duchess Higgins from the night before. With growing horror, Merry realized she sat beside a younger version of herself, and across from them sat Gregory, the seat beside him empty.

How could she openly refuse?

She forced a tight smile and made her way to the empty chair. "Good evening. How do you fair?"

Duchess Higgins beamed. "It's been a wonderful

day! Lady Merry, I'm pleased to introduce you to my daughter, the Lady Wendy. And you said you were slightly acquainted with the prince already?"

Merry pasted on her most friendly smile. "How nice to meet you, Lady Wendy, and to see you again, Your Highness." She made sure not to raise her head enough to quite meet Gregory's eye.

Wendy seemed as genuine and friendly as her mother, the duchess. She had dark brown hair that curled riotously from root to tip. It was piled into a high crown atop her head. She wore a black jeweled choker, and a velvety, violet gown. Her eyes were dark and her skin fair.

"Mother told me you're from Dawson's Edge."

Merry kept her smile in place and nodded. "That's right. My father is a baron there." Or he was.

Waves of tension rolled off Gregory. Was he scowling? Frowning? Drowning his sorrows in drink?

She dared not look his way.

"And how did you and the prince come to meet?"

To speak of him and not so much as glance at him felt wholly unnatural. Social niceties were a necessity if she was going to win this game.

An eternity seemed to pass as she forced her falsely happy gaze his way. To her surprise, he looked at her easily. His gaze was not friendly, but it wasn't wary either. It was more...detached.

"I came with Prince—or rather, Ambassador—Dawson when he came to negotiate a peace treaty between our kingdoms. I became briefly acquainted with the prince then." She smiled once at him, only to play the part of unconcerned acquaintance.

Something flashed behind his eyes as she spoke. Something that made her breath catch momentarily.

He hadn't forgotten her so easily, and maybe he did hate her for it.

"How nice," the duchess said. "Lady Merry, I was telling Wendy of some of your customs in Dawson's Edge."

Merry smiled, and the duchess needed no further encouragement to take charge of the conversation. Merry listened intently, offering clarification where needed and advice when asked. It was easy to be herself amid flowing conversation.

Gregory sat quietly through it all. From across the table, Merry caught Wendy smiling his way several times. He must have smiled back, because she always lowered her eyes, cheeks pink.

Merry didn't speak with him. She didn't look his way, and she tried desperately not to move, afraid that if she so much as accidentally bumped his knee with her own that he would scorch her with a scathing look.

"Lady Merry," Wendy cut into the conversation. "Mother told me all about you, but she never mentioned why you're here. Are you on holiday?"

"Actually, I'm working as an ambassador of sorts for Dawson's Edge." The practiced speech rolled off her tongue like butter. The story was one thing Queen Charlotte had been firm on. "Because of the delicate nature of our kingdoms' relationship at this time, I was happy to help bridge the gap peacefully."

Lady Wendy wasn't quick to catch on. She frowned slightly. It caused a small wrinkle on her forehead between her eyebrows. "The delicate nature?"

"Because of my sister, Princess Roanna." Gregory's masculine voice broke in before Merry was forced to explain.

Enlightenment broke across Wendy's face, and before Merry could think better of it she smiled her thanks at Gregory.

He watched her again, the detached look still on his face.

Her heart erupted in flutters, and she clutched her dress in her hands beneath the table. Would this meal never end?

Someone to the duchess's right asked her a question, and she began a new conversation. They pulled Wendy into the discussion, leaving Merry and Gregory to themselves.

Merry quickly took a bite of her meal, hoping not to seem too uncomfortable. After a moment, she turned to the diner on her left. It was a balding man who had a small patch of white fluff on the top of his head. But he was turned to the guest on his other side.

Slowly, she faced forward again.

"How is your room?" Gregory spoke quietly but clipped.

She could keep her gaze forward, but it was too unnatural and would draw more attention than if she simply looked at him. With resignation she turned his way.

Something burned there behind the blue of his eyes, but she couldn't decipher what it was.

"The room is lovely. Much larger than anything I'm used to, I assure you."

He didn't nod his affirmation of understanding. After a moment, he turned away.

"How did your flight home from Dawson's Edge go? After the ball, I mean." She swallowed her nerves. "You said you were excited to use the personal air ship your father had commissioned for you."

That flash behind his eyes was back. His Adam's apple bobbed as he swallowed. "It was actually quite fantastic." A ghost of a smile tried to break through, but he quickly ironed it out.

"Your mother offered to let me travel here via airship, but I insisted on taking an auto. The thought of flying terrifies me."

He kept her gaze, unblinking, another moment. Then he turned away without another word.

7

Roanna...

Ben had been in Dawson's Edge less than two days, but Roanna had spent barely fifteen minutes with him. Between Roland and the king, they kept Ben swept up in meetings, consults, and brainstorming sessions. For her birth family to dislike her betrothed so much, they sure were taking up a lot of his time.

Besides that, they kept Roanna covered in guards, thanks to the threats they had received. She glanced at them now, standing at each doorway.

Supper ended, and the royal family moved to the sitting room behind the dining hall. One of the noblemen—Roanna still couldn't remember most of their names—cornered King Dawson, and Roland was blessedly absent.

Ben slipped his fingers into Roanna's grip and smiled. "I think our days of hiding away are gone."

She huffed but smiled. "We could always resort to our old tricks."

His eyes crinkled at the edges when he smiled. "Don't tempt me. I want your family to trust me." But he stumbled over the word family.

She wanted to ask him a million questions. Were

his parents against their marriage now? Were they postponing things? What did he make of the threats that had been made against her?

She opened her mouth to suggest they could meet in the gardens once everyone had gone to bed, but before she could speak, a lady approached with questions about Roanna's upcoming engagement party. She spoke as briefly as possible, but as she finished, someone else called for Ben's attentions.

Disappointment swirled through her. This wasn't fair. In Chester's Wake they would be given privacy. But here? Dawson's Edge seemed unnaturally bent on keeping them apart.

Roanna turned to the bookshelf behind them and began browsing titles. Most of the books in the Dawsonian palace held no interest for her, but every now and again, she'd spot one on Dawsonian history, or gardening.

A hand slipped around her waist, and warm breath tickled her neck. "Meet me an hour after this torture ends. The gardens." Then Ben's hand was gone, and he'd stepped away.

Heat crept up her neck. She took a deep breath to calm herself then turned casually. Roland had appeared, and he'd drawn Ben into conversation with a few of the other men.

Roanna's heart fluttered. She could wait a couple more hours.

At last, the evening ended, and she said her good nights as the other guests left the sitting room. Katherine had long since gone to bed, and now, only a few men mingled, Ben included. Roanna approached.

"I'm going up," she said, kissing King Dawson's cheek. Their relationship was easy, if somewhat awkward and new.

"Sleep well, daughter. I've arranged an outing for you and the prince tomorrow."

Roanna raised her eyebrows, and she turned to Ben. He grinned. "We're to visit Lady Gretchen."

"Lady Gretchen?" She was the king's sister, and Roanna and Mother had stayed with her during a storm a couple of months ago.

Ben only grinned. "Fulfilling a promise," he said.

Roanna nodded. She didn't honestly care what they did if she was with him. She dipped her head in acknowledgement. "Very well. I'll see you at breakfast."

She hurried to her room, already counting the minutes until she'd meet him in the garden. She wanted to know what the Dawsons had been so secretly consulting about with him. What his parents thought of her now that they knew she had an anomaly. What the chatter in his kingdom was. Would they accept a Rejected princess? A Rejected queen?

Time crept along. Bette helped her change into bed clothes and take down her hair, and Roanna changed into more casual clothes as soon as Bette left for bed. She looked at herself in the mirror, studying her hair. She hadn't gotten used to the length yet and still wore it up most of the time.

But she wanted Ben to see it. Wanted to know what he thought about it. She left it down.

At last, an hour had passed. The guards would be in the hallway, but Roanna knew how to get around them. She peeked from her room, glancing up and down the empty, dark, and quiet corridor.

She crept from her room and to the end of the hall then peered around the corner. She continued her sneaky dance until she reached the first floor. It was empty, and Roanna easily slipped toward the back of the palace and the gardens. As she reached the doors leading outside, someone stepped from the shadows.

Roanna smiled, eager to greet Ben.

She froze.

Roland shook his head at her, his eyes showing disappointment. "I worried I'd find you here."

She could try to deny it, but what else would she be doing at this hour? "Did I drop my shield again?" she asked, wondering if he'd seen inside her mind.

"No. But you're a woman, and he's a man, and it's not too difficult to read between the lines of your hidden glances."

Embarrassment wormed its way up her neck and into her ears and cheeks.

"I only want to speak to him without being constantly interrupted. I want to know what his parents say about me now that they..." how to describe it? Finally, she said, "Now that they know the truth."

Why did the Dawsons have to be so overprotective? It made her feel like a petulant child.

His eyes narrowed, and he crossed his arms. "Very well, but I'm only giving you thirty minutes. If you're not back in this spot by then, I'm coming after you." He jerked his head toward the gardens. "Your prince is already waiting for you. He crept by without even seeing me." His tone told her what he thought of that.

Roanna worked to keep the anger from her voice. "Fine." She slipped past him and hurried to the warm, moist air of the palace gardens. Ben sat near the fountain in the middle, waiting for her. She smiled and hurried forward.

"Roland caught me. He said we can have thirty minutes."

He shrugged. "He was hiding in the alcove near the door. I saw him and was surprised when he didn't stop me. I suppose it's better than him spying on us outright."

She grinned. Of course, Ben had seen him. She reached toward him, and he immediately took her hands and pulled her against him. "I've missed you." His words warmed her heart.

"I've missed you, too."

He moved to resume his seat on the fountain, but she tugged his hand. "Let's move over there." She nodded toward a slightly more hidden bench. He followed her, and they sat.

"What have they been speaking to you about?" She didn't waste any time in trying to get answers. "The Dawsons, I mean."

She worked to keep her mind closed, shielded against any of Roland's prying. Occasionally, she would forget. Let down her defenses and feel him in her mind. Roland had made it his own pet project to keep watch over her. Protect her. Suffocate her.

Ben frowned and looked down. "The Dawsons fear the rebels still within the country as well as those who support them across the ocean. The rebels have gone deep underground, and if they're not found, they might cause harm later."

Harm, as in killing the royal family. Killing Roanna. She knew the proof of his statements, having seen them for herself.

"Do they have leads?"

He shook his head, and her stomach clenched. "Have you spoken to Gregory? He's been helping

Chester's Wake with their own investigation."

Ben's gaze danced away. Roanna frowned. What was he not saying?

"Ben?"

He sighed. "Gregory is angry. He's angry with both of us for stirring up this thing to begin with. When he speaks with me, it's only out of necessity and always straight to the point. He says they're working on it, but as far as I know, they don't have anything yet. They've been focusing their search on the missing princess."

The thought of Gregory so angry with her pained her. He had barely spoken to her since her heritage was revealed. She had hurt him with her truth. Hurt him more by not telling him the truth earlier when she'd discovered it herself. He was not himself, and she felt largely to blame.

"I need to tell them about Dr. Presnell." She looked to her hands in her lap. "I don't see it's possible that they haven't discovered his involvement."

"We don't even know for sure that he was involved, at least not to the level we suspect."

Roanna thought of the elderly doctor who had attended her mother the night she went into labor. He had been thrown into the dungeon in Chester's Wake after upsetting the queen, and he had known Roanna's true identity. But how had her kidnapping come about? It was still a mystery.

She looked back to Ben. "Still, I should tell them."

"You'll get your chance as soon as they arrive."

True enough.

"Let's not talk about any of that right now."

She thought of Roland just around the corner. If only she could make him go away. Creep into his head and force him to go to his own rooms.

Instead, she leaned closer to Ben. He smelled of sandalwood. "I love you."

He smiled down at her, and a moment later, he kissed her. It was easy, as if they'd kissed a million times—which they definitely hadn't. But this was Ben. She was meant to be with him, and they both felt it.

After a moment she pulled away from him. "I have other questions."

"Can't they wait?"

"Ahem." Roland's deadpan interruption made her jump, but Ben pulled away slowly. "Did you need something, Ambassador?" he asked. His tone indicated his irritation.

"I think it's time we cut this rendezvous short."

"You said thirty minutes," Roanna said.

"And you said you were going to be talking." He held out his hand. "Come along."

Anger burst through her. "Roland, you are my uncle and my instructor, but by no means are you my parent or guardian. I agreed to abide by your thirty-minute suggestion," she emphasized the word suggestion, "but I do still have questions for Ben, and I will see them answered."

Steely anger flashed in Roland's eyes. A painful wave hit her mind, and she realized he was reaching out to her, trying to speak to her.

What? she snapped.

Do you think the king would be pleased with your secret meeting with the boy in the palace gardens?

Heat spread through her. What was wrong with Roland? He was again playing the part of jilted fiancé.

Leave us. And do not come back when thirty minutes is up. Uncle.

She snapped her mind shut with a vengeance. He glared at her then at Ben. After a moment, he stormed away.

Likely he was going to wake the king or perhaps the queen.

Roanna sighed. "That didn't end well."

Ben watched her curiously. "Were you speaking to him?"

She'd gotten so used to it she hadn't considered how it must look to Ben. "Yes. He didn't have anything kind to say."

"Perhaps we should wait to finish our conversation in the morning," Ben suggested.

Roanna sighed. "Very well, we can finish talking tomorrow, but first, will you please tell me about your family? What do they think of all this?" She watched his face eagerly, hoping he would answer honestly.

8

Roanna lay in bed an hour later. She held a simple gold band. A ring. It held no adornment. No jewels. Only the ring.

Ben had slipped it onto her finger only a few moments after Roland left and not fifteen minutes before Katherine had come to the garden at Roland's urging. Katherine hadn't been pleased. She'd explained that she and King Dawson needed Roanna to follow their instructions. If they couldn't trust her, where would any of them be?

Roanna sighed. She shouldn't have gone to the garden. Shouldn't have agreed to Ben's plan. But when had she ever refused one of his schemes? Never. Still, the Dawsons saw it as a sign of disrespect, and she would have to choose more wisely in the future.

The ring shone in the lamplight of her room, almost sparkling. Ben had told her it was a promise ring. He promised to marry her. He'd given her only a few sentences of explanation about his parents and their adjustment to the truth of her heritage. That's when he'd given her the ring, and their conversation had changed to plans for the future.

A slow smile spread across her face. She couldn't wait to marry her very best friend.

A pang pulled behind her left eye, like the beginning of a headache. It was a pang she recognized. Someone wanted to speak to her.

Roanna pressed her eyes closed and ignored the feeling. She did not wish to hear more of Roland's opinions. He had become increasingly protective of her where Ben was concerned these last several weeks. It was frustrating and intrusive.

But the pang persisted. She sighed and allowed her mind to open.

Speak.

The voice came swiftly, and it was not Roland.

You caused such a stir with your antics. Would you like any brotherly advice?

Prince Stefan, and he sounded amused.

Roanna had little experience with Stefan. It was strange to think she had another brother. They had a distant relationship because he and Princess Bella lived in their own palace in the neighboring providence, just outside the capital city. They were only here now in preparation for the engagement ball.

How did you hear about my antics?

Stefan laughed in her ear.

Uncle Roland gave Father an earful about it. I couldn't help but overhear. You may or may not be pleased to know that he used lots of vulgarity.

Roanna frowned.

Can they not hear you now?

A knock sounded on the door, and Roanna gasped. She climbed out of bed in her nightgown, grabbing a robe as she moved. She cracked open the door.

Stefan stood on the other side, grinning.

"Do you always stay up so late?" She let him into

the room and closed the door behind him.

He smirked. "Do you always go to bed so early?"

Roanna studied him, this brother of hers. He shared her dark hair and olive-toned skin. He was older than her by at least ten years, but the cut of their eyes and mouths were the same. Again, she wondered how she had never noticed that she and Gregory did not look alike.

A slight pain in her heart caused her to look away. "What advice would you give?"

"Don't get caught."

Roanna huffed and sat on her bed. "That is not very helpful advice."

He plopped onto the bed beside her, the smell of alcohol in the air around him.

Roanna frowned again. Her new brother did not have the best of reputations.

"Roland does not trust the Prince of Lox. He's only trying to protect you. You will find, as you get to know us more, that we are fiercely loyal to our own."

His words rang true. The Dawsons were strange—different than the family she had grown up with—but they were not bad. They were not villains. They were simply superstitious, and Roland's behavior was in line with that.

"I trust the royal family of Lox with my life. There is no reason for Roland to distrust them."

Stefan nodded, seeming to consider her words. "You know them well. Just remember, we do not. Also, we are not the ones postponing your marriage arrangement."

His words were like a clamp around her heart. Had he heard her thoughts earlier in the day? Did he guess she was worried about this very thing?

"What do you mean?"

He watched her a moment longer, his eyebrows drawn together. "I do not know the Loxians, and while I have no doubt Prince Ben would marry you in a single breath, I do not see the same eagerness exhibited by his parents." He held up his hands. "Speaking from an outside viewpoint only, of course."

The clamp on her heart tightened. Her breaths came in short bursts.

Let it not be so, she prayed. "Did you say there was advice in there somewhere?"

He grinned again. "I like you, sister."

She managed a small smile.

"Advice," he continued. "All right, here's advice for you. Don't marry someone because you get caught up in the moment—at least, not if you can help it."

The words hung in the air between them. They filled Roanna with sadness for her newfound brother. She had noted the lack of relationship between him and his wife.

"Anyway," Stefan said, "my real advice is to remember Roland is watching. And Father is watching. And the servants are watching." He paused and laughed. "You are a princess. You know these things already. Haven't you been watched all your life?"

Had she? Father and Mother were always watching, but they'd given her such freedom. It was a practice she did not find here in Dawson's Edge.

"Don't make the foolish choice to have a rendezvous with a man in the palace gardens." He nudged her shoulder. "Next time, choose a room somewhere where you'll have a bit of real privacy."

Heat burst through her neck and cheeks. "It wasn't like that, Stefan. Roland worries for nothing."

Stefan stood. "I believe you are right, but be more careful, nonetheless."

"I will." She stood too, and Stefan walked toward the door.

Good night, Sister.

She smiled. *Good night, Brother.*

Stefan left the room, and Roanna returned to bed. Nerves twisted her stomach in knots. Nerves over Queen Frieda and King Neville in Lox. Nerves over Roland's overprotectiveness. Nerves over her strange, mind bending anomaly, as well as the rebels within the country who still wished to put an end to her existence.

She wished she understood the anomaly better. Knew where it had come from and why. But why did any of the Rejected have the anomalies they were born possessing? What would happen if the rebels succeeded in their mission?

Where did these awful anomalies come from? The question was more like a prayer. A plea for answers. She may have found the answers to the questions raised by her visit to the dungeon all those months ago, but the answers had only raised new questions.

Her mind worked into the wee hours of the morning. At last, she fell asleep. Her family from Chester's Wake would be arriving soon for her engagement ball. She was anxious to see them.

9

Merry…

Merry sat in Queen Charlotte's office, tapping her foot. What had happened to the queen? She and the king had been absent at breakfast—as had Gregory. A servant had instructed Merry to wait in the queen's office, but she'd been sitting for close to half an hour alone.

The door opened, and she spun around. Instead of Queen Charlotte, Gregory stood in the doorway. His eyes were steely, and he wore pristinely pressed brown slacks with a tan colored shirt. He looked completely professional. Still, something wasn't quite right. She knew it by the way his dark brown hair was parted messily to the side, as if he'd run his hands through it multiple times.

Merry's stomach tightened. She stood quickly and hurried to him. "What's wrong?"

His nostrils flared when he looked at her. It was the same simmering hatred she'd felt fleetingly from him the night before. "Mother is with Father. I'm to escort you to her."

Why this should cause him such consternation, she did not know.

"Very well."

He waited for her to grab the files she'd left on the chair. As she approached him, she realized they were alone. She could apologize for what had happened between them and the hurt and embarrassment she may have caused him.

Instead, she said nothing.

They walked quickly through the palace. Servants scurried in the halls, carrying bundles and bags and other things. It seemed busier than usual. Hectic.

Merry wanted to ask what was happening, but she kept her questions to herself. Gregory was obviously not inclined to speak to her. They arrived at the king's offices. Merry had never been to this part of the palace. She clasped her hands together and tried to attract as little attention as possible.

Gregory led her into the room. The queen sat at a desk and glanced up at her. "Oh, thank goodness you're here." She waved Merry over. "You'll be a great help, my darling."

Merry glanced at Gregory. He looked between her and his mother, his eyes still angry but less so in the presence of Queen Charlotte. Maybe he'd thought the queen was treating Merry like she was a monster, and now he realized he was incorrect.

She tugged her arm gently from his grasp. "Thank you for escorting me," she muttered.

His scowl returned. He marched to the queen's side.

Merry hurried to Queen Charlotte. "How can I help?"

"The Dawsons are throwing Roanna and Ben an engagement ball. It will be in just under two weeks. While the king and I will be travelling there when the day arrives, we have determined it would be a wonderful opportunity for you to begin learning what you can from the nobility there, as far as the identity of rebels still in hiding."

Merry held her breath. Queen Charlotte intended for her to return to Dawson's Edge so soon?

"I'm willing to do whatever you need, Your Highness, but I'm afraid I don't understand." She swallowed her nerves, hoping she didn't waver on the outside the way she did on the inside.

"The nobility will be headed to the capital in droves." The queen looked at paperwork spread across the desk. "It will be the perfect time to speak with many of them. Gregory will go with you, of course. It is natural for him to travel to see his sister. We will stay in touch to make all of the necessary arrangements."

Merry dare not chance a look Gregory's way. Did he know this was what the queen had in mind? Maybe that was why he was so obviously angry.

"I'm at your disposal, Queen Charlotte."

The queen looked at her again. "I know you are, dear. You've been such a help already."

Merry curtsied slightly and took a deep breath. "If I may ask a question, Your Highness?"

Queen Charlotte seemed surprised, but she nodded.

"They'll never believe my loyalty, Your Highness. They know I've been offered asylum by your country and that you're searching for rebels. They'll see my duplicity."

"But your father is still imprisoned by the Dawsons. Your loyalty will always be to your family no matter what. Let them see that, and they will believe you. Tell them you want to free your family."

Merry drew back at Queen Charlotte's words. Did the queen suspect—did the queen know Merry's heart? Had Merry been so transparent?

That was a thought for another day. For now, she must focus. She considered the queen's idea. She had to admit it could work. But the queen couldn't be thinking straight if she was so easily swayed to send Merry back into enemy territory with the guise of wanting to break Papa from prison. That was absolutely what Merry wanted. It was madness for the queen to trust her so soon and so resolutely.

Against her better judgement, Merry nodded. "I will help you. Of course, I will help you. You must tell me what I should do."

Relief washed off Queen Charlotte in waves. "Bless you, Merry." She squeezed her hand one last time before releasing her. "Gregory," she said.

Gregory shifted at his mother's side, attentive but wary. The queen might trust Merry, but the prince did not.

"You will be travelling to Dawson's Edge as we discussed. Merry will be coming with you. You will be her escort, and her guardian, but you must be quiet about it all. Not even the Dawsons are to know she has returned. It must appear as if she is working to free her father."

Gregory's frown could stretch from one end of the earth to the other. "Mother, I don't understand."

"We will set up the contacts." Queen Charlotte turned to her. "You will go under the guise of being in secret. You cannot stay at your family's estate, obviously. And certainly not at the palace. We will arrange everything for you. You will meet with Gregory regularly as he works with the Dawsons to uncover new information regarding the rebels." She regarded both of them as a whole. "This is acceptable to you?"

Merry's throat was filled with cotton. She tried to swallow, but her nerves would not wash away. Instead, she nodded.

Gregory's nostrils flared again. "Mother, I'm not sure this is the best way. Leave this to me. To the military intelligence."

Queen Charlotte's eyes flashed, and for a moment, Merry understood from where Gregory got his fierceness. "I will employ every trick I have up my sleeve to protect Roanna. Even you cannot argue with that plan."

Gregory kept his mother's gaze. Something passed between them. A quiet understanding, perhaps. He nodded once. "When?"

Queen Charlotte angled away, thinking. "It should be soon. Tomorrow, perhaps."

Gregory nodded. "Very well."

"Yes." Queen Charlotte began making notes. "You'll leave first thing in the morning. Take the airship."

The airship? Merry's eyes slid closed as butterflies erupted in her stomach. The idea of being suspended so high above the earth filled her with fear. She took a slow breath and willed her nerves to calm. She could do this. And she would. It might put her in exactly the right position to help Papa after all.

10

The palace was oddly quiet for the rest of the day. Queen Charlotte took meals in her office with Merry in a chair across her desk. The queen pumped her full of information: tips, instructions, specific bits of intelligence to go after. She arranged social outings for Merry, clandestine meetings at parties and operas. At one point, she revealed the Dawsons had received threats against Roanna's life. Queen Charlotte seemed calm over this information, but Merry guessed it was an act.

Who would have expected the prim and proper queen to be so advanced in intelligence and military matters?

But of course, Gregory was advanced in these areas. It must be a family trait.

They did not finish until well into the night. Queen Charlotte dismissed Merry, and she happily left the queen's offices for the solitude of her own chambers. The palace was dim, barely lit by pale lamps through the corridors and main entry. Merry started up the stairs as a guard headed down. She smiled at him pleasantly but continued on her way.

The guard stepped in front of her. She moved to

step out of his way, but he followed her movements. Frowning slightly, she looked up. "Pardon me. I didn't mean to tie you up."

The man stepped closer to her. Close enough for Merry to see the cold glint in his gray eyes. His hair was cut short on his scalp, and his muscles bulged beneath his uniform. "If you think you're fooling anyone, you're wrong. You don't belong here. The queen will see that soon enough."

Merry's heart doubled in speed. She straightened her shoulders and tried to shove her way around him. "Excuse me, sir. I'm going to my room."

His thick hand wrapped around her upper arm. He tightened his grip. "You might be able to charm a few people, but you don't hold any sway over me, rebel." He spat the word like a curse.

Taking a deep breath, Merry willed herself to stay calm. He would let her go any moment, and she would be sure to tell the queen of his behavior first thing in the morning.

If he didn't let her go…

Before she could finish the thought, the guard yanked her forward. She collided with his broad chest and looked up at him before she could think differently. "You're no one here, understand? Not nobility. Worthless."

Worthless? The only one who was worthless was him. Merry had had enough of his bullying. She shoved her knee toward his groin. He groaned and bent forward but did not release her arm.

"You little witch," he ground out.

The look in his eyes put fear in Merry's heart for the first time. He was a royal guard. Surely, he didn't mean to harm her, a guest of the queen.

Suddenly, the guard was yanked away from her. It threw her off balance, and she slipped down several stairs. Her shins burned, but she ignored it, happy to be away. Scrambling to her feet, she glanced around to assess the situation.

"What's this, Gideon?"

Gregory stood over the guard named Gideon. Another guard pinned Gideon to the ground. The mystery guard's face was red with strain as Gideon struggled against him, but his lithe, lean muscles were able to hold the meatier guard down.

Gregory hunched down near Gideon's head. His face was morphed with disbelief and barely controlled anger. "What do you think you're doing, Gideon?" He spit out the words with slow control.

"She's a traitor. You said so yourself!" Gideon managed to shrug out of the other guard's grip. He shot a glare at his comrade but remained free. "I was just letting her know not to try anything stupid under my watch."

"If you're ever caught exhibiting such behavior again, I assure you, your talents in the royal guard will no longer be necessary. I won't tolerate that kind of indecency from my men." Gregory stood to his full height. "Get up."

Gideon and the other guard rose.

"Apologize to the queen's guest."

Gideon's face reddened. Merry's own face grew hot. She didn't want his apology. She certainly didn't need it. But what other choice did she have but to stand there like a frightened doe? The men were blocking her path to her room.

She took a deep breath and steeled herself to meet Gideon's eyes. He looked to her with enough hatred to power a war bot. "My apologies."

Gregory sighed. "I suspect you can do better than that."

Gideon's nostrils flared, but a moment later his expression neutralized. "Please forgive me, my lady."

Eager to get this over with and return to her own room, Merry nodded once.

"Return to your post."

Gideon obeyed Gregory's command without another glance her way, but his shoulders did not lose their knots, and his movements were stiff with anger.

Merry stood still not a moment longer. She moved to continue her climb up the stairs without looking at Gregory. She had not missed Gideon's words. *She's a traitor. You said so yourself.*

He'd made it abundantly clear what he thought of her.

"Escort her, Wesley. Make sure no one else bothers her."

Merry stumbled at his words. For a split second, she allowed herself to look his way. He didn't hold the same hatred in his eyes that she'd seen that morning, though she certainly didn't see warmth there either.

"I'm quite capable."

The guard named Wesley grinned. "Quite. We saw how you kneed Gideon. Trust me. I wouldn't want to cross you in the dark, my lady."

Gregory didn't share Wesley's smile. "It's for your own safety." He turned away as if that settled it all.

Wesley held out his arm to Merry as though he was a gentleman and she still a noblewoman.

Merry considered refusing. Demanding Gregory not treat her so rudely.

Instead, she took Wesley's arm. She was a traitor,

after all. And she just might betray Gregory again if circumstances called for it. She wouldn't add insult to his injury.

"Thank you for your help," she said to no one in particular.

"I am always happy to help a lady," Wesley replied.

They moved past Gregory. Wesley took her to the guest wing then walked her to her door. "Good evening, Lady Merry. We will see you early on the morn."

Her heart had calmed, and she gave him a truly grateful smile. "You will be going to Dawson's Edge, then?"

"I will, my lady." He bowed his head slightly. "Good night."

"Good night."

He left her then, and she slipped inside her room. Fraja was there. She was finishing packing Merry's things. Merry's heart squeezed.

"I'm sorry, Fraja. You had just unpacked all of this."

Fraja shrugged her shoulders as if they carried a heavy load. "We go home. This makes me glad for you."

Home. Or at least, her home country. But she wasn't exactly welcome there. Queen Charlotte even said her presence would be kept from the royal family. That didn't seem at all safe, but what choice did she have?

"Thank you, all the same."

Fraja moved to give her a tight hug. "You are welcome, all the same. Now, let us get you ready for bed."

Merry nodded and obeyed Fraja's commands. Tomorrow she would fly with Gregory and his people on an air ship. She did not look forward to the prospect.

11

Merry was awakened by Fraja early. Her maid dressed Merry in disguise with a smart top hat, a silky scarf, and a pair of dark, round glasses, then herded her from her rooms and toward the auto waiting out front. She and Fraja sat alone in the back of the small, black vehicle. They were driven down the cobbled streets of Chester's Wake toward the air station, which took less than ten minutes.

"Can you see it?" Fraja stretched her neck to peer around buildings.

"Not yet." Merry didn't want to see it. The thought of the airship made her stomach twist in knots. She purposefully kept her eyes downcast as servants came to unload her luggage and take it to the airship. She followed behind an excited Fraja—which was amusing all its own—as the small group made its way to the backside of a metal building.

Once it was impossible to ignore any longer, Merry looked up. The ship took her breath away. The cabin was larger than she'd expected. Fully enclosed, with small, round windows. Chains connected it to the bulbous material above. The material was already inflated with flaming hot air, and it bobbed a few feet off the ground.

She allowed herself a moment to glance around for Gregory. He was nowhere in sight.

Pressing her eyes closed, she sighed. She should stop thinking about him. Stop pining for him as if he might suddenly forget her crimes and forgive her. Her choices had been made. Papa came first. The rest of her family came first. Gregory was nothing to her.

She stepped toward the airship with her chin held high, ignoring the small place in her heart that whispered *liar*.

Cabin chairs lined the inside of the ship, in rows of two deep. One window seat, one aisle seat. The seats were filled with men and women.

Merry frowned. What sort of secret mission was no secret at all?

But then she recalled how Gregory would be going to the Dawsonian palace for an engagement ball. This was his entourage. Only Merry herself was a secret. She would attend outings, but only those people she was scheduled to meet would truly know her identity.

The thought twisted her stomach in knots all over again. Was she afraid? Or thrilled? It was hard to say.

Wesley, the lean guard from the night before, stepped to her side. "Follow me to your seats, please." He led her and Fraja past the large group of travelers to a door in the back. Inside were four seats.

"This is to help keep your presence from being made known," Wesley explained.

Merry nodded. "Thank you."

Wesley bowed. "I will return shortly to ride with you." He slipped out quietly.

"Would you sit by the window?" Fraja pointed to

the seats. "Or the aisle?"

Merry considered. Which would be least frightening? "The aisle," she decided.

Fraja nodded and scooted into the seat next to the window.

Merry glanced around one last time as if there were some secret way out. A free pass for ignoring her fear a little while longer.

If only such passes existed. She would have used hers long ago.

She adjusted herself in the seat then took a few moments to study her surroundings. With interest she noted a window on the wall viewing the rest of the passengers. Only it wasn't a regular window. It appeared to be a mirror. This one allowed her to see those on the other side. She recognized a few of the soldiers she'd seen with Gregory around the palace the last few days. With disgust, she noted Gideon among them, but he hadn't seen her as of yet. She also spotted Wesley moving among the group.

Toward the back of the airship, she spotted Duchess Higgins and her daughter, Wendy. What place did they have on an entourage to Dawson's Edge? Perhaps they were considered close allies of the royal family, the way she and her family had been to the Dawsons. For the Hamiltons' sake she hoped Wendy's family was more loyal.

As Merry turned from the duchess and her daughter, she caught Gregory's silhouette from the corner of her eye. She paused long enough to see him smile at Wendy and bend to speak with her, although he couldn't sit beside her. The duchess held that spot.

Merry turned away smoothly, practiced at hiding her action and intentions. But from whom was she hiding? It was only herself and Fraja.

After several moments, the passengers settled into seats. Energy rumbled in the air tank above them, and Merry tensed. She took her seat. The airship was preparing for flight. She gripped the small bag she held in her lap. Taking a deep breath, she pressed her eyes closed and counted to five. It would be a short flight, barely over an hour. She could do this. Would do this. It would help Papa. Once she was in touch with others in the rebel cause, she could tell them what she knew in order to either aid in Papa's escape from the dungeon at the palace or construct a plan to free him.

It was her fault Papa had ended up imprisoned in the first place. If she hadn't been so enamored with Gregory—so eager to make acquaintance with his sister, Roanna—she wouldn't have invited the enemy right into their home. Urged Papa to trust them.

The door opened and Wesley entered once again. He took the seat across from her.

"Your knuckles are white."

Merry frowned. "Pardon?"

He smiled. "Are you scared to fly?"

She swallowed around her fear and nodded. "This is my first time."

"You might find you like it. Try to relax. Also, it helps to sit by the window."

She frowned, but he held up a hand as if to stop her doubts.

"It sounds counterintuitive, but it's true. Being able to see out the window can help alleviate some of the anxiety." He shrugged. "It's just a piece of advice. You can't help your fears, I suppose."

Merry took a shuddering breath. Sit by the window to alleviate anxiety? It did sound counterintuitive.

Still...

She glanced at Fraja. The maid stared at her with a slightly sad smile. "You wish to change seats?"

Fraja wanted to fly. Wanted to watch.

Merry chuckled. "No, Fraja. You stay there. I am going to try to keep my eyes closed for the entire flight no matter where I sit."

Fraja nodded as if this were of no consequence, but Merry could not ignore the slight sparkle in her nursemaid's eyes. It gave her a small measure of happiness to allow Fraja an obvious enjoyment.

Merry settled against the headrest. Her fingers were still gripped tightly to her bag, but her nerves had settled at least minimally.

12

Gregory…

Anger burned through him. Anger at the rebels who threatened his sister. Anger at his parents for never realizing they had the wrong princess.

What sort of parents didn't know an imposter when they saw one?

He grunted at the thought.

He'd been well enough fooled by an imposter. She sat somewhere on this airship right now.

He looked for her again, as he'd been doing since she arrived at the palace. His gaze landed briefly on the mirror on the back wall.

Speaking of anger, he was angry at Merry Stern for making a fool out of him. His only consolation was that few people knew of his foolishness. The consolation was very small, indeed.

Lastly, he was angry at Roanna.

Guilt burned through him. How could he be angry with her? She'd been wronged. Yet, he blamed her. She'd gone digging where things were better left buried. Insisting on answers where truth brought pain. Fighting for change when victory was unobtainable.

His shoulders tightened as he justified his anger.

She had forced their family to take up her fight, letting it be known she was, herself, an anomaly. What were they supposed to do when faced with such knowledge? How could they explain it to the people?

Wesley moved through the crowd and slipped inside the room at the back of the ship. The room where Merry sat.

Gregory's interests were drawn away. His nostrils flared with self-loathing. How could he wonder about her? Watch for her? Wish so desperately to speak to her? She was a traitor, a rebel, a liar. She was despicable, worthless, untrustworthy.

His eyes slid closed, and he worked to steady his heartrate.

She was beautiful. Enchanting. Beguiling.

Was it any wonder she made such a spectacular rebel? When he'd seen Gideon attacking her the night before it'd taken everything inside him to hold back his anger. He wouldn't—couldn't—let Merry Stern see how much she affected him. But even the memory of it seared his mind.

To keep his restless nerves from driving him insane, he shot from his seat and moved down the aisle. He strode to the cabin and knocked.

The door cracked open before the steward opened the door fully. "My prince, how can we help you?"

Gregory pushed inside. "What's the estimated time of arrival?"

"One hour, twelve minutes, Your Highness."

"Thank you." He gave a curt nod and turned back to the main hold. Things would be hairy once they arrived in Dawson's Edge. He would need to get his entourage to the palace but manage to sneak Merry away. Mother had left that part of the plan up to his discretion.

The problem he faced was that the Sterns were a well-known family in Dawson's Edge. More now than ever. Those at the air station were sure to recognize her. He'd stayed awake most of the night devising plans and recording his thoughts on the matter. It hadn't helped his efficiency that his thoughts constantly strayed toward her.

Mother didn't know of his short-lived relationship with Merry. If Mother had known, she wouldn't have asked him to include her in anything.

He paused and frowned.

Untrue. She would expect Gregory to put aside any feelings in order to bring Roanna to safety. He knew this because it was exactly what he'd expect anyone else to do.

With resolve, he marched to the back room where Merry rode with her maid and Wesley. He kept his eyes on Wesley and leaned close to his ear. "Bring Lady Stern to the conference room."

Wesley nodded and Gregory moved on. He would use the next few moments to compose himself. He was still angry with her. Furious with her. Disgusted by her. But he didn't want to be alone with her.

He needed to brief her on the specifics of the mission, though he had to admit she was good at dealing with things spur of the moment. He could probably keep her in the dark, and she would do just as splendidly at duping the rebels.

She'd done it to him easily enough.

A few moments later, a soft knock sounded at the door, and at his beckoning, Wesley entered with Merry. Her face was pale, her eyes wide. She was terrified of flying, and now he'd asked her to leave the safety of her seat restraint. He remembered the conversation from all those weeks ago very well. She'd wished him well on his flight, her eyes glittering like jewels.

He did not address her fear, even if he minimally admitted to himself that he felt sorry for her. "At the air station, I will lead you to the auto that will take you to the safe house. I will meet you there later this evening."

She nodded. They stared at each other awkwardly.

At last, Wesley cleared his throat. "Is that all, Your Highness?"

"Yes, thank you." Gregory silently cursed himself for not being ready to speak further. What was wrong with him?

Wesley took Merry's elbow and turned her toward the door. Before she reached it, she looked to him one last time. Gregory's heart sped. Her eyes held questions. Pain and questions. Confusion and questions.

Good. Let her wonder. Once they figured out who was behind this rebel mess, he would be done with her and for good this time.

13

Gregory returned to his seat and finished the rest of the flight in silence. Lady Wendy and her mother, the duchess, tried to speak with him a handful of times. He gave them tightlipped smiles, but they did not catch on to his mood. Now, as they disembarked, Lady Wendy approached again.

"Your Highness, I'm quite excited to see the palace. I was hoping we might go on a tour of the kingdom while we're here."

Lady Wendy was a quiet girl, he'd learned. He liked her. Had thought he liked her quite well until Mother had introduced the idea of bringing Merry Stern to the palace. After that, all thoughts of Lady Wendy had fled.

Regardless, in those few weeks, he had learned that Wendy was timid. A tour of the kingdom wouldn't be her idea. It was almost certainly the duchess who suggested it.

"That might be a possibility." He didn't slow his step. "We may have extra time. I will have to let you know."

Lady Wendy's face reddened. "Of course, Your Highness."

He nodded curtly. "If you'll excuse me." He would have to decide about Wendy soon. She didn't deserve to feel hope where there was none.

Though, it seemed he had already made up his mind then.

He veered away from her and strode toward the spot where Wesley stood now with a disguised Merry. Gideon stood several paces away. Gregory caught his attention and gestured for him to join them.

Once he'd congregated them near the black auto parked away from the group, he spoke quickly. "Wesley, you'll travel with Lady—Miss Stern to the safe house. I will come tonight, as planned."

No one blinked at his slight toward Merry. Not even Merry herself.

The jab was much less satisfactory when she did not take the bait. Why couldn't she be offended like any normal person would be?

Wesley nodded. "Of course, Your Highness." He opened the auto door and let Merry inside. Then, he climbed in himself. Gregory and Gideon headed back toward the main group. He had originally intended to send Gideon with Merry, but after last night's spectacle on the stairs, he would not be making that mistake.

"How are we to trust her?" Gideon spat out as they walked.

Gregory balled his fists. "You will make this an issue, Gideon?" Again, he remembered how he felt seeing her in danger.

Gideon grunted, though he didn't argue.

But Gregory couldn't let himself be vulnerable where she was concerned. Not only had Mother begged him to trust her, but he also found himself wanting to trust her, as foolish as it was.

So far, she had done nothing to earn his trust. He would give her the chance, perhaps, but she wasn't there yet. He must be wary.

"We will follow the queen's orders, Gideon." He left it at that as they joined the rest of the entourage and loaded into white autos supplied by the Dawson family. They were whisked toward the palace, and Gregory's mind turned to Roanna. She was an intelligent person. She and Ben had singlehandedly turned two kingdoms on their heads. It could be that she would lend great understanding to their search for rebels.

As the autos drove toward the gates of the Dawsonian palace, Gregory settled his mind. He would find answers here.

The drive took what felt like an eternity, but they had soon reached the Dawson family castle. Gregory climbed from the auto with purpose, Gideon at his side. Queen Katherine met him at the palace entrance, Ben at her side. Ben's face showed he was frustrated over something. His face was unshaven, and his hair combed messily to the side.

Gregory greeted the queen then turned to Ben. "How are you?" He knew Ben would hold nothing back. If something was wrong, he would tell Gregory. Which was more than he could say of the Dawsons.

The rest of the entourage was pouring into the palace entryway, and Queen Katherine had begun to frown. "Let us talk as we walk, shall we?" She waved at a few of the servants who stepped toward the guests, and Katherine ushered them toward the king's offices.

"There is question as to whether the engagement ball should go on as planned," Ben said.

Gregory frowned. "Why?"

"Let us talk with the king," Katherine interjected.

Soon, they arrived at the king's offices. They were shown right in.

King Dawson stood near his desk, red faced and wide eyed, screaming at one of his aids. The aid rushed from the room to do whatever the king had bid him.

Roland Dawson sat in an armchair to the side of the king's desk. He held a report of some type in his hands, and he was scouring it intently.

"King Dawson," Gregory said. "My parents send their greetings and well wishes. They look forward to arriving next week."

Dawson nodded, as if the pleasantries were a minor inconvenience. Right now, Gregory leaned toward agreeance.

"Yes, well, we may have no need for their arrival." King Dawson stood beside his desk, glaring at Ben. "Perhaps your parents should have kept the Loxian prince away from the princess over the years. Perhaps then they wouldn't continuously find themselves in compromising positions!" His voice rose with each statement.

Ben kept his focus on Gregory, and Gregory knew Ben well enough to understand that the young prince was imploring him to see the rabid behavior of the king as nothing more than blame throwing.

Gregory did recognize the behavior, but what compromising position had Ben and Roanna found themselves in this time? And why would it have the king of Dawson's Edge in such an uproar?

"The king speaks truth." Roland Dawson had set his report down, but he still lounged in the chair. "I caught them myself last night in the palace gardens.

The boy has no morals."

Ben's nostrils flared and again his look told Gregory they were blowing things out of proportion. "Roanna and I are engaged to be married," he said flatly. "And the few moments we spent together in the garden were hardly cause for any type of postponement."

Gregory pushed away any thought of what Roanna and Ben might have been doing in the palace gardens. "Can we speak plainly? I have no idea what you're talking about."

King Dawson smacked the desk. "The Loxians have suggested we postpone the ball and return the prince home for a time."

Gregory frowned. All of this because Roanna and Ben were caught alone together? How had Roanna put up with these shenanigans for all these weeks? He shifted awkwardly, afraid Roland would launch into a detailed explanation of his sister's love life.

"I imagine it will all be worked out to everyone's satisfaction. I will contact my parents immediately. Perhaps they can help."

The king seemed appeased at this suggestion, and Gregory quickly began questioning him on their intelligence regarding the rebellion. King Dawson launched into a new diatribe, and Gregory gladly left the original subject behind.

When at last the meeting had ended for the afternoon, Gregory begged off on eating supper with the family. He said he needed time to clear his mind and think. He and his guard, Gideon, would take a drive. He could use the time to think over all he'd learned and to digest the new information.

And then it would be time to see Merry.

"I would like to see Roanna," he said to Ben as they left the king's office.

"I want you to know there was nothing inappropriate going on, despite what the Dawsons are saying."

Gregory gave him a sidelong glance. "Please do not expound. I really don't care to know."

Ben frowned, but he seemed relieved to hear it.

"Roanna?" Gregory reminded him.

Ben sighed. "She is most likely in the palace gardens. I'll take you to her." Ben moved them through the palace with ease, as if it were his own home. It was a strange thought that this was where Roanna lived now. He did not think of her as belonging to the Dawson family, yet she did.

Just as Ben had predicted, Roanna worked with her hands in a small patch of dirt in a small courtyard. Down on her hands and knees, she glanced up as they approached. Her face lit with a smile, and she leapt to her feet.

"Gregory!" She ran toward him and threw her arms around his neck.

For once in the last few weeks, everything felt right again. He felt whole.

He returned the hug. "I've missed you." The words came out without him meaning for them to, but they were true all the same.

She pulled out of his arms. "I've missed you, too. I did not expect you today."

"Mother sent me early. She heard about the threats you've received, and she wanted further investigation into the matter."

Roanna chuckled. "Of course, she did. I'm so glad you're here."

Gregory glanced to the dirt. "What are you working on?"

"Planting vegetables. The Dawsons think it's absurd, but I enjoy it so much." She retrieved a towel from the nearby bench then wiped her hands. "What sort of investigation will you be doing this time?"

Gregory suddenly regretted his need to go see Merry with an update. He wanted to stay here with Roanna as long as he could. He had missed her more than he realized. How silly it had been to be angry at her.

"Mother has set up meetings with a few nobles. People she thinks might have information about the rebellion, even if they're not aware they have the information." He glanced around. "She would rather keep it quiet, though."

"That sounds tedious." She grinned, but her eyes didn't seem as bright. "I wanted to tell you about something else, though." She wiped her hands on the towel again, as if she couldn't figure out what else to do with them.

"Tell me," he prodded.

She launched into a tale of Dr. Presnell, the doctor who attended her birth. Gregory let her finish her story, but he shook his head.

"We've explored the possibilities of Dr. Presnell's involvement. He likely brought you to Chester's Wake, but it is almost certain he had help in taking the other baby away. He did not leave the palace that night." He sighed, thinking of the sibling he had out in the world. Everyone assumed it was a girl, but he had considered that it might not be. What if Dr. Presnell had lied about that and whisked a baby boy away before anyone saw it for themselves?

He'd kept that theory to himself.

Roanna seemed surprised but relieved to hear they had thought of this. "Have you spoken to him?"

"Not personally, but others have. They say he is senile."

Roanna nodded. "Yes, I thought it myself."

He raised his eyebrows. "You've spoken to him?"

"Once, yes." Red colored her cheeks, and she glanced at Ben.

Gregory looked between the two of them. They were so in tune, almost as if they were a single person instead of two. What must it be like to have such a relationship? "You two really have gotten yourselves into a whole lot of interesting situations, haven't you?"

Ben scratched his neck. "You could say that."

"Well," Gregory said. "I will look into it further if I can. For now, I need to head out."

"You're not staying for supper?" Roanna frowned, her eyebrows lowered.

"I have some things to take care of for Mother."

Roanna nodded as if she understood this was information that was to be kept quiet. "Tomorrow there is an opera. We'll be attending. You should come as well."

Gregory considered it. People who could help their cause would likely be there. "That's a good idea. I'll make plans to attend."

He said his good-byes and hugged Roanna one last time. Leaving her behind was harder than he would have imagined.

14

The safe house was less than a fifteen-minute drive from the palace. It was situated east of the castle, nestled in a cul-de-sac of townhomes in the heart of the capital city.

Gregory instructed Gideon to stand guard outside. Trees grew at each corner of the house, giving privacy between neighbors, however slight. They would need to keep things inconspicuous, which he would do good to remember. He didn't need questions as to why he was regularly visiting a townhome in the city.

Wesley welcomed him. An entryway led straight to a stairwell. To the left was a small dining area, and to the right a sitting room. Merry and Fraja sat on a sofa. Their conversation stopped, and all eyes turned to him.

"Good evening," he said.

"My Lord," Wesley said easily. He bowed

Gregory nodded once at his faithful guard. "Gideon patrols outside. I would have you join him."

Wesley bowed again. "Of course." He left the room quietly, leaving behind Merry and the maid.

Unease crept through him. He didn't want to speak with Merry privately, but for the maid's own safety it was best if she knew nothing. Taking a deep breath, he straightened his shoulders.

"Please, madam, give us a space alone."

The old woman hesitated for a moment but relented to the back of the house without argument.

Merry watched him anxiously, not cowering in fear. She seemed eager to know what he knew. Facing conflict head on seemed to be her way.

He shoved aside the admiration that came with the thought. He couldn't let himself become too comfortable with her, although he felt less anger after having spent time with Roanna earlier in the day.

"You've been able to settle in, I trust?"

Merry stood and nodded. "The townhome is comfortable, and Wesley was quite adept at setting up the Messenger. I have already notified the queen of my safe arrival."

"Good."

He stood awkwardly for a moment when she gestured toward the dining room. "We were going to eat. You will join us?"

Would he?

He ignored the offer and instead nodded to the sofa. "Please sit with me. I have ideas that I hope you will be able to use."

She followed his instruction without question. They sat inches apart on the small sofa, and he immediately realized his mistake. He could not concentrate sitting beside her this way. He should have stayed standing, separated by several feet. In fact, he should have kept Wesley inside.

He wouldn't be intimidated. He stood again and paced. "While the Dawsons seem oblivious to the possibility, it appears obvious to me that there must be rebels within the palace. Roanna received a threat placed inside her rooms, which begs the question, how might rebels have access to such an intimate location?"

She nodded, seemingly catching on to his line of thought. "You want me to see what I can find."

"Exactly."

She bit her lip and looked away. Thinking?

He stared at her lips. He'd noticed her nervous habit a time or two over the last few days since they'd been reunited. She hadn't been so nervous when they'd met in the past.

"Please," he finally said, unable to stand the silence. "What are you thinking?"

"The Van Hoosiers are an eastern coast family with a large estate. They're a huge family. The Earl has six brothers, and between them all, there are a dozen sons. Three of them went into the military, last I knew. If any of them are stationed at the palace, it would be an easy way to keep an informant right in the throw of things."

"Are the Van Hoosiers part of the rebellion?"

She shook her head. "That is something I don't know. But the Earl's youngest daughter is a bit of a—" she paused. "Well," she finally went on. "She's known for her loose tongue. If you can get me in the same room with her, I am certain I can find useful information."

Gregory processed her words. She knew so much about this family. How? "You're acquainted with the Van Hoosiers?"

She paused a moment too long, and her gaze darted away. "Only slightly, but if we learn they are, indeed, involved, I have no doubt I would be welcomed by them."

A vague answer, but he would focus on the more important task of finding useful information. "I'll find out all I can as quickly as I can and set up something."

They stared at each other a moment more. A memory of a kiss along the river in Chester's Wake filled his mind. He quickly looked away. "It's settled then."

Merry didn't speak.

He cleared his throat. No one had ever made him so uncomfortable. Put him so on edge. Made his heart beat so hard.

"You're comfortable with Wesley staying here?"

She frowned slightly. "Certainly. He's a perfect gentleman. It's doubtful he's needed, though, if no one knows I'm here."

Gregory's defenses rose instantly. Why was she so eager to get rid of the guard?

"Wesley will stay. You're certain you can learn more from this youngest Van Hoosier girl?"

Now a small smile turned her lips up in a sly smile. "If you but meet her, you will see exactly why I'm so confident. Hattie can't stop her mouth from running."

"It seems people would be tighter lipped around her then."

Merry shook her head. She wore her blonde hair down, and it swayed softly around her shoulders. "Hattie has this way about her." Her eyes took on a faraway, dazzled look. "People trust her. She makes them want to open up to her. It's the most bizarre thing."

Gregory stared at Merry, unable to look away. Yes, he could imagine such a girl.

"Gregory?" Her soft tone awakened him to his

staring.

He cleared his throat again and resumed pacing. "That's all for tonight. We can talk more in the morning."

She stood. "Have you eaten, then?"

"No."

She didn't invite him again to stay, but the implication hung in the air.

Their gazes locked, and he knew without a doubt that staying here would be a mistake. "I need to return to the palace. I'll send word when I've made solid plans." He strode out the door without giving her the chance to reply.

He would allow her the opportunity to rebuild some trust, but he wouldn't allow her to make a fool of him again.

15

Merry…

Merry helped Fraja clean up the dinner dishes—something Fraja protested harshly, but Merry insisted. She wasn't noble anymore, and Fraja wasn't being paid anything to serve her. Wesley had gone out to patrol around the cul-de-sac before anyone went to sleep for the night. He would be bedding down in the sitting room of the townhome while Merry and Fraja shared the bed in the one bedroom.

She'd managed to watch Gregory leave and then get through all the supper meal with her dignity intact. But inside, she was shaking. Gregory hadn't even questioned her about the Van Hoosier connection. Hadn't thought it strange that she gravitated to this family when surely there were other noble families with members in the military or who worked in the palace.

However, Joffrey Van Hoosier was her mother's uncle. She would be welcomed there, and while she had no certain knowledge they were involved in the rebellion, it was almost assured that they knew something about it on some level. The fact that they wouldn't turn her in to the Dawson family also led her toward pursuing them first. They would want to help her exonerate Papa. They would be on her side.

A tiny prick of guilt pinched at her heart. Perhaps she was deceiving Gregory. Freeing Papa was her main wish, but still, she didn't wish to hurt Gregory in the process.

She shook off her guilt and readied for bed. She wasn't deceiving him. The Van Hoosiers would likely offer insight into the rebel cause. That was what Gregory was looking for.

A door closed and Merry figured it was Wesley coming in from watch. A few moments later, Fraja returned to their small, shared room, and they were quickly tucked into bed for the night. Gregory didn't say how long it would take him to make arrangements. She would have to be ready at a moment's notice.

The night passed slowly. Merry tossed and turned, but she did manage to get a few hours of accumulated sleep. As soon as the first rays of the morning's light peeked through the window, she rose and dressed. She wouldn't leave her room until Fraja did, in case Wesley still slept or was indecent, but she needn't worry because Fraja awoke as she was dressing.

A few minutes later, Merry was in the kitchen. Fraja prepared a simple breakfast of eggs and toast. Wesley was already outside, making his rounds. Again, Merry couldn't imagine who would be looking for her here, but she supposed it was better to be safe than sorry.

Just as Wesley came inside to eat breakfast, the purr of an auto rumbled in the air. Wesley remained inside despite the sound, meaning he was expecting this visitor. It was surely Gregory. They must be communicating via Messenger.

Merry's heart sped, but she remained seated and took another bite of toast as if she hadn't a care in the world. What would he have to say today?

A sharp rat-a-tat sounded, and Wesley opened the door.

Gregory stepped inside, leaving Gideon on the porch. Gideon threw her an icy glare as the door closed behind the prince, sealing the guard outside.

Merry quickly looked to Gregory, attempting to ignore the unease that crept inside her at the hatred in Gideon's eyes.

"Mother has set up a rendezvous with an ambassador from Bella de St. Paul's home country." Gregory's voice held no warmth, no greeting of fondness.

"Jakbar?" Merry asked. She hadn't learned much about the countries across the ocean, but she knew enough about Princess Bella to give her a small cache of knowledge.

Gregory nodded once. "The meeting takes place tonight at the opera."

Merry frowned slightly. The opera was such a public place. So open. How would they keep her hidden there?

Gregory seemed to sense her thoughts. "It's a masquerade."

"I have no costume to wear."

"Mother has commissioned a seamstress to come this morning. She should be arriving soon."

Merry couldn't imagine a dressmaker who worked so quickly, but she did not question him further on it. Instead, her mind went toward the ambassador. "Can you share any information about the ambassador? I have no connection with him. How do I know I can trust him, and why would he trust me?"

At least with her own countrymen she might have some pull, but a stranger wasn't likely to offer up pertinent information.

"Hakeem Hidalgo is his name." Gregory paused and looked around. Fraja had left them, and Wesley had slipped outside with Gideon.

"I've never met him," Merry said.

Gregory frowned slightly and shifted.

Unease?

Merry wasn't sure why he would be so suddenly uncomfortable.

"We decided to contact him based on information you provided some months ago."

"Me?" Merry considered what she may have said that could have prompted this. "I told you about the princess's request for divorce."

He nodded slightly. "If Jakbar has fallen out of good grace with the royal family and considered joining the rebellion, there may be information there to glean. In this instance, Ambassador Hidalgo might speak with you."

Merry wanted to know more—how had Queen Charlotte set this up? What was she supposed to ask?

But she wouldn't press him further. Merry knew how to make conversation. How to get people to open up. She would start with that and move forward.

"Very well. I'll be prepared for the seamstress."

He shifted again before bowing slightly. "I'll not accompany you tonight, but I'll be at the opera in case you should need me. Wesley will have everything else you need."

"Very well."

Silence stretched between them.

"Would you like to stay for breakfast?"

He glanced toward the table where food still sat freshly prepared. "No, thank you. Have Wesley contact me if you should think of anything you need."

With that he turned and left the room.

Merry stared after him only a moment before resuming her breakfast. If the seamstress was coming, she needed to be ready. Besides that, she needed to recall everything she knew about Jakbar and Princess Bella. She'd had little contact with Prince Stefan of Dawson's Edge or his wife, Princess Bella, over the years. He was ten years her senior, and she'd not spoken to him since well before he married the princess.

Still, she remembered the celebration well. Jakbar had transported elephants, monkeys, and goats to Dawson's Edge. The procession down the streets of the capital city had gone on for hours. Dancers, acrobats, and other performers kept everyone entertained and cheering—including Merry.

She smiled. What fun that had been. She hadn't known anything of Papa's involvement in any rebellion back then, not really. She hadn't needed to know until she was seventeen, and Papa asked her to help. She was good at making new friends, he'd said, and he wanted her to befriend a noble's daughter in order to spend more time with her family and learn where their loyalties lay.

Merry's stomach turned. She dropped the toast onto her plate. Papa had asked that of her before she had even reached her adult years. Why had she never realized before just how unfair of him that had been?

She did not like this train of thought, so she stood to clean her place. Fraja returned a few minutes later, and several minutes passed until Wesley returned from outside and the purr of the engine restarted.

Merry left the dining room and climbed the stairs to her bedroom to await the seamstress's arrival.

16

The seamstress arrived at exactly ten o'clock. She wore her hair wrapped in a colorful kerchief, and she wore a billowing blouse and full skirts that rustled when she walked. Merry had never seen the woman before, which was by design, she was sure.

"You are the lady of the house?" The woman eyed Merry as if taking mental calculations.

Gregory must not have given a name.

"I am."

"Very good." A slow smile broke across the woman's face. "It will be good to dress you. Much like dressing a doll."

No one had ever said such a thing to Merry. She offered a tentative smile. This seamstress seemed friendly and genuine. She needn't be on her guard so strongly.

The woman went to work, and a few moments later, they got started. Merry stood on a small platform the woman had constructed from pieces carried in a large bag. Her arms outstretched, she waited while the woman measured her chest, waist, hips, shoulders, and height.

"Wait here," the woman said. "I will return

shortly."

She hurried outside. A few minutes later, she returned with Wesley in tow carrying a large garment bag. Wesley did not glance her way, which was good because she was not properly dressed.

Once he had gone, the seamstress opened the bag and began laying out dress choices. "There are four to choose from. I fix any of them to fit you."

Merry inspected her choices. The first gown was deep purple and made of satin. It had a high neck, long sleeves, and a billowing skirt that was shorter in the front and longer in the back. The next gown was blue taffeta, with a billowing skirt and plunging neckline. It came with a smart, tight fitting jacket with long sleeves and a high neck. The other two choices included a black gown with black lace and a red gown with a thick, black belt.

"I like the purple," she said. "However, it's a masquerade. Are there masks?"

The seamstress smiled again. "But of course, miss." She pulled them from the bag and laid them out. Merry's gaze moved immediately to a purple mask with teal feathers, which resembled a peacock.

"I'd like to try this one, please."

The seamstress helped her dress quickly. She pinned and poked and cut then stood back and inspected her work. "Perfection."

A small mirror had been set up in the corner of the room. Merry looked at it and her breath caught. While her family was noble, they lived a modest life. She had never owned anything quite so fine.

"Yes," she said. "This is the one I would like."

The seamstress nodded her approval then helped her out of the dress so she could finish the alterations.

Merry left the woman to work in peace. She moved to the table in the dining area so she could study what she knew of Jakbar and the ambassador in preparations for the night. Jakbar had two seasons—summer and winter. It was either frigidly cold or sweltering hot on any given day. Princess Bella de St. Paul had enjoyed her transition to Dawson's Edge immensely because they often saw four full seasons.

But things weren't always as they seemed. Bella de St. Paul was unhappy here in Dawson's Edge. Merry frowned. What would make her unhappy?

Moving from her seat, she paced the small dining area. Prince Stefan—King Dawson's son—seemed like a kind enough man. Merry had rarely been in the same room with him, let alone spoken to him, though. Did he treat Bella unkindly? Was she simply homesick? Were there certain truces left unfulfilled upon her marriage?

Those were questions Merry did not have the answers to. Perhaps Gregory would know. She would be sure to ask him the next time she spoke with him.

For tonight, she would focus on Jakbar's involvement with the rebellion. Papa had once said that if they could get full commitment from the emperor, they would have enough manpower to overthrow the Dawsons. This indicated the commitment had never been fully realized. Another question without an answer.

A few hours passed, and the seamstress announced the dress was ready. As she predicted, the gown fit Merry to perfection. The seamstress left and Merry prepared for the opera. Fraja helped her use a heated rod to curl her hair. Then they pinned it into tight spirals around the crown of her head. Merry stepped into the stunning purple gown, and they placed the feathered mask on her face.

Merry stared at her reflection in the mirror. No one would suspect it was her. Never had she worn something so fine. Her reflection was stunning. She could certainly get used to this type of finery.

A pang wormed its way through her. What was to become of her? When all was said and done, if she failed in freeing Papa, what would happen to her? She would likely never wear anything so beautiful again. She would need to find somewhere to live. A way to sustain herself. What profession could she possibly apply herself to?

The knot in her stomach tightened, and she pressed her eyes closed. This was too much to consider, and she had no help. Her only friend in the world was Fraja. And there was Wesley, too, she supposed. At least he was kind to her. Gregory resented her, and Gideon hated her.

Merry had no one else with whom to speak. How she longed for true companionship.

She gave herself another moment to wallow in her misery. Then she straightened her shoulders and took a deep breath. She needed to meet Wesley downstairs. Her own feelings could be put away until later.

17

Merry stepped to the landing at the top of the stairs.

Wesley stood at the bottom. He looked up at her as if seeing an angel of light. A grin broke across his face. "I am not sure that every man at the opera will not wish to tell you their secrets tonight."

Merry was glad for the mask to hide her embarrassment. "Clever as you may think you are, you are likely wrong."

He shook his head. "I am never wrong."

She relented and gave him a smile. "You look dashing yourself." He wore a stunning navy suit, complete with Chester's Wake insignia signifying his place in the royal guard. Golden tassels hung off each shoulder.

"Yes, well, your charms won't work on me. I have no secrets to share." He winked, and Merry laughed.

Outside, an auto had been arranged for them. Wesley held the door for her then climbed in beside her as if he were her escort. But inside the auto, he was all business. "Once we're there, I will not congregate near you. The rebels we aren't working with must not realize you're working with Chester's Wake."

"Won't they see us arrive together?"

"We will drop you off at the entrance, and I will remain in the auto with the driver until he has parked. I will locate you once I make my way inside, and from there, I will keep watch over you."

Merry nodded her understanding. This would not be difficult. She had been to this opera house multiple times, and she had mingled with most of these people. Though they would not realize she was herself tonight, she would be perfectly comfortable around them.

They arrived with no fanfare. The auto pulled to the curb outside the opera house, and the driver let Merry out. She approached the doors with little attention and walked inside.

Low lights burned in lanterns around the entryway. It was dim here. Always so dim everywhere in Dawson's Edge. The hall walls were covered in elegant red drapes, and the floor was carpeted with plush red rugs.

People milled about, talking in loud voices. Laughter rang in the air as music played softly in the background, most likely coming from the auditorium. Merry glanced around. Many wore costumes, but not all. She recognized a few nobles from the western border near Lox. They stood at the ticket window. Merry fingered her own ticket, which Wesley had given her in the auto.

Another group of nobles congregated near the doors to the auditorium. These ones stuck close to the capitol, always. They were the king's lackeys.

The thought made Merry frown. Why did she call them his lackeys? It was Papa's term for them, but now that she considered it, she wasn't sure why he called them that.

Gregory had informed her that she would meet the ambassador inside the auditorium once the show had begun. She would be seated beside him, which was what he was expecting.

Now was not the time to mingle. Moving with purpose, she approached the doors to the auditorium, ticket in hand.

A man rammed into her, sloshing some beverage onto her gown. Merry gasped.

"My apologies, beautiful." The man hiccupped, and Merry's eyes widened. It was the prince of Dawson's Edge, and he was very obviously drunken. He did have the wits about him to offer her a handkerchief.

She took it and brushed away the liquid before it could stain. "Thank you," she mumbled. He would not recognize her voice, she knew, but she did not want anyone to overhear her. She had not been shy before Papa was caught as a traitor, and people would more than likely peg her.

She handed back the handkerchief, but the prince caught her hand. "What is your name, lovely? You're stunning, and I make it a point to spend time with stunning women."

Merry froze for a moment. The prince was married. Surely, he was ashamed to behave this way in public.

"Prince Stefan," a voice intervened.

Merry held her breath, taking pains to turn away quickly as Gregory approached. He was saving her, though she had no idea if he realized it. She did not wait to find out but made her way quickly to her seat without fully looking Gregory's way. No one yet sat in the seat beside hers, on either side. The Jakbar ambassador had not arrived.

Merry waited, nerves rushing through her. She breathed deeply, hoping to calm herself. The encounter with the prince was unexpected and disturbing. If that was how he behaved, she could full well understand why Princess Bella would want a divorce.

She closed her eyes and rubbed her forehead, willing away the tension.

"Good evening, my lady," a smooth, deep voice interrupted her thoughts. The slight accent gave him away, and she turned to him.

"Good evening, sir. How do you do?"

He smiled at her, dark curls falling around his black sparkling mask. "I do well. I am lucky to sit beside such a lovely lady."

"You flatter me, sir." She paused then continued. "Whom do I have the pleasure of sitting beside?"

"I am Hakeem Hidalgo, ambassador from Jakbar. It is a pleasure to make your acquaintance."

Merry smiled and offered her hand. "Ambassador Hidalgo, may I call you Hakeem?"

He dipped his head in agreeance. "And what is your name, my lady?"

"But this is a masquerade, Ambassador! Perhaps, though, you shall find out before the night is through."

This seemed to please him. "Very well. Do you enjoy the opera?"

Merry was eager to end the pleasantries and delve into more important matters, but she had learned it was best to allow people to open up in their own time. If she rushed him, he may be less open with his information. They chatted a few minutes more. A tight knot formed in her stomach once again. The feeling was becoming more familiar each passing moment.

It was pressure to succeed. Papa's life depended on her. Could she pull through?

18

Gregory adjusted the silky black strap holding his mask in place. If tied too loosely, the mask slipped. He'd had it tightened, only now it irritated behind his ears.

The mask was black with gold trim, and it covered his eyes and the top of his nose. He hated masquerades in general, but to attend a masquerade at the opera was especially uninviting. Still, the hordes of people around him were equally uncomfortable. That was some consolation.

Gregory left Prince Stefan in a guard's capable hands. The Dawsonian guard would ensure the drunken prince found his seat and, hopefully, his wife.

That prince was now his sister's brother. It was a strange and depressing realization.

He scanned the crowd looking for Wesley's tall frame or Merry's purple peacock mask. Heat spread up his neck at the thought of her. She'd been stunning, standing there warding off the prince's advances. He'd recognized her immediately, which would concern him except he'd been watching for her. Hopefully, no one else would spot her so easily.

Growling in frustration, he turned toward the

auditorium. He should join his entourage as the lights were beginning to dim. A woman bumped into him, and he caught her before she stumbled.

"I apologize, miss," he said quickly.

The woman wore a deep red gown with a black corset. Her black hair was piled on top of her head with a small black hat with a thin black veil to cover her forehead perched to the side. She wore a black eye mask.

Full, red lips smiled up at him. "No apology necessary, sir. It is crowded, do you not think so?" She spoke with an accent, though it was faint.

He was thankful for the mask to hide his surprise at seeing her here. It was the first he'd seen her in Dawson's Edge at all, and he'd believed the rumors that she'd left her husband. "Princess de St. Paul. How do you do?"

Her lips now formed into a pout, but the look in her eyes was friendly and playful. "Boo, my speaking gives away my identity. There is no use for this silly mask."

Gregory put on a light air so as not to be rude, but also to not give away his nerves. "On the contrary, the mask adds a lovely measure of appeal and intrigue. You look stunning, Princess."

She grinned now. "And with whom do I have the pleasure of speaking?"

He considered not revealing his identity, but he quickly realized that wasn't likely to play in his favor. He bowed slightly. "Prince Gregory Hamilton of Chester's Wake, at your service."

"Prince Gregory? What a delight."

Just then, the music from the auditorium grew louder.

"It looks like the show is about to begin. I hope you enjoy, Princess."

She smiled again, nodded, and stepped away. Gregory maneuvered through the crowd to find his seat.

He sat with others in his entourage, including Lady Wendy, her mother, and Roland Dawson. Wendy smiled up at him when he glanced her way. He politely returned the smile then turned to watch the performers. He would need to speak with her as soon as possible about their relationship. He could not in good conscious continue seeing her romantically. He may have no future with Merry, but he certainly didn't have one with Wendy either. He would not fulfill her as he realized now she could never fulfill him.

The lights dimmed, and the actor on stage began a slow, deep song about passionate love. It was nothing out of the ordinary for an opera, yet Gregory felt as if the entire auditorium were waiting to see his reaction. He was being ridiculous.

Ignoring the opera, he scanned the crowd. He found Merry almost immediately. She sat on the lower level beside, he assumed, the ambassador of Jakbar. Their heads were bent close together, and the ambassador's shoulders shook slightly with laughter.

Merry was certainly wooing him as she was so skilled at doing. She really was masterful at putting people at ease. Mother had been right in sending her, as much as he hated to admit it.

He watched them rather than the opera for much of the first act. They talked and laughed quietly while Gregory grew more and more tense. He took a deep breath and forced his shoulders to relax.

The first act ended, and the curtain fell for a brief

interlude. Lady Wendy sat beside him. She smiled at him. "Are you enjoying the performance?"

He gave what he hoped was a natural smile. "I am, and yourself?"

"Yes, it's lovely."

He glanced back toward Merry and the ambassador. Merry had left her seat. Adrenaline surged through him. Where had she gone?

"If you'll excuse me," he said, standing.

Wendy frowned, seeming confused, but she nodded as he hurried from his seat toward the exit.

Where had Merry gone? He didn't think to check for the ambassador to see if he might have gone with her.

Only a few people milled about the corridors outside the auditorium. The dim halls were covered from ceiling to floor in a thick, red velvet. It muted all sound. Glancing around, he spotted her purple gown. She was alone.

He hurried forward and met her in a small, secluded alcove.

He cursed himself for noticing, but the purple gown fit her most attractively. The jeweled belt wrapped around her like she was an actual princess, and the mask with purple feathers finished the look in a breathtaking display.

"Did you learn anything?"

She nodded quickly. "He spoke of Prince Benjamin of Lox. He mentioned that he would be returning home in two days. I thought that odd, as we are here for an engagement ball."

Gregory frowned, considering the conversation they'd had upon his arrival regarding Ben and Roanna's escapades in the garden. Merry wasn't aware of those happenings. "How would the ambassador of Jakbar know such a thing?"

"I don't know, but he was quite sure. He also spoke of a hope to end the marriage agreement between the prince and Roanna."

"Did he give any specifics? Timelines? Routes? Perhaps they plan to attack his entourage."

"No." She frowned, seeming to consider her next words. "He said something else strange. He said they wanted to keep Dawson's Edge weak."

Dawson's Edge, not the Dawson family. If the ambassador worked with Dawsonian rebels, wouldn't they wish to keep the kingdom strong?

"Definitely worth noting."

The music from the second act had already started. Gregory glanced toward the auditorium door. Then he looked back to Merry.

They stood a moment in silence, and the strains of the music from inside the theatre seemed deafening. The tension in the air shifted. His goal-oriented attitude melted like butter, leaving only the two of them standing in its wake.

His gaze met hers, and she watched him silently. He swallowed hard. "You look stunning, Miss Stern."

A blush appeared high on her cheek bones, and she looked away. "Thank you."

His heart sped up. He must get back inside the auditorium. He wouldn't be able to explain such a long absence, should someone notice and ask. Besides that, it was rude.

"I saw Princess de St. Paul just before the performance began."

What a fool he was, giving her useless information simply to prolong their clandestine meeting.

"I found it surprising that her husband would behave as he did with his wife right here in the same theatre."

Merry bit her lip. "I did not see her, but I wondered if his behavior might not be why there are rumors she planned to ask for divorce."

He nodded. "Do you feel this could be why her country is open to rebellious causes?"

She bit her lip again. "It was rumored that her family might help the rebellion, but it seems rather rash that they would go to war over a wayward husband."

He agreed. "I should return to my seat before we draw suspicion."

"Yes, absolutely. Shall you go first, then?"

He nodded slightly, yet still his feet did not move. He swallowed the invisible knot in his throat. "Good evening, Merry. I will speak with you further tomorrow." And with that, he hurried away.

19

Lady Wendy smiled at him again when he retook his seat. He nodded to her then faced the stage, but his eyes scanned the crowd. Where were Ben and Roanna? Roanna had mentioned coming, so he assumed them here. He needed to speak with Ben about the possibility of his returning home.

He caught Merry resuming her seat beside the ambassador. Hakeem leaned in, and they started a new conversation. Was it strictly business, or were they conversing personally now?

It shouldn't matter. She would tell him if anything else pertinent came up.

The music of the opera grated on his nerves. He would much rather be sitting in an office pouring over military tactics or intelligence then he would to be sitting here listening to love songs. Of course, if he were sitting beside Merry instead of Lady Wendy? He must not think that way. He looked to his lap and took a deep breath.

What was he doing? He needed to perform his duties, but outside of that, what was he all about? He needed to decide, and sooner rather than later.

"Are you enjoying the music?" He leaned slightly

toward Wendy and spoke softly.

Relief filled her eyes at his interest, and guilt rammed his chest.

"I enjoy it very much. I'm so pleased to be here with you."

He smiled and returned his attention to the stage. As soon as this cursed performance was over, he would find Ben and question him. Depending on the information he gleaned, they would formulate theories as to how the ambassador of Jakbar had come across the information as well as a plan of action.

And then he would make a plan to speak with Lady Wendy.

Gregory spent the rest of the second act considering various leads they might explore regarding the identity of other rebels. An idea kept coming back to him, something he'd thought about before but had not voiced.

Merry Stern would likely not wish to go along with his idea. His shoulders tensed at the thought of the grief it would likely cause her, but her family estate was most likely to offer good insight. Could they search it?

He would put away that idea for now, but if nothing came of their other leads, he would revisit it. Merry would need to understand, and if she were truly on the side of right, she would understand, indeed.

At last, the music ended. Gregory had still not spotted Ben or Roanna, so he had no other choice but to stay with his entourage as they made their way back to the palace. Two autos made up their group. Gregory, Wendy, and the duchess rode in one auto while Roland and a few others rode in the other. The duchess peppered him with questions as they drove.

"What will be your main area of focus as you move into more responsibilities back home?" she asked.

"I have been heavily involved in learning military matters for several years now." Irritation built in him at her question. He was being unfair, he knew. He was their crown prince, and he owed them respect and kindness. It was a part of himself he used to give freely. Now, less so.

"But now you are refocusing on the rebellion here in Dawson's Edge?" The duchess frowned, as if she were confused and put off by this.

"Not necessarily two separate matters. The rebel forces were responsible for the unrest at our own borders not long ago. For the safety of us all, it is important to stomp out this group."

This seemed to appease her. She continued questioning him, and he worked at being open and kind. Her questions helped him understand how the people of Chester's Wake were feeling regarding their kingdom being thrown suddenly into an alliance with Dawson's Edge. He hadn't truly considered how they felt about it all.

His thoughts turned to the lost child, the one stolen from his family. What did the people think of that child?

It was a nice break from the constant tension in his chest over Merry Stern.

When they arrived at the palace, Duchess Higgins bid him good night, but he stopped Lady Wendy.

"Might we speak a moment?"

She widened her eyes but nodded quickly.

Duchess Higgins smiled in pleasure. "Don't be long, dear." She left them in the great hall.

Gregory watched her go then turned his gaze to Wendy. "My lady, I fear I have been an abysmal suitor. The truth is, I find myself unready to commit to this relationship. I thought it fairer to tell you immediately then to lead you on."

The excited light in Wendy's eyes dimmed.

Guilt coursed through him.

She opened her mouth as if she would speak but then snapped her lips closed. She gave him a slight nod. "Very well." The words were whispered.

She turned on her heel and quickly followed her mother's path.

Gregory watched her go. Should he stop her? Explain further? But no, he wouldn't further insult her. She would be glad for his refusal someday.

With purpose, he headed toward Ben's rooms. He knocked, and Hansen answered the door. Ben hadn't returned from the opera.

"Will you give him a message for me?"

Hansen bowed his agreeance.

"Tell him I need to speak with him, sooner rather than later. It's a matter of secret intelligence."

Hansen nodded. "I will tell him as soon as I see him."

"Thank you."

Gregory wasn't yet ready to return to his room, but he had nowhere else he wished to be. No one he wished to spend time with. Loneliness had become a regular companion for him.

He headed to his rooms in order to change from his opera attire. Once he was more comfortable, he walked to a small sitting area situated in a balcony overlooking a side entry to the palace. It reminded him of home, and he wished he could return.

Soon. He would finish this mission as soon as possible and return home.

But what of Merry Stern? What would they do with her once the rebels had been apprehended? She could not stay in Dawson's Edge—she would never be welcomed by the Dawsons.

But what would she do in Chester's Wake? Be Mother's permanent assistant? That would be exhausting.

He sighed and rubbed a hand over his eyes.

How late would Ben be?

The sound of laughter came from the entryway below, and he peered over. Roanna and Ben had stepped through the doors. Bette, Roanna's maid, followed behind them. She must have been assigned chaperone duty due to their indiscretions.

Gregory chuckled at the thought. All their lives, they'd been allowed to come and go as they pleased, but now that they were engaged to be married, they were kept on a short leash.

He stood and called down to them.

"We're coming, Gregory," Roanna called back with a smile.

He waited for them to make their way up a winding staircase.

"Did you enjoy the masquerade?" Roanna still wore her gown. It was flaming red, and Ben carried her mask, which had tall red feathers like she was fire itself.

He laughed at her question. "Do you think I enjoyed it?"

She grinned and shrugged. "You never know."

He turned to Ben. "I wanted to speak with you."

Roanna bid Bette return to her room. Then they

moved to the sofas in the sitting area.

"What's wrong?" Ben asked.

Gregory had to be careful in how he presented his information so as not to identify the Jakbar ambassador or Merry. "I received information tonight regarding you and your plan to return to Lox before the engagement ball."

Ben frowned. "I'm not returning to Lox anytime soon."

"The source was quite certain of this report, which I knew to be very odd. I wanted to make you aware of it and get your thoughts on it."

"Who told you this?" Roanna asked. Although she seemed concerned about his words, her eyes sparkled with happiness. He realized it was something that had been missing before she had uncovered the truth about herself. Maybe he had been too harsh toward her.

Gregory shook his head. "I cannot say, not yet. But you need to be aware that the rebels may be targeting you, and soon."

Ben still frowned. He looked away. "What interest could the rebels have in me? Something isn't right about all of this. I can't put my finger on what it is that bothers me, but it doesn't add up."

"How so?"

He shook his head. "I don't know. Give me time to put my thoughts together on it. When I do, I'll share them with you."

Gregory nodded and stood. "That sounds well enough."

"Are you going to bed so soon?" Roanna held out her hand. "Stay with us."

He glanced between them. "I don't want to be a third wheel."

She raised her brows. "A third wheel? Why would you think that? You could never be a third wheel."

Gregory searched her eyes for any hint of pity, but he saw none. He sat. "I won't make you twist my arm then."

And for the next two hours the three of them talked, laughed, and reminisced. He told Roanna stories of home, and she told him stories of Dawson's Edge. When at last they parted ways, he fell asleep without tossing and turning, and he realized in the morning that it was the first time in months.

20

Gregory needed to speak with Merry to formulate some sort of plan for what they might investigate next. But his late night with Roanna and Ben had left him wanting to stick around the palace more. See them, speak with them.

At breakfast, he spoke congenially with others at the table.

"You seem to be feeling quite well this morning." Duchess Higgins met his gaze from across the table. Her smile was tight, her eyes boring into him. "You must have slept well."

Gregory swallowed hard. "I did. And yourself?"

"I always sleep well." The words were spoken tersely.

He glanced around, but Lady Wendy was not with her mother.

Ben sat a few seats down. He leaned forward and spoke to Gregory. "What are your plans for the day, Gregory? More errands to run?"

"No. I have nothing planned."

"Come with us, then. Some of the men have arranged a wrestling match later this morning."

"Wrestling?" Gregory had never seen a wrestling

match, though he knew the sport.

"It's a popular recreation here in Dawson's Edge," Roland piped up. "Many of the nobles participate. You're welcome to try your hand at it if you'd like. I can give you a few pointers after the meal."

Gregory considered the offer then nodded. "I would appreciate that. Yes, I'll attend."

Ben grinned. "You won't regret it."

Gregory finished his breakfast, glad for the plans.

Wendy's mother approached him as they left the dining hall. "Your Highness, I wondered if I could implore you to reconsider your words to Lady Wendy last night. I assure you she is most keen."

Irritation surged through him. He knew his own heart on this, and he knew he was not interested in marriage to Lady Wendy. "I'm very sorry for any hurt Lady Wendy has experienced. If you'll excuse me, Duchess." He left her glaring after him to join Roland.

"I'm glad to see you sticking around today," Roland said as they walked. "You were sparse yesterday."

Gregory cut his eyes toward Roland, or more particularly the suspicious way in which he spoke. He would not acknowledge the statement. "Should I change clothes for this sport?"

"We have appropriate attire in our sporting rooms. You're welcome to change there." Roland didn't press him further about his absence the day before, and Gregory let go of his tension on the subject.

Roland led him to a brass elevator at the end of the hallway. Gregory recognized the elevator area, as he had ridden the royal family's personal elevators to an underground bunker during an attack at the palace a few months ago. That was back when he did not yet realize Roanna was not his true sister.

The memory was painful and distant, yet fresh. He pushed it away as they rode to the third floor.

Roland began his tutorial as they neared a large door at the end of the hallway. "The rules are fairly simple at their core. Two opponents compete to take the other down with brute force. There is no hitting or biting allowed, though everything else is typically within allowance. The goal is to pin your opponent to the mat for a specified amount of time."

Gregory was aware of the generalities of the sport, but he did not interrupt. They entered the large room at the end of the hall. All manner of sports equipment had been set up around the expanse: a fencing area in the far left corner, weightlifting directly to the right, and what looked like a boxing arena beside that.

Several men gathered at the back of the room, and that is where they headed. Roland approached a servant and instructed him to bring Gregory something suitable to wear. Roland did not change clothes himself. Gregory quickly changed into the lightweight linen pants. He did not wear a shirt.

Over the next hour, Roland explained various wrestling moves that were popular among players. He modeled lifts, positions, and methods. Sweat ran down Gregory's back as he attempted move after move, sometimes with Roland and other times with other men in the room. Occasionally, he was bested, but overall, he did well.

Roland clapped him on the shoulder, the sting on Gregory's bare skin burning. "We ought to set up a real match soon. You'd do well, is my guess."

Gregory breathed hard, his heart not yet slowed from the activity. "I enjoy it very much. Thank you for teaching me."

Roland nodded. "My pleasure, fellow prince." He left Gregory to clean up with a promise to see him again when the other men arrived later.

He had spoken very little to Roland over the months, and most of their interaction had been tense at best. Yet today, Roland had been kind to him. Perhaps he could see how Roanna had lived here these last few months. Perhaps.

After Roland left him, Gregory decided to stay in the sporting room. He needed to speak with Merry to discuss their options and to learn what else the ambassador of Jakbar had revealed.

But he wanted to do none of those things, and as he'd agreed to attend this match, it was all that was expected of him in this moment.

Standing back, he watched two other men step onto the thick leather mat in the center of the area. The mat was stuffed with some type of feather to cushion it, and the thick brown leather encased it. The two men wore trousers and no shirts. They crouched in front of each other. When the man officiating their skirmish waved a hand, they moved toward each other.

Gregory studied the way they moved, how they ducked in and out of each other's reach, how they gave and took blows by their opponent. It was no different than his war games, really. Strategy, tactics, execution, victory.

He narrowed his eyes as he considered that. It was the approach he needed to take with catching the rebels. He was so focused on Merry Stern that he hadn't used his cool head and his trained military logic. He would need to remedy that, and soon.

"You from Chester's Wake?" A man stood beside

him now. He was a few years older than Gregory, with blonde hair and bulging muscles. His blue eyes seemed friendly.

Gregory looked him over. He wouldn't mind having someone like that on his royal guard.

"I'm Prince Gregory Hamilton. Whom do I have the pleasure of speaking with?"

The man grinned. He was missing a canine tooth, but it didn't detract from his intimidating form or, Gregory had to admit, his good looks.

"My name is Henri Van Hoosier. I'm in the royal guard here at the palace." He nodded as if he were speaking to himself and answering himself.

Gregory watched him in amusement.

"I enlisted in the military to show my support for king and country, though I am noble born."

Suddenly, his name resonated in Gregory's memory. Van Hoosier? This was the family Merry had mentioned.

Careful to keep his revelations off his face, Gregory nodded to him. "Good to meet you, Henri. The Van Hoosier family, you say? What does your family do?"

Henri had said he was loyal to king and country. Not an odd statement to make, no matter which side he was on. He wouldn't want to draw speculation if he was a rebel, and he wouldn't want to associate with the rebels if he was a loyalist. It told Gregory nothing.

"We're landowners," he said. If it were possible, his muscles bulged even more. "We lease the lands to farmers—mostly tobacco, but other crops, too."

"Where is this?"

"East."

Gregory nodded. "I should like to see it, Henri."

Henri's eyebrows rose, and he grinned again. "If you mean that, Prince Gregory Hamilton, I can arrange it. My family would be honored."

"I do mean it. The sooner the better. Does your family have a Messenger?"

"No, afraid not. But it's only a few hours' drive. We can send a message the old-fashioned way."

Gregory smiled. "I would like that very much."

The officiant on the mat shouted, and all heads turned toward him. One of the opponents had won the match.

"Henri?" Gregory held out a hand. "It was a pleasure to meet you."

21

Merry...

An entire day had passed without word from Gregory. Merry had worked with Fraja to clean the safe house until it shined. She walked with Wesley on brief jaunts around the cul-de-sac. She played number games to keep her mind busy. But she couldn't deny she was going mad. What was keeping Gregory? And what was happening at the palace?

Wesley glanced at her across the table as they ate their evening meal. "There's no reason to worry, Miss Stern. The prince will come."

Merry worked to keep the frown from her face. She was practiced at keeping in her feelings. She had, apparently, failed in keeping her feelings hidden this time. She sighed. "I'm restless. I want to learn more. I want to make things happen."

As she finished her words the sound of a motor rumbled from outside. Wesley practically flew to the door, but he quickly held up his hand to appease her. "It's Prince Gregory."

Finally.

Merry retook her seat at the table—part of the ruse of being in control of herself and her emotions—but she wanted to rush outside and demand an update.

She almost laughed at herself at the thought. What would Gregory do if she started demanding things of him? Grumpy, grumpy Gregory. He'd not laugh, certainly.

Wesley went outside. Merry tapped her fingers on the table. She swirled her silver fork in the potato mash that Fraja had cooked for supper. She watched the door.

She needed to hear what was happening. Being on house arrest had been bad, no doubt. But being stuck here when she was on a mission was beyond reason. It was as if she were a prisoner, yet not a prisoner. Which she supposed was at least partly accurate.

She glanced toward the door again. What could be taking him such an eternity? At last, the door swung open and footsteps sounded. A moment later, Gregory stepped inside the dining room.

Merry released a rushing breath which she hoped he wouldn't notice.

He scanned the room, and in a moment, his gaze found hers. He quickly looked away as if seeing her didn't affect him at all. But Merry was an expert at reading people. Skilled at gauging situations and determining the best ways to bring about the desired end.

She did not miss the slight pink in his cheeks as his gaze moved away from hers. The knowledge both exhilarated her and frightened her.

"I believe I've found something that can be useful to us." His words were directed at her. At least, she supposed they were. He faced her but did not look at her.

Fraja still bustled about the room, but now she

hobbled back to the kitchen—to give them privacy, Merry supposed.

"Oh?"

"You mentioned the Van Hoosiers."

A ball of nerves lodged itself in her throat. She swallowed and straightened her shoulders as if she hadn't a care in the world. "Yes?"

"I met one of them today." His words came quickly, excitedly. Finally, he looked at her. He moved toward the table and sat down.

Merry barely knew what to do with herself.

"Who?"

"Henri. He told me about his family and their estate. He has made arrangements for us to visit there. I waited until we could finalize the arrangements before speaking with you."

Henri. He was her second cousin, she believed. It was doubtful he realized she had been to Chester's Wake at all, so he would not have mentioned their relation. In fact, they had barely spoken that she could recall. For now, her secret was safe. She could speak with Hattie, learn if anyone in the Van Hoosier household could help her free Papa, and she could still gather some type of info for the Hamiltons.

"When do we leave?"

"We will leave early in the morning, travelling by train." He paused, as if unsure of his next statement. "There will be a small entourage going, which will complicate things where you're concerned. We will need to keep you out of sight as much as possible."

Merry waited, but he did not explain. She frowned. "Yes, of course. Whatever you need."

"Excellent." He seemed happier today than she had seen him since she had arrived in Chester's Wake.

Something was different, refreshing.

"Did you speak with Prince Benjamin?"

"Yes. He has no plans to travel to Lox anytime soon." Gregory shrugged. "We are on alert, though. It's all very strange."

He paused. "Did the Jakbar ambassador have any other information?"

"He confirmed in general terms what we already knew—the country planned to join the rebellion but had not done so yet. He did imply it was still a consideration, but he gave no specifics. I'm to speak with him again soon, or so he said."

Gregory raised his eyebrows. "Interesting."

"Yes."

They sat another moment in silence. Then Gregory stood. "I'll leave you to prepare for our travels tomorrow."

"Yes, tomorrow." She stood, too.

Gregory nodded to her and exited the room, left her standing alone.

Merry bit her lip. She wrung her hands together then took a calming breath. He hadn't pressed her for more information about the ambassador, and she hadn't offered up anything he didn't press for. She wasn't sure if that meant he was beginning to trust her, or if it only meant he didn't trust her at all and saw no point in insisting on information that may or may not be spotty.

And what of this entourage he mentioned? Why would he be bringing others with them?

Unless it was less conspicuous to bring a group than it was to travel alone. Most likely it would include Henri Van Hoosier. Who else? Almost certainly Lady Wendy and her mother. Princess Roanna? Prince

Benjamin?

Thinking of Roanna and Ben brought longing. She had gotten along with them so well, just as she had fallen in with Gregory so quickly.

She rubbed her forehead, easing an aching tension that had begun months ago and rarely let up. Was she that girl who had become fast friends with them? Or was she this girl—rebel and spy? Could she be both?

This mystery wouldn't be solved tonight, so she headed upstairs to prepare for the morning's journey.

~*~

Wesley woke them early the next morning. Merry dressed as he instructed, in nondescript clothing—a brown skirt that fell in ruffles just below her shins, white stockings, a white blouse and a brown corset. She pulled her hair into a common bun and wrapped a shawl around her head instead of wearing a hat.

She looked no different than any other woman they might see today.

They left the safe house in a black auto and drove to the train station near the palace. Merry saw no one as they boarded the train. Gregory and his entourage must be arriving later. He must have wanted her to arrive early to remain undetected. It made sense. He hadn't clued her in, though, which gave her a partial answer to her mental question the night before—he was not starting to trust her; rather, he did not trust her much at all.

She hardened herself against the indignation that arose. She was glad to know he did not trust her. It would help her remember that they were not friends. Rather, they were working together to bring about separate goals. She would have to be cautious in her manner around him, as he was to her.

Wesley made sure she was comfortable in the train car before moving through one of the interior doors to another car. Now she was alone, Fraja staying at the safe house. She moved to the window and peeked out, watching for other passengers. Before long, two autos approached. Henri Van Hoosier climbed from one followed by Gregory, Lady Wendy, and the duchess. The other auto carried two men who seemed vaguely familiar, though Merry couldn't place them, and finally two more figures emerged. A man and woman—not Roanna and Benjamin.

Merry frowned. It was Prince Stefan and Princess Bella. Why ever would those two come to visit the Van Hoosier estate? She couldn't image, but now she would need to rethink all her actions and be on special guard. What if Hattie wouldn't dare utter a word about rebellion with them around? Even Hattie had to have some measure of good sense and self-preservation.

Merry returned to her seat. She assumed Gregory would present himself at some point throughout the ride. At least, she hoped she wouldn't be riding in solitude.

After some time, the train lurched. A piercing whistle ripped through the air, and they began moving. The entourage must have made it on board safely.

Time passed as they sped down the tracks. Merry stayed in her seat grateful, at least, that they were not flying in an airship. She gripped her hands in her lap. She considered what she would say to Hattie and how she might approach the subject of the rebellion without putting her cousin on the defense. She imagined different possible scenarios for how the day would go, and the longer she sat alone in the train car the more she wondered if Gregory truly did mean to leave her to solitude for the entire trip.

Regardless, all she needed was a chance. A single chance to gain any piece of helpful information. The Hamiltons wanted more names to add to their list of known rebels. Merry did not have that information, but if she could find it—if she could please the Hamiltons—perhaps they would offer Papa asylum the way they had offered it to her.

Her other option was to find the rebels and work with them directly to free Papa from within Dawson's Edge.

Nerves erupted inside her at the idea of working with the rebels all on her own instead of only under Papa's guidance. Was that a step she was willing to take?

She took a slow, steady breath. She would not take that step unless it appeared the only option.

The door to her compartment opened and Merry gasped.

Wesley peeked in then stepped through the doorway. He grinned. "I didn't mean to frighten you."

She smiled and laughed at herself. "It's all right. I'm a little on edge." She didn't expound. Let him think what he would, but she didn't like being left to sit alone this way.

"I apologize for the long absence." He sat. "Prince Gregory informed me that plans have changed somewhat. He did not expect that Prince Stefan and Princess Bella would be travelling with us. That could hinder the overall mission. He hopes to speak with you as soon as he can slip away from them."

Understanding dawned. Yes, that made sense. It was her own duplicity that caused her to be so suspicious and unnerved. "Thank you for explaining. I understand."

Wesley sat back and crossed his ankle over the opposite knee. "You grew up here in Dawson's Edge? It's very beautiful. How far did you live from where we're going?"

"An hour's drive in an auto. I've never been by train."

He nodded, glancing out the window. "Chester's Wake has open spaces, of course, but it's much smaller than Dawson's Edge, and there are more cities. More people, more crowds. I like it here."

Merry smiled, finding herself very comfortable with Wesley. He was kind and accepting and easy to get along with. "When I visited Chester's Wake, I enjoyed it for exactly the reasons you described. I suppose it's natural to enjoy what you've not grown accustomed to."

"True."

"What about you?" she asked. "How did you grow up? Are you noble born, the way Henri Van Hoosier is? He grew up to work in the royal guard, after all."

Wesley shook his head. "Not me. I grew up in the capital city, and I learned to fight on the streets. I was raised by my grandfather, and he took pains to teach me hard work and character. I met the prince as a child when he began his training in working with the people. As we grew older, he helped me get the proper training I needed in order to advance."

Gregory did that? For a poor boy to whom he owed nothing?

It hardly matched up with the frustrated, angry Gregory she had seen so often these last several days. But it did match up with the Gregory she had met months ago. Was she part of the cause for his anger? A stab in her heart caused her to shift.

"What a wonderful story," she said. "Very inspiring. My family was noble born, but we did not have a large estate." It felt odd speaking in the past tense of her family's position and wealth, but she felt no judgment from Wesley. "Still, I could not imagine the life you must have lived. Do you enjoy the royal guard?"

"Very much." He said it without hesitation. "I couldn't ask for a more noble profession. Outside of the clergy, of course."

Again, he said it as if it were the most natural thing in the world. The clergy—a religious term used in Chester's Wake and even Lox. Dawsonians did not practice religion—and even though the rebels wanted to overthrow the Dawsons and their anomalies, it did not mean they wanted to go so far as to accept religion.

"Will you tell me about your religion?"

Wesley's eyebrows rose. "Now that's not a question I get asked every day." He grinned then shrugged. "It's not all that complicated." He started in with a brief explanation of a Higher Power—a God. A loving God, who was interested in the lives of his children. The children were those who trusted Him, and believed He was who He said—that being Lord of all.

Wesley didn't go into deep doctrine or any absurd-sounding beliefs, but Merry took it to understand there was more to it but that he wanted her to understand the basics.

"And these are your personal beliefs?"

"They are."

She nodded quietly, considering. She and Gregory had never discussed religion during their times together, but she had to assume he held the same beliefs. Merry had spoken to Roanna about beliefs, very briefly. Roanna believed in this God Wesley described.

It was something that helped Merry understand them better, if nothing else. Whether it meant anything deeper to her, she would need to consider later.

"Thank you for explaining."

"Anytime, my lady."

Wesley was always so kind to her. She opened her mouth to tell him so, but the train lurched, and the wheels squealed. They were slowing.

Merry and Wesley glanced out the window together. The train station rose in the distance. They had arrived at the Van Hoosier estate. It was time to prepare herself.

"We'll stay here until Prince Gregory calls for us." Wesley watched out the window as if assuring himself all was well for the prince to leave the train.

Merry watched him, considering what it must be like to be in the royal guard. Stressful, most definitely. It would take someone dedicated and loyal above all. Gregory was never without Wesley or Gideon. If any of the royal guard was part of the rebellion, they would need to be very good actors.

The realization gave her pause. It was certainly possible, and obviously someone within the castle staff was part of the rebellion, but it might be much harder to find them than she had at first thought.

From the window, Merry watched the entourage head down a wooden walkway toward the Van Hoosier's sprawling mansion. Gregory, Henri, and Prince Stefan walked ahead, and Princess Bella walked with Lady Wendy and her mother. Gideon brought up the rear.

"I wonder how long we'll be waiting."

Wesley scratched his head. "Hard to say. The prince's main goal will be getting you inside to determine whatever information might be available, but he'll need to find a moment when it won't draw suspicion."

Merry nodded. Hattie would not turn her in if she saw her. She and her cousin had a good relationship. Henri, on the other hand, had little relation with her. If he saw her and recognized her—which he no doubt would, considering she had been part of an ongoing investigation—he would most likely make a scene.

Only moments passed when the messenger at Wesley's side pinged. Merry glanced to him expectantly.

"That was fast." He stood. "Are you ready?"

22

Merry nodded to Wesley, keeping a tight rein on her nerves, and he led her from the train and down the platform, walking at a quick pace. Merry knew where to go, but she followed the plan and went where Wesley indicated. Once inside the mansion, he turned right and brought them into a small library. "Wait here, Lady Merry."

He left her in the library, she presumed to go speak with Gregory.

But only moments passed when Hattie arrived, breathless. "Merry?" She rushed forward, her blonde curls bouncing around her shoulders. Hattie was short, and to make up for it she had a tendency to dress in bright and absurd clothing. Today she wore a blue blouse and purple vest along with a full, silky, red skirt that fell just under her knees. A red top hat rested on her head.

Merry smiled at her cousin and hugged her tightly. "Good morning, Hattie. How are you?"

Hattie's hug was tight and welcoming. "I'm doing well." She pulled away. "How is it that you're here?"

Merry took a deep breath. She glanced around the small library, noting the shelves of books, the winged chairs, and a few tables scattered around the room. They were alone. "I have been commissioned by Chester's Wake to help sniff out rebels in hiding," she explained. She watched Hattie's expression closely to determine her reaction to this blunt information.

Hattie's face remained interested and innocent. She did not seem surprised or suspicious by the confession.

Now was the time to give Hattie the information that might make her story believable to true rebels. "I have agreed to help, but it is only because I wish to work toward Papa's freedom."

Now a pained expression passed over Hattie's face. She grabbed Merry's hand and squeezed. "It pains me to think of Uncle locked in the dungeon."

It pained Merry, too. She strengthened her resolve and pushed forward. "I need help, Hattie. I don't even know where to start."

Hattie frowned. She directed Merry to a set of chairs, and they took their seats. "I don't know how I could help, Merry." She shook her head, curls swaying. "When Uncle was arrested, I was flabbergasted. The whole family was in an uproar, saying it must be a mistake. Father stormed and paced every night after supper, and I feared for Uncle Patrick, Henri's father, as he nearly drank himself to death. But as more evidence came to light, we knew with sinking surety that it was true. I'm so glad that you have been released and freed of charges."

Hattie rambled on, not bridling her tongue at all, as she was wont to do. But Merry listened closely, reading between the lines of Hattie's words.

"Father listened to the news coming from the palace every day. He was on pins and needles."

"I'm sure it was so stressful for all of you." Merry leaned closer. "How did you get the news from the palace?"

"Henri, of course, and our second cousin, Fredrick. You remember him, of course. He is the son of our first cousin, Jamison. I'm not very familiar with either of them as Jamison is so much older than we are."

"Yes, I don't know them well, either. What were people saying?" But Merry already had information that would be useful to Gregory.

"Jamison visited at one point. He chided Father and Uncle Patrick, telling them that traitors couldn't be trusted anyway, family or not." Hattie froze, a hand to her mouth. "Oh, I'm sorry, Merry! I shouldn't have said that."

Merry smiled and patted Hattie's leg. "Do not worry. I've heard worse."

She kept Hattie going for another half hour, wanting to pressure her to help free Papa, but she had gleaned through their conversation that Hattie was innocent and knew nothing outright. She had not been used for the cause the way Merry had.

When enough time passed, she gripped Hattie's hand and pulled her into another hug. "It has been wonderful to chat with you. I've missed everyone so much."

"As I have missed you!"

"I have to ask you to keep our visit quiet, though." Merry paused, hoping she was coming across as sincere. "Until all of the rebels are caught, and until I can help exonerate Papa, I need to be as discreet as possible." It was doubtful her plea would be heeded, but at least it would be no surprise to others to learn Merry Stern worked to free her father.

Hattie nodded, her eyes wide. "I understand."

"Please don't let it slip even to your father or brothers. We cannot let the Dawsons know I am here questioning people. They know I'm working with Chester's Wake, but they cannot realize I want to exonerate Papa." It was partially true.

"I promise, dear Merry!"

Merry smiled. "Thank you, Hattie."

Hattie left a few moments later so she would be free to eat with the other visitors. Before long, Wesley returned to her with a servant carrying a tray. They ate their midday meal in the library. Then Wesley returned them both to the train to await a time they could speak with Gregory.

"I don't expect we'll see the prince until we've all returned to the capital and we're back at the safe house." Wesley pulled something from a pocket and grinned. "Do you play?"

Cards. He wanted to play cards?

Merry chuckled. "I play. Not well, but I can play."

Wesley shuffled through the deck, grinning wider. "Well then, let's pass some time, shall we?"

~*~

Gregory...

Gregory enjoyed spending the day with Henri and Prince Stefan despite the prince's many inappropriate jokes. Honestly, the man appeared to have no moral code at all. They had lunch in the main dining room with the ladies—including Hattie, whom Gregory presumed had spent the morning speaking with

Merry. Hattie and Henri were cousins, he learned while eating.

After lunch, the men retreated to the men's parlor where they played billiards. Then, it had been time to head back to the palace.

"Thank you for hosting us." Gregory held Hattie's hand and bowed slightly.

She smiled and curtsied. "It was such an honor, Prince Gregory. Meeting you, along with Prince Stefan and Princess Bella, and Lady Wendy and Duchess Higgins has been an immense pleasure."

"But seeing me has been the best part of the day, hasn't it, cousin?" Henri winked, and everyone chuckled.

Hattie rolled her eyes at him, and soon they were making their way back to the train. Henri walked ahead, speaking with the princess. Lady Wendy walked behind them, speaking quietly with her mother. She hadn't said three words to him the entire day. This suited him fine, except he did feel badly that she had come to Dawson's Edge at all.

Prince Stefan walked directly beside Gregory, and he leaned toward him now. "Smart idea, coming to speak with the Van Hoosiers." He spoke quietly, so no one could overhear.

Gregory frowned. Had they been so transparent? "How so?"

"Their relation to the Sterns makes them a likely suspect for the rebel band. I hadn't thought of it before."

Heat rose up the back of Gregory's neck. His ears burned, and he flared his nostrils. He took a moment to be sure he could speak calmly. "What, exactly, is the relation? I'm not entirely up to par on the Stern family tree."

"Baron Stern's wife was a Van Hoosier. I believe that both Henri's father, and the girl Hattie's father, were brothers of hers. She died some years back, you know."

Yes, Gregory did know. Merry had mentioned it once, months ago. Her relation to the Van Hoosiers she had not mentioned, however.

He nodded. "I shall keep that in mind."

They boarded the train, and Gregory moved away from the prince. He needed space to think. To sort this out.

He took a seat away from the others. "Call Wesley."

Gideon hovered nearby, and he moved immediately toward the other train car.

"Your Highness." Wendy stood in front of him.

He nodded politely.

"Did you enjoy the outing?" he asked.

She smiled, seeming relieved he was speaking to her. "Very much and seeing so much of the countryside has been lovely." She glanced at the empty seat beside him. "May I join you?"

Her lower lip trembled, and she twisted her thumbs. Her mother must have put her up to asking. Despite not wanting to get her hopes up, he could not stomach the idea of crushing her either.

"Please, sit. I may have to excuse myself for a few moments to discuss some matters with the guards, but I shall return."

Color flushed her face, and she smiled brightly as she sat. "Did you enjoy your time with the Van Hoosiers?" she asked.

He had enjoyed it until Stefan had revealed

Merry's secret.

He kept these thoughts to himself. "It was a good time, to be sure." He paused. "Lady Wendy, I want to apologize again for what we spoke of a few nights past. Though I cannot see us moving forward with a relationship, I hope we, and our families, can remain friendly."

Her smiled faltered, but then she nodded and smiled. She did not answer him.

Gideon returned a moment later and whispered to him, "Wesley is ready to speak with you."

Gregory turned to Wendy. "If you'll excuse me for just a moment."

She nodded. Was it his imagination, or did she seemed relieved to see him go? He moved toward the other rail car and met Wesley in the empty space between the two.

"Did she say anything to you?"

"No, we've been playing cards and chatting. Nothing about the day's events."

Gregory looked away, watched the passing landscape as they rushed back toward the capital. He couldn't trust her. He'd known he couldn't but now that it had been confirmed, he needed to determine the best way to handle it. Anything she told him could be a lie or only partially true, at the very least. He wouldn't be able to adequately determine fact from fiction.

"Your Highness?" Wesley prompted.

"Do you trust her, Wesley?" His personal guard was a good man. A trustworthy friend. Gregory valued his opinion.

Wesley studied him, seeming to try to gauge from where Gregory's question was coming. Did his guards suspect his former relationship with Merry? Maybe.

He'd ditched them when with her a few times, but they'd probably figured things out. It was their job, after all.

Finally, Wesley nodded. "She's keeping a few secrets to herself, no doubt. That is to be expected."

Gregory frowned. To be expected? He supposed Wesley was right about that. "But do you trust her?"

"I don't have the safety of the kingdom resting on my shoulders, but I think I do trust her. At least, right now. She hasn't been given the opportunity to betray anyone yet. If things start moving toward that opportunity, I believe we'll have ample time to stop it. For now, listen to what she has to say and weigh it, decipher whether she's lying. Or not lying."

Listen. Yes, he could listen. Decipher. Try.

"I'll speak with her then."

He stepped around Wesley and into the car with Merry. She looked up at him, and her expression changed from a relaxed smile to a guarded look.

"Wesley filled you in on our unexpected guests, I suppose."

"Yes, and I saw them when you all boarded the train." She paused. "Why did they come?"

How much to reveal? He would only give her rudimentary information. It was all she was offering him, after all. "I believe the Dawson family is suspicious of my intentions here in Dawson's Edge. If I learn anything about the rebels, they want to learn it alongside me."

He would not tell her it also had to do with a relation between the Van Hoosiers and other known rebels. Maybe she would reveal that relationship on her own—and prove her trustworthiness.

"Did you learn anything helpful?" he asked.

Merry sighed. Her usually impeccable posture dipped for only a moment. "I am almost certain her father and uncle are involved. Hattie is clueless, but her description of their behavior during the investigation into my own family implicates their guilt. She said they were on pins and needles, angry, edgy, and reckless."

She was being forthright. This was a good sign. "You believe their behavior implies guilt. They were scared they would be ratted out during the investigation."

She nodded. "She also described behaviors by her cousin, Jamison. He and his family appear—at least to me based on her descriptions—to be innocent. Again, Hattie is clueless. I told her I was trying to help Chester's Wake solve this mystery in order to win Papa's eventual freedom." She looked to her hands, gripped tightly in her lap. "I tried to appeal to her feminine side as she is very close with her own father."

Gregory listened to her words, his mind at war with his emotions. Merry did want to free her own father. She wasn't being deceptive about that and was willingly admitting it to him. Yet, she continued to keep her relationship to Hattie a secret. Why?

"What else did she tell you?"

Merry looked back to him. "Nothing concrete. As I said, she has no idea. I do wonder if there would be evidence somewhere on the estate, but without significant proof of their guilt, I'm not sure how feasible it would be to go searching their mansion."

Her words stirred a reminder of his previous idea in his mind. He paused, considering the possibility. He would not bring it up yet, but it might be a possibility for the future. "Thank you for your efforts. This gives us a starting point, if nothing else."

"You could try crossing paths with Hattie's father or Henri's father." She cocked her head to the side. "Do you find Henri suspicious?"

He raised his eyebrows. Henri? He hadn't given the guard much personal thought other than the initial first moments when they met. But if Henri's father was involved in the rebellion, it might serve him well to have a son in the royal guard, stationed at the palace.

"I don't know just yet."

She accepted his words.

Gregory had nothing else worth saying. He needed to return to his seat before anyone grew suspicious of his absence. Yet, he wanted to stay here. Let Wesley take his place beside Wendy.

"I'm sorry you had to stay cooped inside this train for so long."

Her eyes widened slightly as if his words surprised her. "Wesley is excellent company."

"I agree." He managed a smile, but his insides twisted. Something about her behavior pained him. She was so practiced. So poised. She could fool anyone.

Yet, he suspected something else in her posture. Some pain in her perfect manners. In her too-ready answers.

"I shall speak with you soon."

He left the train car, passing Wesley on his return to Lady Wendy. She smiled at him as he sat, and they made small talk for the rest of the ride to the palace. But his mind was back in the other train car with the possibility of new names for their rebel roster, the possibility that he was being duped, and the possibility that he would never get over it.

23

Roanna...

"Have you seen Gregory?" Roanna had searched the palace high and low but had not found him.

Katherine looked up from her desk where she was filling out papers. "No, I haven't seen him." She paused. "Though it seems I remember hearing something last night about an outing with Stefan and Bella."

"Oh." Her two brothers together. They did not invite her? "Thank you, Katherine. Any word from the Bellevues?"

"No, nothing."

Ben's parents had instructed they would attend the engagement ball, but Ben had not heard from them in a few days. After the love they had shown her over the years, it seemed odd that now they had grown cold.

Odd, or a statement.

She left Katherine to her work and headed toward the palace gardens. She had been working on her powers with one of the maids there. The maid could speed or halt the growth of plants though no one in the palace knew it of her. Roanna enjoyed their training sessions together. It wasn't quite time for their normal rendezvous, but Roanna didn't mind an early start.

As she moved through the palace corridors, a male servant approached her. "Princess, a message."

Roanna paused and took the letter he offered. Ben's familiar handwriting greeted her.

Roanna,

We must speak immediately. My family has asked I meet them in Lox.

Much love,

Ben

Roanna frowned. Gregory had asked Ben if he planned to travel home. Something about a contact mentioning it.

Who was Gregory's contact?

She narrowed her eyes and considered. Gregory had been gone frequently. Working on his spy missions? With whom? Surely, Stefan and Bella weren't working with him. It seemed too bizarre to be true.

Changing directions, she headed toward Ben's suites. She would not go inside—she had been practicing more caution since the fiasco in the garden—but there was a sitting room situated in an alcove near the rooms. She would meet Ben there.

As she approached, Ben waited for her already. A servant and a guard stood nearby. She hurried toward him. "Is something wrong?"

He shook his head. "Father said Mother is ill. They would like me to return immediately."

Roanna studied him, gauging his belief of this story. She did not want to accuse his family, especially as it could be honest and true. But she could not forget Gregory's questions from nights ago.

"You will go?"

He took a deep breath and flared his nostrils as he released it. "I don't know. I want to speak to Gregory."

Roanna let out a pent-up breath. So, he wasn't entirely believing.

"Katherine said he is on an outing with Stefan and Bella."

He raised his eyebrows. "Odd choice."

She gave him a sideways glance. "Agreed. I'm a little suspicious."

"I need to talk to him about any information he uncovers." Ben sat on the couch and sighed. "I don't know how I'm supposed to do that easily from Lox."

She wished he would not go, but she wouldn't tell him that. If Queen Frieda really was ill, Roanna would not keep him away.

"You've spoken to Baron Stern as well as the Maynes. Have you ever asked them directly about me? About my birth?"

Ben frowned. "No. It's not that easy. I've asked if they have information regarding your birth but never directly if they were involved in you being taken to Chester's Wake. They claim no knowledge."

"And you've brought in Dr. Presnell."

His frown deepened. "No. He's an old, senile man. We've been hesitant to upset him and cause him any sudden stress. He might have a stroke or heart attack."

Roanna wrapped her arms around her middle. She joined Ben on the sofa and scooted close to him. "I can't help feeling as if knowing the truth would bring closure. To me, yes, but also to my family. Mother and Father are driving themselves insane in their search for their true child." She looked into his eyes, hoping to see compassion there. "What if she's been killed?"

Ben drew her close. "We're going to solve this. Even now, Gregory works to find answers. We will find them."

He was so sure. So determined.

"For now, I'm going to assume I'm going to Lox. As soon as I can speak with Gregory, I'll know."

"You'll let me know?"

"Of course."

Roanna stood. "I should go then. I'm meeting someone in the gardens."

"More practice?"

He was so accepting of her anomaly. So comfortable with her powers. She smiled. "Something like that. You won't leave without saying good-bye?"

"Never." He stood and took her hand. He kissed it gently. "Until we meet again, princess."

Heat rushed to her cheeks. She smiled one last time and hurried away. The guard looked away, but the servant watched them nosily. Roanna ignored him.

In the garden, she met the maid just as she arrived.

"Princess! I thought you would be here already." The maid was young, maybe fourteen years old. She had bright red hair and freckles on her nose. Her name was Mindy.

"I received a message I needed to take care of. Are you ready?"

Mindy nodded. She showed Roanna how she had learned that if she shut her eyes, she could better close out distraction. She told her how she spoke silently within herself to bring about greater results.

Her instructions sounded like prayer. Roanna smiled to herself. Soon, she had forgotten—at least temporarily—about Gregory's strange outing, Ben's upcoming trip to Lox, and the truth behind her past.

Gregory did not arrive in time for supper that evening. What was keeping him? She couldn't even guess. Ben said that if he didn't arrive by breakfast, he would need to make the decision to leave.

Roanna waited until long shadows danced across her room from the fire, but Gregory had not returned yet. She lay in bed, considering the future. What if she and Ben were never allowed to marry? It was absurd. Of course, they would be allowed to marry. Wouldn't they?

In the morning, she hurried to breakfast. Ben sat beside Gregory, their heads bent low in conversation. The seats on either side of them were taken, so Roanna moved to the seat across from Ben. Lady Wendy and her mother sat across from Gregory. Roanna remembered them from home, though she hadn't conversed with Wendy with any regularity.

"Good morning, Princess." The duchess smiled at her.

"Good morning, Duchess."

"I was disappointed that you were not with us on our outing to the Van Hoosier estate yesterday." She watched her with narrowed eyes, as if gauging her reaction.

Roanna shifted. "I hate to have missed it."

The duchess babbled on about the mansion, the countryside, the family. Roanna listened, but the woman offered nothing to lead her to believe they had been on a mission for information. The duchess also mentioned, in hushed whispers, the budding relationship between Prince Gregory and Lady Wendy.

Roanna raised her eyebrows at this information and made a mental note to ask Gregory later.

At last, Gregory rescued her. "Can I speak with

you, Roanna?"

They left the table, Ben in tow. They walked from the dining room and toward a small sitting area near the library.

Gregory seemed uncertain. Nervous.

Odd for Gregory.

"What is it?" she asked.

"I was at the Van Hoosier estate yesterday. Do you know of them?"

Roanna knew of no one. "No, I've never met them."

"One is Henri Van Hoosier. He mentioned he was sometimes assigned to your security detail."

Roanna frowned and thought. "The tall one, with blond hair?"

"That would be Henri."

Roanna nodded slowly. She did know him, though she hadn't spoken with him. "What about them?"

"I have reason to believe at least some of them are part of the rebel band. I wondered if you could speak with Katherine to ensure they are invited to your engagement ball."

The engagement ball? "You plan to turn my ball into an investigation?"

He smirked. "Come now, sis. You don't expect me to believe you actually object to this."

A slow smile spread across her face. "No. I don't suppose I do. I can ask, though she is likely to find it strange, don't you think?"

Gregory frowned slightly but then shook his head. "Tell her you've met Henri Van Hoosier, a palace guard of noble birth. I don't think she will find that strange."

Roanna shrugged. "Very well." She paused,

glanced around, then spoke. "Gregory, are you forming an attachment to Lady Wendy?"

Gregory drew back, his eyebrows pulled together. "Lady Wendy? Why would you ask?"

"Her mother told me it was true."

He sighed. "I had hoped—rather, I had tried. But I've spoken to Lady Wendy and explained that it is not to be. Her mother is finding it difficult to accept."

Roanna watched him. His pink cheeks, and his quick answer. Mother had mentioned asking Merry Stern to the palace in Chester's Wake. Was this why Gregory had given up a relationship with Wendy?

Ben cleared his throat, drawing attention away from her brother's love affairs. "Gregory believes it best if I return to Lox."

The statement clamped around Roanna's stomach and clenched it. "You believe it's safe?"

Gregory sighed. "The rebels have orchestrated attacks and kidnappings. It would be no hard thing for them to poison the queen. Ben should see his mother."

"Of course." Roanna reached for Ben's hand. He gave her a small smile.

"I won't be away for long. Only enough to see her and be sure she's on the mend. I'll update Mother and Father about what's happening here."

Roanna snorted. "What's happening here is almost nothing. No wedding date, no movement as to the rebel bands."

"That's not entirely true." Gregory looked around as if to ensure privacy. "We're making progress. It's just not something we've shared."

Roanna itched to ask more, but she knew Gregory. He would not share more until he was ready and certainly not simply because she had asked.

"I'll go and be back as soon as I can." Ben squeezed her hand. "I'll likely leave later this afternoon."

Roanna nodded. She understood whether she liked it or not.

Later that evening, Roanna sought out Katherine at supper. The dining hall was boisterous and glowing, lit with the flickering flames of candelabra and chandelier. Diners sat around the large table, and the seat directly to Katherine's right was open.

Ben had left earlier in the day hoping to make quick time home, and now Roanna approached Katherine and took the empty seat. "Katherine, I wondered about the guest list for the engagement ball."

Katherine turned from her other dining partner and gave her full attention to Roanna. "You wish to invite someone specific?"

"Gregory told me how he'd visited the Van Hoosier estate and how much he enjoyed it. He said a palace guard here, Henri, was part of that noble family. I wondered if they had been invited as Gregory enjoyed them so much."

Katherine smiled and patted Roanna's hands. "That has been taken care of, and yes, the Van Hoosiers have been invited."

"Oh good. Gregory will be pleased to hear it."

Katherine restarted her conversation with her other partner, and Roanna scanned the room for Gregory. She did not spot him. Out again?

She hid her frown and made idle conversation with some of the other diners. Duchess Higgins again approached and attempted a conversation. She mentioned they were thinking of leaving the entourage unless Roanna thought Gregory would object. The duchess said they were homesick, but Roanna thought jilted was the more likely description.

At last, Roanna begged out of the conversation by complaint of a headache. She hurried back toward the family wing of the palace. A pang behind her eye halted her.

She opened her mind, gently at first but then wider. Roland hadn't pestered her in days. Perhaps it was someone else.

You're always running off.

Roanna smiled. *Another brotherly bit of advice? What have I done this time?*

Stefan's laugh sounded in her mind. *I'm sure you've done something, but I'm not aware of it, whatever it is. I was looking for Gregory.*

Roanna paused. She didn't wish to admit she found Gregory's behavior suspect. *I haven't seen him.*

Stefan, too, paused. *Odd hours your brother keeps. And he's always sneaking away.*

Roanna didn't answer as she didn't know what to say. Gregory had his mission, but it seemed more than that.

Has he found a love here in Dawson's Edge?

She frowned. Had Gregory found a love? Or had he brought one with him from Chester's Wake? It certainly wasn't Lady Wendy, despite the duchess's hopes.

You'll have to tell me if you find the answer to that. She hoped it came across playfully, rather than suspiciously.

Stefan chuckled. *I'll leave you to your thoughts, then, Sister.*

Roanna said good night then closed her mind once

more. She would ready for bed and hope to see Gregory in the morning to discuss what Katherine had told her.

24

"Wake up, miss!" Bette's frantic voice pulled her from the dregs of sleep.

Roanna sat up, frowning. "What is it?"

Bette pulled at her arm. Her eyes were stretched wide in panic. "We must hurry! The palace is under attack!"

Attack?

Roanna bolted from the bed and grabbed her dressing robe. "Tell me what you know."

"I don't know anything, miss. I only know the guards awoke me and instructed I get you to safety. We have to reach the passageway in the hallway to get to the bunker."

Roanna had taken the secret passageway to the underground bunker once before when the palace was under attack. She quickly slipped her feet into slippers and grabbed Bette's hand as they raced for the door.

The hallway was empty as they raced from her room. They ran hand in hand, but as they turned toward the passageway at the end of the hall, loud footsteps pounded behind them. Before she had time to scream or run, hands wrenched her backward.

"I found the princess!" someone hissed. For a

fleeting moment she hoped it was one of the palace guards. But the hope was short lived. A palace guard would have urged her forward, not yanked her back.

She struggled against the brute holding her. He was big—huge really. He stood head and shoulders above her, and the breadth of his shoulders was intimidating. He only dug his fingers into her skin tighter.

"You're coming with us."

"Let me go!" she said. "Bette!" But she couldn't even turn to see what had become of her maid.

"None of that now," the brute said. He held a cloth against her mouth and nose. Its sickly-sweet scent made her stomach roll and her mind swim. And then she knew nothing.

25

Gregory...

Gregory woke, the sound of rushing footsteps giving evidence that someone was in his rooms. He sprang from the bed, noting the darkness that hung in the air. He met the visitor just as he reached the doorway to the sitting area.

A palace servant. The servant bowed slightly. "Prince Gregory, His Highness the King has sent for you. It is urgent."

Gregory nodded and quickly changed into more appropriate clothing. Then he followed the servant down the halls. The servant did not lead him to the king's office. Rather, they headed toward the elevator that led to the underground bunker. The same one they had occupied months before when the palace was under attack.

Surely, the palace wasn't again under attack. The royal family had taken care to secure it better against future attacks.

But they stepped onto the metal elevator and headed into the belly of the earth. The cage rattled slightly as it descended, but a few moments later, they had arrived.

The underground bunker bustled with bodies, all moving and talking over each other. Chaos. Gregory did not need direction on where to go. He remembered the War Room well enough. He found the king along with Roland and Stefan pacing.

The king spotted him immediately. His eyes were wild, and his hair stood on end. "Prince Gregory. Something terrible has happened."

Gregory's muscles tensed. His heart stilled then thundered. He waited.

The king rubbed a hand over his haggard face. "They've struck again. They took Roanna."

Gregory's mind reeled. Took her? After threats were made and the king assured she was safe, they still managed to get inside the palace and take her? Anger exploded inside him, but he kept himself in check.

"There's more." Roland glanced at the king, as if gauging whether he would tell the tale. "We've received word. The prince of Lox was attacked in his airship on the way to Lox."

Gregory widened his eyes. He leaned forward slightly. "They attacked an airship as well as a palace all in one night?"

Roland flinched. "It appears so."

"Ben was taken?"

"No."

Relief washed over Gregory as Roland continued.

"Not taken, only injured slightly it appears. He is well and in Lox now. We have not alerted the Bellevues of our situation here."

"And my parents?"

Roland glanced again at the king, who was apparently too overcome with emotion to explain the situation. "No. Please feel free to do this." He nodded at an aide, who approached with a Messenger.

Gregory took calming breaths as he prepared to speak with his parents. How could this happen? He contacted his parents, giving them what little information he had. They wept, and his heart wept with them.

"I will find her," he promised.

Mother and Father implored him to be quick about it.

When they finished the communication, Gregory turned to the Dawsons. "You must tell the Bellevues as soon as possible. They need to understand what we're dealing with."

Stefan stepped up. "I will do that. I can make myself useful every now and then."

Gregory nodded to him, wondering at the king's lack of action. King Dawson leaned against his desk, his head bent low. He was filled with sorrow, Gregory understood, but he was the king, and his palace had just been attacked. He must move to action.

Gregory pressed Roland for more information. "They moved quickly, taking Roanna and leaving behind her maid."

"Bette."

"Yes. She was found in the hallway, unconscious."

"They hurt no one else?"

"No, it appears they knew exactly where to target."

Gregory flared his nostrils in anger and frustration. "Has there been any contact? A ransom asked? Demands made?" Surely, if it was the rebels, they would be demanding the Dawsons step down from the throne.

Of course, it would be ridiculous for them to

demand such a thing. Rarely would a ruler risk their entire kingdom to save one member of their family. If that were the case, royal kidnappings would happen rampantly. No, there was no negotiating with terrorists, and for good reason.

The rebels would surely know such a thing.

Except Roanna was different. The king and queen had only gained their long-lost daughter recently. One could deduce they would do anything to keep her.

"No contact so far," Roland said.

Gregory nodded his understanding, but suspicions raged in his mind. There was someone who might know something about this. He meant to speak with her immediately.

26

Merry...

Merry had heard nothing from Gregory since they had returned from the Van Hoosier estate. She had busied herself over the last day with going over the family trees she had made with Queen Charlotte while in Chester's Wake. Earlier that morning she and Wesley had taken a walk around the cul-de-sac. They had spoken about Chester's Wake, and Wesley had told her about the Rejected Homes there. He'd told stories of visiting the homes with Princess Roanna when she would make her monthly donations. He told her of the children who lived there, as well as the young adults who were either Terminated or set free upon reaching adulthood—all depending upon their condition.

The idea of the homes both fascinated and appalled Merry, and she determined to visit them when they returned to the northern kingdom. How did these children grow up knowing the uncertainty of their fate? Merry felt strongly related to their uncertainty.

The walk with Wesley had ended, and now she had nothing with which to occupy her time. She sat in the small parlor room, looking at a book without really reading it.

The rumble of an auto caught her attention. Wesley was already outside, and as was the usual routine, she expected them to converse for a few moments before Gregory would come inside.

But moments later the front door burst open, and Merry jumped in her seat. She stood and hurried to see what was happening.

Gregory stood in the entryway. Fire burned in his gaze. Red stained his cheekbones. His nostrils flared.

"There has been an attack at the palace here in Dawson's Edge." He spoke low but heatedly.

With horror she realized that he suspected she knew of this. Perhaps even believed her involved. She shook her head. "When? How?"

He stepped closer and clasped her upper arm. The pressure wasn't enough to harm her, but it was certainly enough to frighten her. "They took Roanna." His voice broke as he said his sister's name, but the fiery look didn't leave his eyes.

"I know nothing about it, Gregory. I swear it to you. I know nothing outside of what my own Papa arranged weeks ago. My involvement is over. I am committed to helping you." She had nothing to convince him but her own word. Would it be enough?

But he didn't release her arm. "How can I trust you when you withhold information at will?"

Fear wrapped around her like a claw, but she didn't fight him. "What are you talking about?"

He kept her gaze another beat then looked to his own hand still holding her arm. He released her as if just realizing what he was doing. He paced away, and she watched as he took several deep breaths.

"Henri Van Hoosier is your cousin. Hattie Van Hoosier is your cousin. You did not feel this was relevant to share?" He shook his head. "I am not a fool. You knew you should share it but didn't, which tells me you are not wholly committed to helping me, as you said."

Anger danced in his gaze. But more than anger, hurt.

She had done that, now for a second time. He would certainly never forgive her.

She looked down, heat blazing up her neck and into her cheeks. But she had to face her actions. How could she fix this and still save Papa?

She met his gaze once more. "I knew I could get information from Hattie, but I was afraid that if you knew of our relationship you would not allow me to speak with her. I knew it would appear suspicious if you learned the truth, but it was the only place I knew to start."

His expression did not change. He remained angry and distrustful of her. "There is more."

Merry held her breath. What would he reveal now?

"Prince Benjamin was also attacked, though he escaped unscathed."

Merry frowned. "Attacked? Where? In the palace?"

"No, on his way to Lox."

"It is as the ambassador from Jakbar said."

Gregory lowered his eyebrows as a deep frown engulfed his face. He paced once more. "I suspected the rebels had somehow poisoned the queen of Lox when I heard Ben planned to travel. They must have planned it so Ben would be gone, and they could take

Roanna." He stopped and shook his head. "But why?"

Merry had theories—to hurt the Dawsons, to cause unrest, to show their power in the face of the capture of their leaders. But they were only theories. She did not voice them.

"It doesn't feel right." He stared away as if thinking.

She considered the pain he must be feeling at the idea of his sister being harmed. She had an idea that had presented itself before, but she had dismissed it as unlikely to be heeded. Now, however, things were different. "I have thought of someone else we could question."

He turned back to her, his eyes narrowed and suspicious. Still angry. But he nodded. "Go on." His words were harsh.

"While I imagine you have spoken to Dr. Presnell, I think it would be worth our time to speak with him again. Rather, if I spoke with him."

Gregory shook his head, frowning. "Why? He is old and senile."

"He is old, yes. He is not senile. He is…forgetful. I know how to make him remember."

Again, his eyes narrowed. "How?"

"I have been conversing with him all my life. He is a precious old man who needs gentle care. I know how to give that gentle care."

His nostrils flared and he turned away. He paced several turns then turned to her. The color had not left his cheeks, but he straightened his shoulders. "Very well, but I will not let you speak with him alone. I only agree because at this moment the priority is finding my sister."

"That is my priority, as well." His words stung,

but she deserved them. And she knew in her heart then that her own words were true. Roanna had been kind to her. Kinder than she had needed to be. She was innocent and did not deserve to be used by the rebels this way. Merry wasn't sure what she believed, but she did not believe in hurting innocent people to come to a certain end.

Gregory said nothing else. He stomped outside.

No sounds of an auto rumbled to life from the outdoors. She peeked out the window and saw Gregory, Wesley, and Gideon hovered together in conversation.

She frowned. They might at least come inside where they would be hidden from anyone passing nearby. When would they go to see the doctor? This afternoon or the morning at the latest. It was no quick trip to visit Dr. Presnell. And it would be no easy thing to extract information from him. It would be time consuming. Tedious. Arduous. It would take patience and a gentle kindness that most were not willing to invest when it came to speaking with an old man.

But Dr. Presnell knew all the secrets of the rebels for he had been guiding them for decades.

Merry hurried upstairs to prepare a few things to take along in case anything extra was needed. She found a small carpet bag and packed an extra set of clothing, and she changed into more comfortable boots that had no heel. Just as she finished lacing them, the door downstairs closed.

She grabbed her bag and hurried down.

Wesley stood at the bottom of the steps. He glanced at the bag in her hand then looked to her face. "You have gathered we will be leaving soon, I see."

"Yes, I thought it necessary."

He nodded. "How clever you are, Lady Stern."

She smiled at him gratefully. "Shall we go then?"

He bowed slightly. "Indeed."

Merry quickly found Fraja and told her she would be going out and not to worry if she didn't return quickly. Then she met Wesley at the front door. He led her to the auto, where Gideon sat in the driver's seat and Gregory sat in the back. Wesley opened the door to the back, and Merry hesitated only a moment before climbing inside. It was likely to be a long, uncomfortable ride.

Gregory worked with his head bent over his Messenger screen as they drove. Occasionally, Wesley peered over the front seat and spoke with her, peppering her with questions about the countryside, or her childhood, or her opinion on fruit tarts and whipped desserts.

At other times, Gregory interrupted their conversation to ask Wesley tactical questions or security questions. When needed, he scooted forward to speak quietly, she supposed to keep her from overhearing.

During those times, such as now, Merry's mind went to Roanna's kidnapping. Prince Benjamin, attacked. Princess Roanna, taken. The Queen of Lox, ill.

All at the rebels' hand, in one orchestrated attack? She frowned. Did their reach extend so far?

"Do you think so, Lady Merry?"

Merry looked to Wesley. He and Gregory stared at her. "Pardon?"

"We're getting close, I believe. But you know better than I."

Merry glanced out the window. The land had begun flattening out, and the smell of sea salt hung in the air. Moss-covered trees lined one side of the road. "Yes. It won't be long now."

At last, they rounded a bend and a small lane stood out on the right. "That's it," she directed.

Gideon turned them onto the quaint pathway that ended at a modest cottage.

"I will go with you." Gregory watched her now, suspicious.

"I don't believe I can get him to open up if you are present." She knew the words would cast doubt on her, but they were truth.

Gregory hesitated.

"What if I accompany Lady Merry?"

All eyes turned to Wesley.

Merry's heart buoyed. "Yes, that is a magnificent idea."

Gregory let out a long breath. "Yes, you should accompany her."

Wesley quickly exited the auto. He opened the door for Merry, and together they approached Dr. Presnell's cottage. Their knock was greeted by an elderly butler. He was tall, towering over them both, and he had thick tufts of hair atop his head. His skin was pale and sagging, but his eyes were bright.

"Gerard." Merry smiled. "I am here to see Dr. Presnell. Is he in?"

Gerard straightened. "Lady Merry Stern. You will be most welcome by the doctor." His gaze darted to Wesley. "Come inside, and I will fetch him."

They followed the butler inside, and he led them to a small sitting area. The walls were lined with bookshelves, and various medical instruments littered the tables that were placed throughout the room. Thick curtains covered the windows, but Gerard pulled them back to let in more light.

"Make yourselves at home." He made his way to the doorway. "I will return shortly."

Merry and Wesley sat on the single sofa, leaving two winged armchairs empty.

"You've known the doctor long?" Wesley asked.

"From my infancy. Papa always had dealings with him."

"And do you know much of his involvement in the rebellion?" These words were spoken softly.

Merry paused. She frowned. "I thought I knew, but I am beginning to suspect I don't know much of anything at all."

Wesley's eyes showed understanding and compassion. Did he suspect her inner struggles regarding what she felt about the things she had been raised to believe?

Gerard returned, followed immediately by Dr. Presnell. Merry smiled brightly and rose to meet him. "Dr. Presnell, what a pleasure to see you again." She moved quickly to hug him.

A grin broke across the man's face. He was short and balding, though a few white hairs remained. He had grown thicker in the middle, but his smile was just as jolly. "Lady Merry." His voice wobbled. "This is a most pleasant surprise." He returned her hug, albeit slowly.

"Come sit with us, Doctor." Merry tugged his hand gently. "I have brought my dear friend, Wesley, with me. I hope you do not mind."

"No, no. I do not mind at all."

Wesley moved to an armchair, and Merry sat with Dr. Presnell on the sofa.

"To what do I owe the pleasure of your visit, Lady

Merry?" Dr. Presnell asked. "Do I remember wrongly or were you not put on house arrest when your father was taken in that unfortunate matter regarding the royal family?"

Merry gripped Dr. Presnell's hand. "You do not remember wrongly. I was, indeed, put on house arrest, but that has been lifted. I was overjoyed when I realized I would get to come and see you."

Dr. Presnell's eyes brightened. "That is good to hear."

Merry chatted with him for a few moments. She asked after his health and his humors. Then, leaning forward slightly, she went on. "Dr. Presnell, do you know that Papa is still in the dungeon?"

The light in his eyes dimmed slightly. "Yes, yes. I believe I remember this."

"I would very much like to free him. Have you heard of anything being done in this regard?"

Dr. Presnell frowned. "In what regard, my dear?"

"In regard to freeing Papa. Is anyone working to free Papa?"

Dr. Presnell sighed. "I am too old to free him, Lady Merry. Though I wish I could."

"I know you do." Merry smiled. "So do I."

Dr. Presnell asked after Wesley and what family he came from. Wesley—ever congenial—explained he had come from a poor working family, which seemed to impress Dr. Presnell.

After a time, Merry pressed him further. "Has there been any new developments since Papa's arrest? I worry over the cause, and the mission, without Papa or the Maynes to oversee things."

Dr. Presnell scratched his head. "Things seem to have stalled with the mission of late."

He didn't elaborate.

"Have they, Dr. Presnell?" Merry asked softly. "Is there no plan to continue to stir the people or to disrupt the royal family? A plot to take the princess, perhaps?"

"No, no. That was an old plot. We took the princess years ago."

Merry froze. She had not expected such a confession, and Wesley was taking note, no doubt.

"Yes?" Merry tread carefully. She could lose Dr. Presnell's line of thought too easily. "When did you take the princess? I can't quite remember that story."

"That was years ago, when the baby was first born. I didn't want to do it. I couldn't get rid of the baby, no matter what they said." He sighed. "I made sure she lived." He nodded absently, as if remembering. "I made sure they both lived."

Dr. Presnell glanced back to her, his eye keen. "I'm a doctor, you know. It is my preference to uphold life, no matter my orders."

Merry quickly smiled. "Of course. And you are a man of integrity. I would expect no less." But her mind worked. By whose orders did Dr. Presnell move? He was the leader of the rebel movement.

"Thank you, my dear. You are too kind."

"So, there are no new plots against the princess, then."

Dr. Presnell frowned. "No, no. We took the princess years ago."

"I understand." She squeezed his hand again.

"You should check with your father. He likely kept the order. He keeps everything, you know."

Merry frowned, but before she could consider his words Dr. Presnell hollered. "Gerard! Bring us tea. I'm an old man, and I'm thirsty."

"Tea sounds marvelous. Thank you, Dr. Presnell."

They spoke pleasantly for a lengthy time, but Merry could not seem to hold his attention long enough to get any further information. No matter. They had enough. At long last, she gave him another tight hug and said good-bye.

Wesley didn't speak as they approached the auto, and once inside, he continued to keep his peace. Merry was grateful. It appeared he trusted her.

Gregory watched her with impatient eyes. It must have been torture for him to stay outside for the entire visit.

"According to Dr. Presnell, there was no plot to kidnap the princess."

Gregory narrowed his eyes. "But she was, indeed, kidnapped."

"Indeed." She spoke the word softly, considering herself what it meant. "If Papa and Duke Mayne are in the dungeon, it is possible no one is keeping Dr. Presnell up to date on the happenings within the rebellion."

"But?"

"But I feel that is unlikely. He has been at the head of the thing for many years."

"So, you do not believe it was the rebels who took Roanna and attacked Ben?" He deduced her meaning quickly enough.

She shook her head. "I do not know yet what to think. Dr. Presnell had a lot to say, and it does involve Roanna." She glanced at Wesley who only looked straight ahead. Gideon drove stoically as seemed to be his normal persona.

"What is that supposed to mean, then?"

"He says he was ordered to take the princess as a baby. He was supposed to kill her, but he couldn't do it, so he made sure she was safe. Then, he said he made sure they were both safe."

Gregory's eyebrows pulled low. "Both safe?"

She nodded slightly, allowing him time to process everything they had discussed.

Gideon spoke. "Your Highness?"

"What is it?" Gregory was impatient now. Irritated.

"We are being followed, sir. I noted an auto that passed the lane while we waited outside the cottage. It passed by several times. Now it is a way behind us."

Gregory growled and glanced to their rear. Merry couldn't help but do the same. As noted, someone on the road followed them from a considerable distance.

"Speed up, of course. We'll see if we can lose them." He turned back to the front and closed his eyes. "So, the rebels took Roanna as a baby and deposited her in Chester's Wake. And Dr. Presnell took the other baby—a girl, indeed—" he paused, as if considering this. "And he did something else with her. Something to keep her alive."

Merry watched him. Studied him. She didn't want to cause him further pain, but he would be hurt no matter what. "That is what he said. But that is not what I find the most peculiar. He said he was following orders. He said my papa would have record of these orders." She shook her head. "Who was giving them these orders? Dr. Presnell was in charge of everyone."

He looked to her once again. His expression was blank. He shook his head. "I don't know."

The auto vibrated with speed as they zipped along. Merry looked out the back window again, but their chasers had not relented. "What could they want?" she asked.

Wesley watched, too. "It's hard to say. They may have recognized the prince. They may want nothing more than to rob us."

Gideon grunted. "Or it could be whoever attacked the prince of Lox and kidnapped the princess."

A chill rushed over her, and her skin prickled. Truly? She hadn't considered they might be in real danger.

"Go faster." Gregory's command put his driver into action, and the auto sped even faster. They took a curve, and Merry was thrown against the door. She didn't complain, and no one asked after her. A moment later, the other auto followed.

The trees thickened as they drove. The flatlands varied into slight hills, and the auto behind them drifted from sight, only to reappear moments later.

"Turn onto one of the dirt paths," Gregory instructed.

"They'll see the dust." Gideon had a point.

"We'll never lose them like this."

Gideon didn't argue further. As soon as they had crested another hill, Gideon jerked the wheel to the right, and they sped down a different path. The cloud of dust behind them kept Merry from seeing whether they were followed. A moment later, they turned again.

A loud clank filled the air, and the auto shook.

Merry gasped, and Gideon's nostrils flared as he gripped the wheel.

"Go as far as you can," Gregory said. "We will stop when it becomes necessary."

They drove for long minutes, but Merry no longer

saw anyone behind them. Two more dirt paths crisscrossed their drive, and each time they took the new road. At last, the auto refused to go farther. It sputtered and shook until it stopped.

27

Merry chewed her bottom lip. Frustration was nothing new to her, but this was something else altogether. Fear. Uncertainty. She had never known these feelings quite so poignantly.

Well, almost never.

There were things at work here that she must not be aware of, the same way things were at work when she thought she was bringing Princess Roanna into the fold of the rebellion. She hadn't known the truth about Roanna, and that knowledge cost them dearly.

What was at play here that might wreck her future?

Gregory worked manically with Wesley and Gideon to fix the auto. A large sheet of metal had come off the bottom of the chassis. It had twisted and snapped and hung by only a screw. The men worked to salvage what they could and reattach it.

Sweat pooled on Gregory's light-colored shirt and dripped down his forehead. He shouldn't have come. The crown prince shouldn't be here putting himself in danger this way. All of Chester's Wake could be in danger because of her plan to speak with Dr. Presnell.

Looking to the south, a billow of dust moved in

the distance. Was it their chasers catching up? They would be caught if the men couldn't get them moving, now.

"It's fixed!" Wesley shouted. He and Gideon snatched the tools from the ground and tossed them into the auto, while Gregory grabbed her arm with one hand, his other hand holding the offending metal sheet. He hauled her to the door.

"Climb in," he barked.

She didn't need any further instruction. Wesley was in the driver's seat and pulling away before Gregory had even shut the door opposite hers. They sped away, racing toward a side road she hoped would give them enough headway to lose their trackers. Gregory still held the broken piece of metal in his hands. He caught her looking. "I didn't want to leave any trail behind us." It came out more like a growl.

Merry looked away. He blamed this on her. Of course, he did. As much as she'd tried to earn his trust, he obviously held her poor judgments against her. Not that she could blame him.

Wesley took a sharp curve, and Merry was tossed sideways. She landed against Gregory and gasped. The metal shards he held sliced through her blouse and into her left shoulder.

She quickly pulled away from him and rearranged her position to keep the wound hidden. The last thing they needed was to slow down because of worry over her. There would be time to care for the injury later.

Gregory constantly glanced behind them, and she picked up on the habit. She never saw another auto following.

They drove for an hour straight, Merry ignoring the pain in her shoulder and working to keep pressure on it without drawing too much attention. As the sun dipped below the horizon, they finally slowed to a more reasonable pace.

"We should stop and figure out where we are," Wesley said. "I can hide us, and we can get a bearing on our location."

"I know this area," Merry said. "There's a fresh spring and pool about a half mile down the road. It's hidden among an outcropping of small cliffs. I would appreciate stopping, however briefly." She wanted desperately to clean the wound and create a makeshift bandage.

"Do you know your way back from here?" Gregory asked. He still barked it at her, but he didn't sound quite so accusatory.

"Yes, but there are multiple routes. I'll leave you with a few to consider while I freshen up."

He nodded, and they easily found the deserted springs ahead. Merry climbed out, carrying the small bag she'd brought along with her. She quickly explained the various options they had at getting back to the safe house. Then she stepped back. "I'll be at the pool for a few minutes. I would appreciate privacy." The men only stared at her a moment, seeming confused, but they nodded and turned away to discuss their plans.

She dashed toward the pool and immediately stripped off her corset. She pulled one arm out of the sleeve of her blouse to expose her injured left shoulder. Blood still oozed from the deep wound, but it wasn't gushing. She dug inside the satchel and found a piece of cloth she could use to gently clean the wound. The cool water stung at first but then soothed her. She worked slowly, being careful not to restart the bleeding. Fraja could stitch her when she returned to the safe house.

Once she had cleaned herself sufficiently, she stripped off the entire shirt and quickly worked to replace it with one from the satchel. It was surely almost time for them to depart.

28

Gregory...

They decided in a few moments which route to take, but after further inspection of the auto, they weren't certain they would be able to make it. Gregory wandered off a few paces to dip his hands into the stream. He splashed the cool water on his sweaty face.

That chase had been too close. Things hadn't gone the way they'd planned, not at all, and it was unlikely they would ever know who had chased them.

He frowned. Had someone else been working against them, or had Merry herself sabotaged the efforts? He hated himself for having begun to trust her, only to find himself in the same place of anger and resentment all over again.

Still, sabotaging this plan wouldn't help her free her father, so he could only conclude she hadn't been the responsible party in this catastrophe.

He scowled. He didn't want to defend her against his own mental accusations.

Glancing back at Wesley and Gideon, he saw they were bent over the map and intent on their tasks. It was nearly time that they needed to be on their way. How far could they go with the darkening sky and little clear path? Still, they had to do something.

He didn't want to leave without assuring himself they were in the clear. He looked to the top of the small cliffs. That would be the perfect place to see the road.

Making quick work of hiking the small, rocky incline, he'd soon reached the top. He kept himself low to the ground so as to not give away their position if someone happened to be travelling their way, but nothing moved along the dusty road. They were safe, for now.

He turned to make his way back to the men, but a soft groan caught his attention. Just over the next rocky surface was a pool of water, and Merry sat on a ledge at its bank. Pink water surrounded her, and she held a bloody cloth against her shoulder.

Panic gripped him, but he quickly pushed it aside. She wasn't in danger or she'd be in more distress. But when had she been injured?

The metal shards in the auto? She'd fallen hard against them, but she hadn't complained. Hadn't said a word.

No, Merry wouldn't say anything. She was like that.

Frustrating admiration for her rose up again. He watched another moment as she gently cleaned the wound. But then, without warning, she stripped off her blouse.

He quickly turned away, but he couldn't help the burning in his cheeks.

Closing his eyes and taking a deep breath, he willed his heart to slow. He began the descent to the road and the auto below. They would give Merry her privacy. Then they would be on their way, but he would be sure to ask after her wellbeing.

~*~

Merry's shoulder ached as she returned to the men. They stood huddled around the auto, as she'd left them.

"We likely won't make it back to the capital with the auto in this condition." Wesley shook his head. He rubbed his forehead.

"What do we do?" Gregory sounded tired. Defeated. He looked between his guards.

"We're in the middle of a long stretch of forest." Gideon crossed his arms, his legs hip width apart. "What about the Messenger?"

Merry closed her eyes and took a deep breath. The Messengers wouldn't work out here. It was too remote.

Wesley confirmed it. "I tried as soon as we stopped. I can't get anything on it."

"It's dark." Gregory looked to the sky. "We can sleep in the auto."

"Unprotected?" Wesley raised an eyebrow. "I wouldn't put my prince in that situation unless absolutely necessary."

Gregory raised his arms and looked around. "Waiting for a better situation to drop out of the sky?"

"There are people who live nearby." The words burst out. She didn't want to say them. Didn't want to tromp through these trees at night and speak to the people who made their home deep in the forest. But they might be able to help.

All eyes were on her.

"Who?" Gregory demanded. He obviously hadn't

regained trust in her.

She rubbed her shoulder, the ache growing. The scene in front of her wobbled slightly, and she closed her eyes for a moment. When was the last time she'd eaten? "They're odd people. I've never seen the villages, but I've heard of them. People live there who are said to possess great powers. They don't socialize."

Gregory quirked an eyebrow. "That doesn't sound safe."

Wesley laughed. "That is quite the understatement."

Merry shrugged then winced with the pain.

Wesley frowned. "What is it?"

She quickly shook her head. The action increased her dizziness. "I'm fine. I am only trying to help."

Gideon scowled at her. "How do we know you're not leading us straight to danger? No. You can't go there, Your Highness."

Gregory glanced at Gideon. "Check yourself, Gideon." He rubbed his forehead again. "We have two options. Sleep in the auto or go see these people with anomalies."

"Lady Merry." Wesley took a step toward her. "Do you believe these village people are dangerous?"

She swallowed hard, her throat suddenly dry. No one had ever asked her opinion on anomalies or powers. No one had ever challenged her to formulate a belief on any of the major goings on in the world. What did she think?

She swallowed again. "I don't believe they're dangerous, no." The words were breathy. Stars danced in front of her eyes. Would a confession like that make a person dizzy?

"Merry?" Wesley's tone held concern.

"Merry." She realized Gregory's hand was on her arm. "She's lost too much blood."

Merry frowned. How did he know?

The world went black.

~*~

When she awoke, she lay on the seat of the auto. All four doors were open, and Gregory stood at her head, outside of the auto. He squatted beside her.

"You didn't tell us about your wound."

Her mouth was dry. She licked her lips. "How did you know?"

He looked away. "I saw you. At the ravine." He glanced back to her, his eyes wary. "I looked away as soon as I realized, but I saw the blood."

Heat rose to her cheeks, and she was glad for the darkness. "I'm thirsty."

He quickly retrieved a small flask and handed it to her. "It's water."

He helped her sit up and sip from the flask. "What do we do?" she asked.

"You need help, but we have to balance the reality here. Can we make it through the dark forest in a reasonable amount of time, and will these people even help us? Or would it be better to have you rest here overnight and find help in the daylight?"

"Am I in actual peril?" She glanced at her still-covered shoulder. "I don't feel that poorly."

"Wesley examined your wound. He is trained in first aid. He says the wound is deep. It needs cleaned and stitched, but you are not in peril."

She lay back on the seat. "I know the village people exist, and I know they have powers. I know their powers vary greatly. I don't know, however, if they're trustworthy." A headache started at the base of her neck and quickly inked its way to her temples and forehead. "I only know what Papa said." She looked up at Gregory. He was listening to her, and for once, his guard seemed down. This was Gregory. Not the offended prince, the angry man. Only Gregory.

"Papa did not trust those who were different. He spoke about the villages often enough, and I know they're here. They're not far."

"Do you feel it's worth it?"

She kept his gaze. It was the longest he'd gone without looking away in the weeks she had worked with him. His look changed, and he shifted. His Adam's apple bobbed as he swallowed.

"I'm sorry you were hurt." He spoke softly.

"It's nothing."

He shook his head, finally breaking her gaze. "It isn't nothing. You've been extremely compliant, and I haven't treated you with respect. I should have known the moment you were injured, and instead, you've endured bleeding and pain for hours."

She kept quiet because his words were truthful. He had not treated her with respect. But she was not wholly innocent. "Then I should apologize as well."

He looked back to her, frowning slightly. "How so?"

"I did not mean for any of this to happen." She forced her tone to remain even. "I did not know the things I know now, and I blindly followed the orders of others. It was real between us, Gregory, and I'm so sorry for the way things worked out."

Pain passed behind his eyes, but in a moment, it had disappeared. He looked away. "I will speak with the guards. We will decide what to do."

The aloof Gregory had returned.

He strode away, and Merry sighed and lay her head back. No matter if he accepted her words, she had said them, and the burden was lifted from her shoulders.

She waited for their instructions as to whether they would go or stay. Her lightheadedness had passed, but she was of no use to them in their discussions. She would only make Gregory uncomfortable and Gideon angry.

Minutes passed, and at last, Gregory approached her. "We will try to find these villagers you mentioned. If they can offer any aid, and help keep you more comfortable, it is for the best."

She pulled herself up to a sitting position. "As you say." She climbed from the auto, and Gregory took her elbow to assist her.

"I'm quite well," she said. "Don't take any unnecessary care on my behalf."

But he watched her uneasily, his brow pulled low. He did not release her arm as she arranged herself. "I would rather be sure. You did faint."

The guards pushed the auto to the side of the road behind some bushes. With any luck that would keep it hidden.

Gideon took the lead, picking through the brush with as much stealth as was possible in the dark. Gregory walked close beside Merry, reaching out for her any time the ground seemed uneven or slippery. Wesley brought up the rear.

Trees rose around them like mountains. The

evening air was hot and damp, but the ground was surprisingly solid and dry underfoot. Merry's strength had come back sufficiently while she had rested, and now, despite hunger, she felt well enough to tromp through the forest.

They had been walking for quite some time when Gideon stopped and held up his hand. They halted.

Why had they stopped? Were they in danger? Merry's heart thundered, and she looked around. Nothing stood out. Every shadow looked the same.

But her ears detected something. A faint rustling.

A moment later, a furry creature burst through the brush, raced in front of them, and continued on its way.

Merry let out a rushing breath, but Gregory shook his head. There was more.

She frowned.

A piercing screech filled the air. Before she had the chance to scream, they were surrounded by people. It appeared they had found the villagers.

29

Merry stayed beside Gregory and Gideon as they walked. They followed Wesley who stepped forward and took the lead. He greeted the people, explaining they had become lost on the road and had an injured member of their party.

The villagers did not seem swayed by his explanations, but he was very diplomatic and gracious—as he always seemed to be—and they did agree not to kill them on the spot.

Gideon, Gregory, and Wesley seemed unsurprised by the villagers' behavior. She supposed they had anticipated this. She likely would have realized it as well had she been thinking clearly. Her injury had left her feeling vulnerable and confused.

The villagers led them through the dark, barely making a sound. The village was not far, but it was covered in brush. It was doubtful she could have led the others here in the darkness. Homes had been constructed in a circular pattern, with a large common area in the middle of them. Candles burned through the dingy windows of the houses that were little more than huts made of mud and straw. Grass and leaves lined the pathways between houses.

The villagers led them to a small building to their right. One of them—a tall man wearing simple linen pants and a tunic—stepped inside the building while the other villagers kept their stance around Merry, Gregory, Wesley, and Gideon.

A moment later, the man reappeared. "You may enter."

Gideon stepped inside first, followed by the rest of them. An old woman sat on a stool. She was dressed in the same type of linen pants and tunic as the man who led them. Her mostly gray hair still held remnants of the black that it used to be, and her darkly tanned skin was wrinkled and dry.

"Who are you?" She spoke simply, looking at them as a group.

Wesley spoke. "We are travelling back to the capital city as guests of King Bartholomew Dawson. Our auto broke down at the road, and we would have waited there for help except one of us is injured." He gestured toward Merry.

The woman's gaze moved to her shoulder. Her eyes were black, piercing. They met Merry's gaze.

"How did you come by such injuries as a guest of the king?"

"We were in an accident." Merry spoke softly, but assuredly. She needed to convince this woman. "I was thrown."

"By a horse?"

"No, inside the auto."

The old woman's gaze moved between the men. Then she looked back to Merry. "You were thrown inside the auto, and injured, but none of these strapping fellows were injured?"

Merry frowned, but she did not waiver or look to

the men for help.

"Let me see it."

Merry paused. "I would request privacy, if I may."

A small smile touched the woman's wrinkled face. She nodded her consent.

The man who led them inside gestured for Gregory and the others to exit. Gregory frowned and looked at Merry, but she shook her head, and he left with the guards.

Merry moved forward and unbuttoned her blouse. She pulled it off one shoulder so the woman could see the wound.

The woman's touch was light. She caused Merry no pain.

She met Merry's gaze again. "What is your name?"

She quickly determined honesty was the only way to deal with this shrewd woman, spy or not. "Merry."

The woman's eyes narrowed slightly, but she did not question her further. "And the men. Do they have names?"

"That should be for them to tell."

The woman grinned this time. "Secrets, secrets. Why should we help you?"

How to answer? While she excelled in social settings, this was hardly an environment she had been trained for. "We are at your mercy." It was truth, which seemed the only way to move forward.

"You want something more than that. I can see it." This woman spoke in riddles.

"What do you mean?"

"Let me touch your shoulder again."

Merry met her eyes. Her heart fluttered, but she saw no reason to refuse. She stepped forward and the woman touched her.

A slight pang pierced Merry's shoulder. She gasped.

"Hold still, Merry." The woman frowned in concentration, and a moment later the pain subsided.

Merry looked at her shoulder and gaped. Despite the blood, the wound was drawn closed.

"What did you do?" Her words were dry, breathless.

The woman looked back to her face, her eyes calculating. "What did you think was going to happen? Don't you know who we are?"

Fear bubbled inside her, but she shoved it away. She had not been harmed, only ministered to. There was no need to fear. "Yes, I am aware of who you are."

The woman held out her hands and stood. "Well then, why should my gift surprise you so?"

"Your gift?"

"Gift." She emphasized the word, her eyes blazing with some unspoken meaning.

Merry considered the woman's behavior. What answer did she wish Merry to give? Working through the possibilities, Merry settled on a question.

"Who gave you this gift?"

A grin broke across the woman's wrinkled face. "There we have it. You're a smart girl."

The air in the hut seemed to dissipate, making it hard to breathe. Merry's throat tightened. She stood on a precipice, yet she knew not what lay beyond. Desperation washed over her.

"Please speak plainly."

"Gifts must come from somewhere, no?" The woman nodded. "Aye, they must come from somewhere. My gift comes from above. Every person here who is gifted? It comes from above. Even the king himself has a gift that has come from above."

Above? She knew to what the woman referred, though she wasn't sure she believed it. "How do you know this?"

"How do you breathe? Can you see the oxygen? The wind? No. You cannot see them, yet you know them well. I cannot see a Creator above, but I know him well."

Merry watched the woman critically. She did not seem crazy, yet her words were foreign. "The Creator told you He gave you these gifts?"

"No. I know it all the same."

"How?" Merry's heart pounded, and sweat beaded at the small of her back. This hut was stifling, and her mouth felt as if cotton had invaded. Why were they having this conversation? She had only just met this woman, having come here for help. Why did the woman deduce so easily that this was the discussion they should be having?

"The Creator gave the first wave of gifts during the wars. He gave them sparingly."

Merry considered her words. The woman had to be telling her these things for a reason. Did she know Merry had been struggling of late with the beliefs she had been taught? If so, how did she know?

Something deep inside whispered that the woman told truth, but Merry needed to understand more. To know with certainty. "The original Dawson was not in the wars."

"The original Dawson was not the first to have powers. The original Dawson was his father's child—and his father was in the war, no?"

Anomalies were passed through bloodlines, she knew this. It served to reason that if the father had been gifted, that gift was passed to the original Dawson.

She swallowed hard, willing her heart to slow as the woman continued. She would listen, as strange as this entire meeting was. Perhaps she could glean something from the woman that would help her later.

"Others were threatened by the powers, but the Creator gives no gift without a purpose. The gifts were given to preserve his people. Healing, communication, great strength and speed. They were all given in order to survive the battles, to survive the war."

"Why is this history lost on us, then?"

The old woman shook her head, her hair swaying slightly. "The Dawsons became prideful and bitter. Belief in the Creator fell away, as you well know. But not everyone forgot."

Not everyone forgot. The people in this village, then?

"Why are you telling me this?"

"You believe me already. I can feel it. But that is not the only reason I tell you. You are meant to pass this along."

Her words did not startle Merry. Somehow, she was right. Merry did believe already. Perhaps she had begun to believe months ago when Princess Roanna first spoke to her of her religion. And again, when Wesley had mentioned his beliefs, Merry had warmed up to the idea even more.

Papa had not subscribed to religion, but that no longer meant Merry couldn't if she so chose. Papa's beliefs were increasingly clashing with her own.

But what had the woman meant by passing the explanation along? Pass it along to whom?

She did not ask. "Thank you. For healing my

wound."

"Button your blouse, Merry. The men return." The woman resumed her seat as Wesley's voice came from outside the hut. Merry quickly covered herself, and a moment later, the men stepped inside. Gregory's gaze found hers immediately.

"Are you well?"

Merry nodded.

"Well," the woman said. She looked to the man who had led them. "Let us feast, shall we?"

30

The woman's name was Margaret, but everyone called her Margie. The man was Jacob. The other villagers seemed pleased to see the outsiders, once they had been deemed safe. They stoked a bonfire in the small circular clearing, and the smoke drifted in the air, tickling Merry's nose. A few of the villagers brought out stringed instruments and drums, and the noise echoed in the night air.

Villagers lined up in the grass and danced, clapping, stomping, and twirling. It was nothing like the refined dancing done in the royal ballrooms.

Merry and Gregory stood at the edge of the clearing, watching. Wesley smiled and spoke with those around him while Gideon stood away from the crowd, scanning constantly. She supposed someone must do it.

"What did the woman say to you?" Gregory stood beside her. He still seemed wary of the villagers, but less so than before.

"She healed my shoulder."

He raised his eyebrows and looked to the place where her wound would be. "Healed your shoulder?"

"Yes. She called her power a 'gift.' She said it

comes from the Creator."

He watched her, his expression unchanging.

She burned with questions as to his thoughts on this subject. She knew the stance of Wesley, Roanna, and now Margie. But not Gregory. What did he believe?

She wouldn't ask him. What right had she?

Instead, they stood in silence, merriment all around them. Men roasted meat over the fire while musicians started another song. Merry remembered the times she and Gregory had danced together, laughed together.

Now their acquaintance existed in awkward silence.

"Merry." Gregory still did not look at her. He shifted, as if he were struggling internally. "I—"

"Do you dance, my lady?" A tall and lanky man stopped in front of her. He held out a hand as he grinned ear to ear.

She hesitated only a moment. She would not offend these people. Instead, she returned his smile and held out her hand. "Thank you, sir. Though I fear I do not know the steps."

"There's nothing to it, I tell you." His smile never wavered, and soon she was dancing and spinning in step with the others. She clapped so hard and so often during the dance that her hands stung. When the music ended, she laughed breathlessly.

"Would you go another round, lady?" the man asked.

Merry shook her head. "I cannot, sir! I'm a bit lightheaded." Margie may have healed her shoulder, but she could not account for the blood loss.

The man bowed slightly. "Let me bring you a

drink then."

She nodded her consent then moved away from the dancing. Gregory still stood as he had before, and Merry rejoined him.

"Their dances are quite lively." She worked to control her breathing.

He looked at her, an emotion in his eye like none she had seen from him since their reacquaintance. He seemed open. Unguarded. Timid.

"What do you believe about what the woman said regarding her gift?" He stumbled over the word gift.

Merry kept his gaze long moments, considering her answer. Finally, she looked away. "I believe her."

Gregory did not reply, and they returned to silence.

A few moments later, the man returned with the drink he had promised her. It was a type of fruity cider, though Merry couldn't place it. She thanked the man, and he moved on to another dancing partner.

A young girl—maybe ten years old—approached Wesley. She looked up at him and grinned. "Will you dance with me, mister?"

Wesley placed his hands on his chest and raised his eyebrows. "Me, my lady?"

The girl giggled.

Wesley bowed low. "I would be honored." He held out his hand and when the girl took it, he led her to join the other dancers. Merry couldn't help smiling.

Gregory fidgeted with the clay mug he held. "Merry?"

She looked to him again, her breath still coming in short bursts but this time from anticipation over what he would say rather than exertion from her dancing.

"Will you sit with me? May we talk?"

She hid her shock with a neutral expression. "If you wish."

He held out his hand, and she took it. The warmth of his skin sent flutters through her stomach.

They found a log at the edge of the clearing and took their seats.

Merry took a sip of her drink, and Gregory watched her closely.

"Are you sure you're all right?"

"I'm well. I'm happy to be in a place where I don't have to hide."

He raised his brows. "I hadn't thought of how that must be. Do you wish to stop working on this mission?"

Merry frowned. "No, not until Roanna is found and the rebels stopped."

The music changed, and the dancing continued. Wesley had found his way near them, quietly standing guard but from far enough away to give them privacy.

"We must talk about Dr. Presnell, and what he revealed."

Merry's gaze snapped to his. This was what he wished to speak about? Disappointment washed over her.

He drew back, his eyes wary. Was he surprised at her reaction?

But then he looked away. He rubbed a hand over his face. "I'm sorry. I'm just afraid."

"Afraid? Of what?" She prodded him to speak. Perhaps he needed to share.

He returned his gaze to hers. His eyes were weary and sad. Defeated. "I'm afraid I will never see my sister again. That we will never stop the rebels and return to peace. That this tension will last forever. I'm afraid of many things."

Merry took in his words, considering them. Gregory would not confide in someone lightly. He had not spoken to Wesley or Gideon, his closest friends. He had confided in her.

Her heart squeezed, and she wished to comfort him somehow. What could she say? She could make him no promises.

Taking his fingers in hers once again, she squeezed them and leaned against his shoulder. They spoke no more, watching the merriment until they were called to eat.

The village people were kind and welcoming, though she saw many strange things—speed and strength like she had never witnessed, on top of Margie's healing. She considered the powers as gifts, given for a purpose. If that were so, why were so many gifts being used astray? Or rather, why were so many gifts being hidden, or stomped out all together in other kingdoms?

Why did Papa wish to stomp out the gifts if they were meant for good? But then, Papa was not religious. He did not subscribe to the belief in the Creator, and Margie had said bitterness and unbelief set in, casting the beliefs in doubt.

Merry bit her lip as she considered the story. She had told Gregory that she did believe. It was a freeing realization that she could have this belief apart from Papa and the rest of her family. It saddened her that so many lived with a lack of knowledge on these truths.

The festivities went well into the night. Wesley and even Gideon danced merrily.

Merry's limbs felt heavy as Margie led her to the same hut they'd occupied before. "You can sleep here with me. Your men will be with Jacob."

"Thank you for your hospitality."

Margie smiled. "Think nothing of it."

~*~

Morning dawned dimly in the forest. Mist hung in the air, but the villagers were no less active than they had been just hours before. Folks washed clothes in large tubs, chopped wood, or cooked at fires. Even children helped with the chores.

Merry waited while Jacob and a few others helped Wesley, Gideon, and Gregory with the auto.

She had offered to help with chores, but Margie had advised her to let her shoulder rest.

While she waited, she thought on Dr. Presnell's words, and how she would relay them to Gregory. More than ever, she wanted to help Gregory find Roanna.

But there was something else that weighed on her. The envelope Papa had given her was back at the safe house. Should she read what was inside?

Merry had never opened it. She was not positive what information it contained, but she suspected. If she were correct, it meant Papa was not who he claimed. The mission was not what the rebels claimed. It was all a lie.

Tears welled in her eyes, burning and blurring the world before her.

"Lady Merry!" Wesley caused her to blink. She quickly wiped at the wetness on her cheeks and stood. "Is all well?" she asked.

"The auto is fixed and ready to go." He studied her a moment but did not comment on her tears.

"I'm ready." She quickly sought out Margie and thanked her one last time.

Margie gripped her hand. "I am thankful the Creator sent you to me."

Merry smiled a wobbly smile, then said good-bye.

Wesley led her to the auto, which waited exactly where they'd left it. The time had come for them to return to the capital. Merry had no idea what awaited.

31

Gregory...

The need to know if there had been word of Roanna's whereabouts burned in Gregory's chest as they drove away from the villagers. He glanced at Merry, who rode silently, watching out the window.

The woman, Margie, had healed her. Closed the wound. She claimed anomalies were a gift.

He ground his teeth and looked away. It might be true. But then, what of other anomalies? What of those who were born deformed or terminally ill? Those were not a gift.

But no, that was an entirely different type of anomaly. It felt brutish to think they should be Terminated. And to think Roanna should be Terminated? No, that was wholly unnatural for him.

Where did that leave him? Perhaps Roanna was right. Perhaps the only true way to move the society forward was to do away with Termination altogether. But how?

He looked back to Merry, watching her out of the corner of his eye. He didn't have to figure out the entire future all in one drive. And perhaps there would be those who would refuse his beliefs. What then? He had to live in peace with them, regardless.

Merry lay her head against the back of the seat. Her eyes slid closed.

He imagined what it had felt like to sit with her. Speak with her and hold her hand. It had felt so…right.

He looked away, his thoughts in disarray. Merry was a criminal. She was not to be trusted. She had been excommunicated from her own country. Even now, he could not be sure he believed her fully. If Wesley had not gone into the doctor's cottage with her, would she still have given him the entire truth?

Regardless, he did know the truth of what the doctor confessed. Besides what she had revealed before their chase the day before, Wesley had given him information from the conversation as he had heard it. He had said Baron Stern would have kept record of an order to kidnap the princess.

The Dawsons had searched the Stern estate. They hadn't come across any such orders. He had to believe that if they had, they would have shared such information.

Mother and Father would be eager to hear whatever he had learned, and it would surely help them find their own lost child if such an order existed.

"Does anyone follow us?" he asked. He glanced out the back window. The road was clear.

"None that I have seen," Gideon answered.

"Good."

He closed his own eyes and reclined in the seat. He had considered it a handful of times and put it off every time, but now it seemed obvious he would need to move forward his idea of searching the Stern estate. He could bring Merry along. She might be able to think of secret hiding locations. She might hold the key to the information that would unravel every mystery.

At some point, he drifted to sleep. He awoke when Wesley called to him. "Your Highness, we've reached the capital city."

He blinked, looking around him. "What is the time?"

"It's time for the midday meal."

There would be questions at the palace. They would wonder where he'd been all day and night. There would be rumors, but he would endure them if it meant he could keep his secrets until Roanna's attackers were captured.

Merry watched him, her eyes sleepy and her hair falling softly around her face. Their gazes met and something inside him twisted.

Last night, he had confessed his fears, but he hadn't fully revealed them. He was also afraid he would never be happy without her.

He spoke to Wesley as Merry prepared to climb from the auto. "I will come for you later this afternoon or first thing in the morning at latest. Be ready."

Wesley nodded and climbed out then opened the door for Merry.

She looked to him, her eyes questioning. What did he expect of her? She seemed to ask silently.

For a moment, his thoughts fled. He wanted to speak with her. Stay with her. But he had too much to say, and too many responsibilities that pressed upon him.

He gulped. "Thank you for your help, Merry."

She dipped her head in the slightest of nods but did not reply. She climbed out, and then she was gone.

When they arrived at the palace, Gregory attempted to make it to his room to change before he had to speak to anyone. He was unsuccessful. Roland spotted him as he climbed the dimly lit staircase toward the guest wing.

"Prince Gregory."

Gregory stopped. He wasn't prepared to explain himself fully. Not here, standing in the open.

"You've made yourself scarce in the face of your sister's disappearance."

"I have been investigating. Please tell me what you've found."

Roland paused, but then he shook his head, his face weary. "Nothing. You?"

"I have information, yes. I would rather not share it here on the staircase."

"Of course. My brother will want to speak with you immediately." He gestured for Gregory to follow him, and they descended the stairs and headed toward the king's offices.

"What of Ben?" Gregory asked. "Have you heard from him?"

"The prince of Lox will return any time now. He found his mother well. They did not wish him to travel so soon following his own attack, but he agreed to take extra precautions."

He left it at that, and Gregory glanced at him. It was the first he'd heard Roland speak of Ben without insulting him. Ben must have finally done something to impress the Dawsons. Perhaps because he insisted on returning to find Roanna.

King Dawson glanced up when Gregory and Roland walked through his office door. His eyes narrowed. "Where did you disappear?"

Prince Stefan stood nearby. He held a flask and took a drink from it.

"I've been gathering information. I have reason to believe Roanna's kidnapping wasn't the work of the rebels."

Roland scoffed. "That's absurd."

Gregory glanced at him then back to the king. "I followed a lead in the south. The source said there had been no orders to kidnap the princess. At least, no recent orders."

"Who is this source?" Roland asked. The familiar sneer was back in his voice. "Why do you talk in riddles?"

"What do you mean by recent?" King Dawson crossed his arms, seeming more intrigued than angry.

Gregory leaned against the arm of a chair. "He admitted to an order to kidnap Roanna as a baby and to dispose of her. He said he couldn't do it, so he took her and ensured her safety—as well as the safety of the other baby."

"Who is this source?" King Dawson asked.

Gregory considered outing the doctor, but he wasn't ready to show all his cards just yet. "I will tell you this information but not yet. First, I need to follow every lead he gave me. I beg your trust and ask you to believe that my deepest wish is to bring Roanna home safely."

The king flared his nostrils, his usual temper presenting itself. Finally, he gave a sharp nod. "I will grant you this, but briefly. I expect answers soon."

"You will have them."

The king opened his mouth, as if to speak, but then he snapped it closed. He looked at Stefan and Roland. "Out, both of you."

Roland frowned, but Stefan strode to the door without question or any hint of a care. Why was the prince here at all? He had never shown care in the workings of the kingdom that Gregory had ever seen.

Maybe Roanna had changed the Dawsons more than he realized.

"Go." King Dawson's voice took on a hard edge, and Roland left the room without putting up further fight.

Whatever the king wanted with Gregory was a mystery to him. Gregory had no worries other than Merry's presence. If he had learned of Merry's help on his missions—and that Chester's Wake was behind her involvement in the investigation—their newfound and still shaky alliance could be jeopardized.

The king moved behind his desk and sank into the chair.

Gregory forced himself to sit opposite, though he much wanted to pace. "I take it you have information you would like to share?" He kept his tone cool and calm; the opposite of his raging emotions inside.

An uncomfortable expression washed over the king's face. Not quite a frown, but a look of indecision and confusion.

Intrigued, Gregory leaned forward. He kept quiet, waiting for the king to speak.

"I wish to speak to you privately. I am counting on your discretion."

"I am very discreet. I assure you."

The king nodded absentmindedly. "Yes, of course."

Again, Gregory waited. He'd never seen the man so confounded. Confused. Befuddled.

King Dawson's gaze finally met his. He took a deep breath. "My council members—my brothers, especially—would not approve of this conversation.

Hence, the secrets. I want Roanna back in my safe care. I am desperate for her safety, in fact. Nothing we have tried has turned up a solid lead, and I am at my wit's end. My council may not understand or agree, but it is not their daughter whose life it at stake."

Whatever Gregory had expected, it wasn't this. Royals in any country had to be solid. Brutal. Firm. If an enemy suspected they could manipulate the royals by abducting family members it would create constant chaos. Because of this, no budging was ever permitted by the royal family.

Here was King Bartholomew Dawson, expressing true, raw emotion over the loss of his newfound daughter. And to a neighboring royal, at that.

"What can I do to help?" It wasn't an offer of service so much as true confusion.

"We are not a religious people."

The statement hung in the air.

"But in Chester's Wake, you welcome many religions," Bartholomew continued.

Realization dawned in Gregory's mind. Bart was looking for spiritual guidance. He was desperate for his daughter's return. For Roanna's return.

Something akin to guilt washed over him. Not even Gregory—a believer in a Sovereign presence— had thought to seek spiritual guidance on Roanna's behalf. He'd been so caught up in his anger, frustration, and confusion over Merry Stern that he hadn't thought to turn to prayer.

"I do subscribe to a belief system, yes."

The king nodded solemnly. "Can your—your—" he paused, as if the words were difficult for him to speak. "Can your God help us find Roanna?"

Gregory kept the king's gaze for long moments. At

last, he nodded. "It is always wise to use whatever methods are at our disposal, eh? Praying certainly couldn't hurt."

A strange sort of relief filled the king's eyes. He nodded quickly. "You will guide me in this way?"

Seeing the emotion on King Dawson's face, feeling the obvious care and concern for Roanna coming from the man, stirred something in Gregory's gut. He'd been so angry at everyone. At Roanna. At the Dawsons. At Merry Stern.

He had not welcomed change. Had not wanted to accept that there was a need for a life any different than the one they'd been living previously. Now, however, he saw something else. He saw a father desperate for his daughter.

Perhaps Gregory had been wrong in his feelings all along. He'd been stubborn. Foolish. "Yes, of course," he agreed. "I can help you."

He realized after a moment that the king meant immediately. He wanted Gregory to pray now.

Embarrassment and discomfort filled him, but he pushed them away and focused on bringing comfort to the king. He prayed a short but heartfelt prayer for Roanna's safe return.

When he had finished, King Dawson seemed pleased. Some of the fear had left his gaze. "Can we speak more on this later? Discreetly, of course."

"Yes, always."

The king nodded again then stood. "Thank you. It is not often I have felt the need to seek such aid."

"It is not often I have been asked for such aid. You are quite welcome, I assure you."

They parted ways and Gregory left the office. He made his way to his suite of rooms, eager to wash and change into a fresh suit. But his mind was now befuddled. Why the confusion?

He knew the answer. First Merry and then King Dawson. They had both had the good sense to seek guidance from above, while he—the supposed believer—hadn't even considered it. What shame.

At last he sunk onto a chair in his room. He put his head into his hands, and he did what he'd promised to try aiding the king in doing—he sought the aid of the Sovereign.

32

That evening after supper, most of the dining party retreated to the library. Gregory hoped to speak to the king or even Roland Dawson. He needed permission to visit the Stern estate, and he wouldn't mind a word with the baron.

The men were absent. Gregory frowned as he looked around the gathering. Who might have the authority to help him?

His gaze fell on Prince Stefan. The prince stood with two women, laughing and drinking. His wife was not to be found.

Gregory approached him. "Stefan, might I speak with you privately?"

Stefan watched him a moment, as if calculating, but he nodded to the women. "Good night, ladies." He stepped to the side with Gregory. "To what do I owe the pleasure?"

"I want to speak with Stern in the dungeon. I have questions for him."

Stefan frowned. "Haven't the rebels already been questioned?"

"They have, but I have specific questions based on new information."

Stefan nodded slightly. "I admit, I haven't been very active in helping to rule Dawson's Edge. I haven't cared all that much." He took a drink from the thick glass he held in his hand. He shrugged. "When we learned of Roanna's place in our family, things felt different for me. I was no longer the lone heir of King Bartholomew Dawson." He rolled his eyes, and Gregory wondered about the relationship Stefan had with his father. It seemed no healthier than the one he held with his wife.

"I've tried to become more active these last couple of months." He scratched his head. "I suppose I can take you to the dungeon if you'd like."

And just like that, Gregory had gained access. He needed to remember to seek Stefan's help more often.

They left the after-dinner gathering immediately. Stefan led him toward the back of the palace, down a dim, narrow staircase. The dark walkway was lit only by the occasional wall sconce, and the walls were so close Gregory continuously bumped his elbows.

They descended farther into the belly of the palace until they reached a landing. The more they walked, the cooler the air grew. Gregory suspected they had left the confines of the palace and were now completely underground.

"It's just around this corner." Stefan nodded ahead, and as they rounded the corner a stone wall stood in front of them. A large metal door blocked the way through.

No guard stood watch, and Stefan pounded his open palm on the metal door. A moment later, the door squealed on his massive hinges as it swung open.

The guard glanced between them then bowed slightly to Stefan. "Your Highness."

"Take us to Stern."

"Right this way." The guard led them inside.

The scent of refuse hung in the air, rotten and pungent. The dank, gray walls held years of grime, and the random torches on the walls offered little light.

Gregory squinted in the dim as his eyes adjusted. The guard led them through the corridor. They stopped at the end of the cell block, and a man lay on the ground, an arm thrown over his eyes.

"Get up." The guard raked his baton across the bars and a loud clang rang out.

The prisoner didn't move.

"I say get up!" The guard's yell echoed.

Like a sloth, the man moved his arm. He rolled over and pushed himself onto an elbow then up to sitting. He groaned as he moved, as if it took much effort. At last, he stood. Grime covered his face, and his hair hung in shaggy knots.

Gregory recognized the former baron, unkept though he now stood.

"You may leave us." Stefan spoke softly to the guard.

Gregory glanced his way at the tone. Was it compassion he heard in his fellow prince's voice?

Stefan gripped the bars. "Baron, we would ask you a few questions."

"Former baron." Stern leaned forward, wracked with coughs.

Gregory wanted to take over. Leave off the effort to gain information through kindness. His sister was missing, and this rat might have information. Yet, he held back, giving deference to Stefan and his methods.

"Be that as it may, I would ask your help. The princess has been taken. Our intelligence suggests this was not a move of the rebel forces. Can you confirm this?"

Stern turned a contemptuous gaze on Gregory. "That would explain your presence." He sneered.

Gregory remained silent. He would gladly rip through the bars if he thought it would help their cause, but Stern had not given any indication he was inclined to offer assistance thus far.

"Your intelligence." Stern sneered again. "My daughter? Is she your source? She's a traitor, and she knows nothing."

Anger crept through Gregory. How had he heard Merry was helping them? Besides that, Stern had not asked after Merry, only condemned her as the supposed source of intelligence. He would not keep silent any longer.

"On the contrary, your dear friend Dr. Presnell gave you up." Gregory stepped close to the bars, gripping them while glaring at Stern. "He said you had proof of a former plot to kidnap the princess as a baby."

A flash of uncertainty danced across Stern's features, but in the space of a heartbeat it was gone. "My estate has already been searched."

Gregory kept his expression neutral, but Stern's answer was a distinct tell.

"Are you confirming there was no current plot to kidnap the princess?" Stefan leaned in, his eyebrows raised.

Stern barked out a laugh, then another. He broke into a chorus of manic laughter, but once again coughs wracked him. His whole body shook with the effort.

Gregory frowned. What was wrong with the man? Cared he nothing for his own welfare?

Stefan looked to Gregory, eyebrows raised in question. Gregory shook his head slightly.

At last, Stern's coughs subsided. His chest moved in and out, wheezing.

The silence stretched between them. A desperate edge trickled into Stern's gaze.

"Do you care to hear how your daughter fares?" Gregory hated to reveal so much information in front of Stefan, but it couldn't be helped. If he could appeal to Stern's fatherly instincts, he might open up.

"If she agreed to help your lot, why should I care?"

"What makes you think she's helping?" Gregory spoke confidently as if he hadn't a care in the world.

Stern did not speak, and the unanswered question hung between them.

At last, Stern straightened his shoulders. He lifted his chin. "She's helping you. I can see the bluff in your expression. Young man, you forget I've been doing this longer than you've been alive."

Gregory's hopes fell. He looked to Stefan. "I got what I needed."

Stefan gave a single nod, and they left Stern standing in his cell. Gregory did, indeed, get what he needed. There was no doubt in his mind that there was information hidden in the Stern estate that the Dawsons had yet to recover. The question was, where?

33

Merry...

By the next day, Merry had regained her strength after all the dancing. While her shoulder ached slightly when she rotated her arm in a wide arc, overall, she was much improved. She studied the slightly mottled skin in the space where the wound had been. It was scarred but healed.

Most impressive.

She had spent the previous evening considering Papa's beliefs. Thinking over what he had imparted to her over the years, and the paths of thought to which he had introduced her.

Had he been wrong?

She hadn't fully decided, but she did know she no longer agreed with him on the main points. She did not believe the Dawsons were evil. She did not believe those with anomalies should be Terminated. She did not believe she had done right by participating in the rebellion.

But she did believe there was a Creator who watched over them all.

A soft knock sounded at the bedroom door, and Merry quickly covered her shoulder. "Who is it?"

"Wesley, my lady. The prince is downstairs to speak with you."

"I'll be right down." She hadn't heard the auto, but she had been rather preoccupied with her thoughts.

She finished dressing, adding a simple black vest to her white blouse and black skirt. Then, she laced up her boots and hurried downstairs. Gregory stood in the parlor, twirling a top hat in his hands. He looked to her as she entered, meeting her gaze without shying away.

His eyes seemed different today. More open, perhaps.

"Any word on Princess Roanna?"

His lighter expression dimmed slightly. "No, no word."

"I'm sorry."

He nodded. "Thank you." They stood awkwardly for a moment. Would he mention their talk from two nights ago? Her apology for the hurt she had caused him?

"Miss Stern, please sit."

Their formalities had returned. Irritation bubbled inside her. He was irrationally stubborn. "No, thank you. I'll stand."

It was unlike her to let her emotions shine through, but she had so hoped he might have forgiven her fully.

He raised his eyebrows at her words. Or maybe at her tone. But he did not press her.

"I have our next move lined up, but I warn you it may not be pleasant."

Pleasant? "You mean I might be injured or end up tromping through the forest in the dim of night? Getting healed by a strange village woman?" She offered a small smile.

A ghost of amusement shone in his eyes, but it departed just as quickly.

"You may or may not be comfortable with my plan, but you would be of great help to us in this situation."

Merry pulled her eyebrows low. "What do you mean, Gregory? What is it?"

"I've gained access to your family estate. I would like to search it for clues. King Dawson insists he's already searched it thoroughly, but I would like to see the place myself. Prince Benjamin would like to come along."

They wanted her to investigate her own home? She had not expected that. Her stomach churned.

Swallowing her nerves, she took a deep breath, doubting she was hiding her feelings well, but at least she now understood why he wouldn't return her playful smile.

"Whatever I can do to help." She forced the words. He had to have noticed, but he didn't scoff at her. Instead, he dipped his head in a single nod.

"I believe you could shed light on the search we would not have otherwise." He paused. "I know it will not be easy for you, and I apologize for that."

Merry searched his face. His eyes were clear, his gaze imploring. He was sincere in his apology.

Courage swelled in her heart. She straightened her shoulders. "When will we go?"

"Today." He paused, and his Adam's apple bobbed as he swallowed. "I have seen your father."

Papa?

Merry held in her gasp. "How did you find him?" Her voice shook slightly, but she didn't allow the tears that burned her eyes.

"He looked unkept, but mostly healthy otherwise."

She waited for him to go on. To pass along kind words. To say he had asked after her.

But nothing else came.

She turned away from Gregory. "I will be ready to leave whenever you give the word." She left the room without waiting for his permission.

A few hours passed. Prince Benjamin arrived, and together they made the journey to the countryside. The men talked as they drove, and Merry watched the familiar sites pass by. Nostalgia swelled inside her—a longing for the lack of cares she once had.

"It is good to see you well, Lady Merry," Prince Benjamin interrupted her musings.

"Thank you, and you as well." She recognized that he did not have to show her kindness. She had tried to enact a plan that would have killed his beloved. Yet, he did not seem to hold anger toward her.

They made small talk as they drove. Gregory kept to himself for the most part. As they neared her family home, tension seeped into her shoulders and neck. How could she do this thing they had asked?

A moment later, Wesley cleared his throat. "Your Highness, we've arrived."

Merry looked out the window to view her childhood home. It was two stories, with a large portico that wrapped around the home. Papa's weather devices still hung from the beams of the overhang, and black shutters hugged the windows.

It wasn't a mansion, as they had never been inordinately wealthy, but it was big enough for her and Papa.

Butterflies like large birds fluttered in her stomach.

She climbed from the auto and waited for Gregory to lead the way. He instructed Gideon to stand watch outside. Then he marched to the portico and the front door.

"Is there anywhere inside that you feel would make a good hiding place? Somewhere no one else would know?" Gregory asked as they entered the estate house.

Merry had considered it all afternoon. She swallowed the tears clogging her throat. "Once, when I was a child, Papa showed me a door. It was a panel in the wall, and it opened up to a hallway. He said we should hide there if we were ever in danger."

Gregory listened intently. "Go on."

She shook her head. "That is all. It was the only time I ever saw that space. But I can at least show you where it's located."

"Thank you." Gregory kept her gaze, his eyes kind.

It had been weeks since she had been inside. As they stepped through the doorway, Merry drank it all in. Dust motes danced in the air, which smelled musty and stale. Nothing had been disturbed. All was exactly as she had left it. She had heard the Dawsons searched it previously before they had allowed her to return home on house arrest. Now, however, it had been deserted.

Gregory turned toward her. "We shall follow you."

Again, she swallowed the tears clogging her throat. Would she ever live here again? Return to her things? Her memories? Her family possessions?

Her heeled boots *clip-clapped* across the wood floors of the entryway. A moment later she stepped onto the soft carpet of the hallway. The corridor was narrow, and each small room they passed brought back a thousand memories: the library where she'd read her favorite books. The pantry where she'd sneaked sugary treats. The staircase leading upstairs to her bedroom. And at the end of the hallways stood a door. It led to Papa's office.

Merry stopped a few feet from the door. Pale green panels lined the wall. "It's one of these, on the right."

She, Gregory, Ben, and Wesley ran their hands over the panels, searching for clues that would lead them to the hidden passage. Dust covered the walls, and Merry's fingers slid across the gritty paint easily.

"What's on the other side of this wall?" Gregory asked.

"The kitchen is somewhere back there, and the pantry of course. But I'm sure the panel Papa showed me was here in this hallway."

Ben began working the panels she had already checked. She shifted to a different section further from the office door. Perhaps it wasn't exactly where she'd remembered it. Her finger hitched on a tiny gap in the panel, and she gasped. Using both hands, she shoved the wall section. She pushed again, slow and steady. The panel groaned as it swung inward.

She turned a triumphant gaze Gregory's way.

He smiled.

34

The air tasted stale, as if it hadn't moved in some time. Merry realized it likely hadn't. Not even the Dawsons had moved it when they performed their search.

Gregory lifted the small lamp he carried. "There on the wall is another lamp. Help me light it."

She moved to the wall and lifted the glass covering, and Gregory used his own lamp to transfer the flame. The dried-up wick on the wall lamp sputtered a moment. It may have no oil left to burn.

But then it caught fire and burned to life. As light illuminated the space, Merry saw that the room was much larger than she'd remembered. It snaked off down a long hallway and appeared to go to the left. The walls were a dark wood, lined with shelves overflowing with books, glass beakers, and dead potted plants.

"Was this a lab?" Gregory leaned his head around the corner.

Merry shook her head. "I have no idea. Papa only showed me once, and I never saw it again. I always wondered what kind of danger we would ever be in."

She fingered a dead, crispy leaf hanging out of a

small brown plant. "I don't understand any of this. Papa is not a scientist. What did he do in this room?"

Gregory took her elbow and led her around the corner while Prince Benjamin stayed in the first room. Wesley stayed in the hall to keep watch.

The second room opened into a decent sized library complete with armchairs and lamps. On a small table, between two armchairs, sat a large book.

Like a moth to a flame, Merry moved toward it. It was a hard cover with gold lettering and leafing, though she couldn't read the title for the dust. Gently, she cleared the dust away.

History and Laws of Spells

Fear, cold and hard, gripped her. She sank into an armchair and pulled the tome onto her lap then, gingerly, she opened the first page.

What would Papa be doing with a book about spells? Wasn't the whole rebel movement to get rid of those who used conjurers, magic, and powers?

"What did you find?" Gregory squatted beside her, his attention on the book.

"It's a book about spells."

His eyebrows lowered and he leaned closer, reading the first page. It was a history of sorts, speaking of the use of magic over the last couple of centuries. Merry skimmed the page then flipped to the next.

"It says spells have been in use for millennium." Her voice was breathy, and she quickly swallowed. It was the dusty air. The closed space. She was feeling claustrophobic.

He glanced up at her. Was that…compassion she saw in his eyes?

"It mentions the Dawson family's rise to power,

and how they didn't require the use of spells." She looked back to the book and flipped farther into the pages, hoping to pass the history section. Around the halfway point, the pages broke into spells and laws. She couldn't look at them anymore, and she slammed the book shut.

"I don't understand any of this. How could he have this book here?"

Gregory reached out and took the book from her lap. "We don't need to look at this right now." His voice was soft, and she sought his eyes.

Yes, it was compassion she'd noticed.

Pushing off from the chair, she began to pace. "So, is this what the rebellion is and has always been? Men who did not have the powers they wished to have? Men with a bitter agenda to be just as powerful as the royal family?"

Gregory didn't speak, only let her work her frustrations out on the tattered carpet as she moved back and forth.

She wanted to defend her thoughts against themselves. Convince herself that she was wrong. But the beakers, the plants, the spell books—they pointed to one obvious thing. Her father had tried to produce the powers he claimed to fight against. He'd been a conjurer all on his own. He'd been fully and completely wrong.

She spun to Gregory. "He lied to me. To us all." The words hung between them and made her feel foolish. It was a wholly unwelcome feeling.

"I'm sorry, Merry. What can I do?" He stepped toward her, slowly at first but then quickly closing the gap. He took her hands and rubbed them gently with his fingers. "I would do anything."

Her gaze moved to his and her cheeks warmed. This was the Gregory she remembered. The one she'd been drawn to and whom she cared about. She allowed him to draw her into his arms, and she pressed her eyes closed.

They stood that way for long moments, unmoving.

A soft knock sounded at the wall, and Wesley's voice carried through to them. "Your Highness, we should go soon."

He still held her hands, and heat crept up her neck and ears. She stepped away. "I would like to take the book with me."

He nodded his understanding and retrieved it. "Help me look for anything else that might be useful information."

They scanned the shelves and tables for anything that stood out.

"Here. These are some kind of lists." He pointed to a small stack of papers that had been placed neatly between a lamp and a book.

She moved to his side and glanced at them as he shuffled through.

"These aren't lists," he said. His voice betrayed his confusion, and she caught his lowered brow. "They're letters."

Merry's eyes trailed back to the letters and the signatures at the bottom. She shook her head in disbelief. Was nothing as they'd been told?

~*~

Once they left her house, Merry rode in silence.

217

Prince Benjamin poured over the letters as they rode back to the safe house. His face ashen, his brows lowered, he did not speak. He sat across from Merry and Gregory in the back of the auto, and Merry chanced a look Gregory's way.

He watched her the same way he had watched her back in the hidden room—with eyes that finally saw her again. It was as if she'd been behind a curtain and had only now come out.

Heat crept into her cheeks, and she looked back to Prince Ben instead. He was conflicted, certainly. The letters proved beyond any shadow of doubt why the princess had been taken as a baby.

But what about today? What about Roanna's whereabouts this very moment?

No one spoke as they rode, and when they arrived at the safe house, she, Gregory, and Prince Benjamin went inside while Wesley and Gideon stayed out to stand guard. Fraja shuffled into the entryway at the sound of the door.

She looked between the three of them then turned a questioning gaze toward Merry. She had learned these last couple of weeks that it was likely she would be asked to give them privacy.

"You would like to eat?" she asked.

Merry squeezed her hand. "Soon, likely. Thank you, Fraja."

Fraja returned the smile and nodded then shuffled back to the kitchen.

Prince Benjamin paced the small entry. He gripped the letters in his hand, crushing them. "How can this be?"

"We cannot take this to the Dawsons." Gregory leaned against the bottom post of the staircase, his arms crossed.

Ben widened his eyes. "You're right. War would start." He rubbed his forehead. "What are we supposed to do with this?"

No one spoke, the quiet belying the heaviness in the air.

"We cannot take it to the Dawsons," Gregory repeated. "But I fear we cannot take it to my parents, either."

Merry agreed. The King and Queen of Chester's Wake may not be biologically related to Princess Roanna, but they were certainly as in love with her as if they were. This information would prove catastrophic.

"These letters provide no helpful information in the present unless they lend evidence to today's predicament." Merry stood straight, pushing aside her own hurt and anger at Papa. "Where is Roanna today? Who has her, where is she, and how can we return her safely? This is our goal right now. We can wait to deal with this issue later."

"Could it be that this lends a clue into who kidnapped Roanna this time?" Gregory looked to Prince Ben. "If it wasn't Dawsonian rebels, could it be your parents?"

Ben turned away and paced. "I have to go home." He clenched and unclenched his fists. "I have to confront them."

Merry's head reeled with the knowledge that Papa had been working under the bidding of the Queen of Lox. That Queen Frieda had commissioned the kidnapping and disposal of the princess of Dawson's Edge many years ago.

Ben continued to pace. "I don't understand why

the rebels would have recently attacked at Lox's border when they've been working together."

Merry frowned. "Just because they once worked together doesn't mean they still do. Their alliance could have ended long ago.

Lox was supposed to be advanced. Accepting, loving, and kind.

Peaceful kingdom? Righteous kingdom? Lies, all of them.

"Mother wouldn't hurt Roanna, not after all these years. If she's in Lox, I will find her." Prince Benjamin stood tall, seeming confident of these facts, but the defeat in the air remained.

There was more they could do, surely. There had to be something.

"We have other leads, as well," Merry reminded them. "We need to set up an interrogation with the Van Hoosier patriarchs. Discover if any palace guards or other servants corroborated with her kidnapping. Even if her kidnapping was at the urging of Queen Frieda, she had to have had help. We can come at this thing both ways."

Gregory stared at her, his eyes fierce. It was no longer hatred she saw there. This look was altogether different. It caused a return of the butterflies from earlier.

"We should hurry." Gregory pushed himself off the banister and moved toward the door. He flung it open. "Wesley, bring the Messengers."

Merry led them to the dining room, and Wesley helped them set up three Messengers. Merry had never owned such a device. The strange, bulbous red lights that flashed across the tops of them lit the room with an eerie glow.

Gregory contacted his parents and asked if they had any contacts with the Van Hoosier family while Prince Ben reached out to those he had met while in Dawson's Edge. Merry watched them, helping when she could or answering questions about family trees when they asked.

She paced the room, antsy with irritation because she couldn't do more.

Fraja brought food, and they ate while they worked.

It had been several hours when a knock sounded at the door. She, Gregory, and Prince Benjamin looked at each other. Not once in all the weeks she had lived in the townhouse had someone knocked on the door other than when Gregory had arrived or when she had expected the seamstress.

"Where is Wesley?" Gregory muttered as he stormed to the door. Merry followed closely behind him.

Gregory peeked outside. "Stefan." The shock in his voice was evident, but he opened the door.

Merry peered around him and saw that Wesley and Gideon stood behind Prince Stefan. Gideon's red face gave evidence to his obvious anger, but Wesley seemed serene, as always.

Stefan's gaze danced to Merry, and a flash of surprise moved in his eyes.

He looked back to Gregory. "I want to help."

Gregory opened the door to allow Stefan entrance. They couldn't very well leave the prince of Dawson's Edge standing on the doorstep, but Merry couldn't imagine how he knew to find them here, let alone how they would be able to integrate Stefan's help without revealing the truth of the things they had discovered.

They would simply have to find a way.

Stefan took in the dining room, presently set up to work as an office. He met each of their gazes. "Now I understand why you've been so secretive, but it was easy enough to follow you. What can I do?"

Gregory frowned and stepped close to Merry. The action was charming, but she didn't see it as necessary. Surely, Prince Stefan wouldn't accost her right here and now.

"We're attempting to find General Van Hoosier, Henri's father. As you know, we have reason to believe he is part of the rebellion. He may be able to offer clues as to Roanna's whereabouts." Gregory spoke easily, as if he and Stefan had developed some sort of relationship.

Stefan nodded. "I can help with that. Father sent General Van Hoosier on a recon mission at the border. We expect him back any day."

Merry frowned.

"Which border?" Gregory spoke what was on Merry's mind.

"The Loxian border. Relations have been tense."

Gregory lifted his brows. "That would have been helpful information to have. Why have relations been tense?"

"You shouldn't be so surprised. You have obviously been keeping information to yourself as well." Stefan turned again to Merry. He nodded toward her. "The Stern girl, correct?"

Gregory stepped yet closer to her. "Your family is aware that we enlisted her help in tracking the rebels."

"But we were not aware you brought her here to Dawson's Edge." Stefan shrugged. "I do not care about that. My point is, we keep the secrets we must."

They faced off in a silent battle. Finally, Gregory nodded. "Very well, then. How can we meet with General Van Hoosier?"

Ben gestured to the table. "Let's sit together and discuss this, shall we?"

As they worked through the details, Merry's mind spun. The royals of Lox had arranged for the kidnapping of the infant Dawsonian princess. The reasoning was obvious. Their son had become betrothed to this princess, and once they learned the Dawsons had powers, they didn't want their son marrying into that family. Now that Princess Roanna had been revealed as one and the same, did they want to dispose of her for good? Prince Ben didn't seem to think so. They knew Roanna personally.

Merry bit her lip and frowned. Surely, they couldn't be so coldhearted.

Stefan helped Gregory and Benjamin arrange for General Van Hoosier to report directly to the palace upon his arrival. They would question the General— her uncle—at that time. But time was growing short. Roanna had been gone now for several days. There had been no word, no ransom asked. That implied the kidnappers did not intend to return her.

Princess Roanna had found favor once before when Dr. Presnell had a move of the conscious for her life. Could she find such favor a second time?

35

Gregory...

A day later, Stefan sent word that the general had returned and would be arriving at the palace shortly. Gregory dressed for the meeting. He pulled on his waistcoat and kerchief but left off the top hat.

His hands shook with the anticipation. Roanna was strong. She would not go down without a fight. Wherever she was, he had to believe she was protected and would return to them soon.

Today they would learn something pertinent, he was sure. Though, there were still things he did not understand. Why would King Dawson send General Van Hoosier to the Loxian border in the first place? If General Van Hoosier was the relative of a known rebel leader, why trust him?

He shook his head. The Dawsons made no sense to him at all.

Taking one last look in the brass mirror in his dressing area, Gregory left his room and made his way downstairs to the dining room. Stefan had seemed unconcerned to find Merry in Dawson's Edge. It didn't mean Gregory could trust him, however. If he told his father, the king could insist he take Merry away immediately.

Gregory hoped the man was too preoccupied to worry over such things, though. His future with Merry was a question mark. Her eyes were burned into his memory. Her tears, her distress—he wanted to wipe it all away. If he could throttle her father for the pain he had caused her, Gregory would do it without regret.

Yet, Gregory could not. And he could not even fully protect Merry at this point. While he had finally seen for himself that she was trustworthy and respectable, it certainly did not mean they could have a future together. Chester's Wake was in turmoil, and he was their future king. They did not fully respect his family at the moment, and it was doubtful they would accept a criminal and traitor as their future queen. It only made sense that a match from a more conservative family within Chester's Wake would help bring about some measure of peace for their kingdom.

The knowledge pained him.

As he neared the dining room, the din drowned out his thoughts. He ought to be focusing on his meeting with the general and recovering Roanna.

He stepped into the dining room. Servants bustled about, serving food and filling drinks. The table was full and boisterous. Gregory glanced the length of it. Soldiers sat, dining. General Van Hoosier had returned, and he'd brought his troops with him.

Gregory spotted an empty chair near Stefan, and the Dawsonian prince waved him over. "Gregory," he said, "allow me to introduce you to General Van Hoosier, who has just returned from the Loxian border. He's brought a handful of men with him, as you can see."

Gregory nodded to Van Hoosier. The man was tall

and meaty like his son, Henri. His dark hair swathed his head, and medals adorned his uniform. "It is a pleasure to meet you, General. I've been wanting to speak with you."

Van Hoosier drew his brows together. "Me, sir? Well, now you've found me. How can I be of service?"

"Let us speak after breakfast. I wouldn't interrupt our good meal."

"Very well," Van Hoosier agreed. "After breakfast will be fine."

Conversation around the table never slowed. Men discussed border relations, ladies discussed politics, others discussed dancing. Gregory began to understand it was carefully cheerful talk, all of it. Gazes constantly skittered toward the king, who stared solemnly at his plate, twirling his utensils.

Pain pierced Gregory's heart. The Dawsons grieved for Roanna. They loved her. She wasn't only his, and his family's, or Ben's.

She was theirs, too. They had only just learned of her as their child, yet she had already been ripped from them. Now he held the secret of how it had happened the first time—devastating information for all involved. Soon he hoped to know the secret of how it had happened a second time. He would eventually share it all with them, because they must know the truth. They deserved to know the truth.

As he listened to the banter around the table, he considered the Dawsons. He might not see eye to eye with them on many things in life—he might not even like them all that much—but he could treat them respectably. He could treat them as human beings, certainly.

Roanna would make an argument for them, as she

would for anyone. As she had done not ten days ago.

Please let us find Roanna. The prayer rolled over the recesses of his mind easily as if he had never stopped praying months ago. His heart lightened, at least fractionally. There was still the business of getting information out of General Van Hoosier.

Gregory straightened his shoulders. It was time to settle this once and for all. Van Hoosier would tell him what he needed to know, or he would not be going home to see his family.

Stefan caught his gaze and nodded almost imperceptibly. Gregory returned the nod. They were in agreement. This ended now.

"Please follow me." Stefan led Gregory and General Van Hoosier toward the king's office suite.

"I am most interested to hear what you could wish to speak with me about, Prince Gregory." But General Van Hoosier's tone wavered ever so slightly.

Gregory kept his smile to himself. Let the general sweat a little.

A few moments later, Stefan gestured to a door at the back corner of the suite. The door was partially hidden by a large beam that ran floor to ceiling. That, along with the dark coloring in the Dawsonian palace, kept it somewhat hidden from view.

Gregory bowed slightly to Van Hoosier. "After you."

Pink tinged the general's cheeks. He scurried into the office. Gregory followed, and Stefan entered last. He closed the door behind him.

"General, I've asked you here under grave circumstances. As you know, Princess Roanna has been kidnapped." He paused only long enough to gauge Van Hoosier's initial reaction.

His expression did not waver.

"We have been using all the intelligence at our disposal, yet we seem to be constantly led down paths that end in knots."

Van Hoosier's lowered eyes darkened. He nodded, a wrinkle forming between his brows. "Tragic, that."

"It is more than tragic." Gregory stepped closer. "It will be devastating to the peoples who are found responsible. And we believe we have a better idea now of who was involved."

Van Hoosier's downcast gaze snapped up. "Oh?"

"Your son is a palace guard, is he not?"

Van Hoosier's expression froze. A moment later, he drew back casually as if he hadn't a care in the world. "A fine guard if I do say so."

"Someone led the kidnappers into the palace. Told them where to go." Gregory stood erect, his arms crossed. "Your brother-in-law, the former Baron Stern, rots in the dungeon this very moment. Perhaps the uncle had passed rebellious ties down to his nephew."

"If that were your belief, odd though it would be, I would presume you would be questioning him and not me."

"I spent the day with Henri Van Hoosier only a few days past."

"And?"

"He failed to reveal his personal ties to Stern. He also let slip that he had been on the princess's detail since Prince Benjamin's arrival. These things lend themselves to motive as well as opportunity."

Van Hoosier's gaze drifted lazily toward Stefan then back to Gregory. "What does this have to do with me? If you believe Henri is guilty then arrest him."

Though Stern and Van Hoosier weren't related by

blood, both obviously felt no shame in sacrificing their children for their own sins.

"He is in custody as we speak." Gregory had made sure of it that morning, confirmed by Stefan's nod. "Which leads us to you, General."

The silence in the room lengthened. Gregory steeled himself. Van Hoosier wasn't leaving this room without giving them something.

A guttural growl came from Van Hoosier's throat. "What do you expect me to tell you? I don't know the princess's whereabouts."

"Who does?"

He snorted but stayed silent.

"Perhaps you'd like to join the rebels already in the dungeon?"

"You'll put me there anyway."

"The king is very interested in the safe return of his daughter. I think you might be surprised." Gregory didn't look at Stefan. He had no idea if King Dawson would be willing to work a deal or if he would feed all rebels to the alligators. At this moment, he didn't particularly care.

Van Hoosier wavered. "Henri is innocent."

So, Van Hoosier wasn't as heartless as Stern, after all.

"Tell me how to find her."

War raged in Van Hoosier's expression as he seemed to calculate his next move. "I want the assurance the king will not lock me up, demote me, or punish my family."

Stefan quickly spoke up. "I will speak with my father personally."

"The guards from the south wing took her. I do not know their orders, only that they were involved."

Stefan stepped to the door. He gave a sharp whistle. Guards appeared.

"No one enters this room." Stefan glared at Van Hoosier. "No one leaves this room."

The guards nodded, and Gregory followed Stefan out.

"I'll alert my father immediately. We'll have the guards from south block questioned right away."

"What will happen to Van Hoosier?" Gregory asked as they walked.

Stefan glanced at him as if he were ludicrous. "He'll be dead by end of week."

36

Roanna…

Roanna lay on the bed in the small room, where she'd been for a week. The room was clean and well lit, with windows lining the tops of the high walls. The walls were made of slats of wood and unpainted. No decorations adorned them, and the simplest of water closets had been erected in one corner.

She stared at the ceiling. What was she going to do to get out of here? There was little indication as to her whereabouts, though she had a clue.

Copper-headed songbirds had been landing on the windowsills high above her head. Roanna had only seen copper-headed songbirds in one location.

Lox.

The guard who brought her meals rarely spoke. The servant girl—dressed in a nondescript black dress—kept mostly silent as well. But occasionally, she had gotten a word or two out of them.

Their language patterns revealed nothing, but those copper-headed birds said much.

Tears burned her eyes. What was she doing in Lox? Why would anyone here wish her harm?

She hadn't been mistreated in any way. At least,

other than being kept locked in a room for days on end. The guard brought meals three times a day. The servant girl brought fresh water to wash.

She sighed again, considering her options. It was nearing the noon hour. The guard would likely be coming soon with a tray. She hadn't used her powers since arriving. Mostly because she did not know for certain where she was and if she would be welcome. Also, because she did not like using them when not in a controlled atmosphere such as the palace gardens. King Dawson, or her parents in Chester's Wake, or even Ben would be coming for her soon. Wouldn't they?

But it had been a week.

Closing her eyes, she concentrated and reached out with her mind.

She felt no one close by.

But someone would be coming soon. She could force them with her powers. They would have no choice but to let her go.

She wouldn't get far, though, at least not in a place like this where she didn't even know where she was. She would be faced with multiple captors between this room and safety. Would she be able to use her powers on each of them? She wasn't sure she was strong enough for such a thing. Besides that, she didn't want to violate people by forcing them to do her bidding.

Her throat tightened, and she swallowed hard.

At least, she didn't want to force them unless she was in actual danger. She would be justified in using her powers if she were in danger, wouldn't she?

Pain shot behind her eyes just thinking about it.

There were other options. Perhaps if she could manage to push the meager furniture in the room—she had a bed, a side table, and an empty chest—she could stack the pieces and reach the windows.

The windows were higher than normal windows, and she was barely above average height.

Again, she closed her eyes and reached out with her mind.

There. A guard was close by. He carried a tray as he drew closer. She tried to discern his whereabouts, but without knowing exactly where they were, it was hard to decipher the fuzzy images that leaked into her mind.

This guard's will was resolute. Thick. Solid.

She would not be able to escape from this one.

She released her hold on his mind and relaxed. Minutes passed before he reached her door. He knocked once. Then a key jingled the lock. The door opened, the guard set the tray on the ground, and he closed the door and was gone.

Based on the simple information she had gathered these last few minutes, she knew more than she had known before. Wherever the guard came from with her food was quite a walk. It had taken him long minutes to reach her after she had first sensed him.

Tears burned her eyes and clogged her throat. The palace at Lox was enormous, but it could not be as she suspected. Queen Frieda would not do such a thing to her. She loved her.

Didn't she?

Roanna considered the way Ben's family had reacted to the news of her heritage. They hadn't spoken a word to her since. They hadn't encouraged the marriage between her and Ben. It was like they never knew her at all.

Did they hate her powers so much that they would

take her out of the picture? She could not reconcile what she knew of the Bellevues with the actions done to her.

She could be wrong. Wholly wrong. She might be in Dawson's Edge still, only near the border with Lox. There could be a powerful noble who was part of the rebellion. This noble could be keeping her hostage.

But deep in her soul she felt it wasn't so.

She lay on the soft bed for a few more minutes before getting up to retrieve the food from its place near the door. The savory scent of soup wafted toward her as she picked up the tray. She carried it to the small bedside table, and there she ate her meal of soup, bread, and cider.

After she ate, she paced the room simply to stay active. She was going mad cooped in this room for hours on end. She considered the windows again, and how she might reach them. If she had one more piece of furniture, she might be able to make it.

Several hours passed. Roanna regularly reached out with her mind, searching for anyone nearby. At last, she felt someone coming her way. A servant girl would be most likely as had become the routine. The girl would take away her tray while delivering fresh water and towels for washing.

Roanna closed her eyes and felt with her powers. The girl's resolve was soft. Uncertain, perhaps. It would be easy to force the girl to stand still while Roanna simply walked out.

Roanna opened her eyes and stared at the ceiling. It wouldn't hurt the girl. At least, not immediately. What would happen when Roanna's absence was discovered, though?

What then?

A creak sounded as the door slipped open. The girl came inside and quickly closed the door behind her. She moved fast, setting the pitcher of water on the desk. She carried towels over one shoulder, and she lay them beside the pitcher. She moved to the food tray and retrieved it.

"Please, can you at least tell me your name?" Roanna had tried several tactics with the girl over the last few days. None had worked at revealing pertinent information so far.

The girl lifted the tray and started toward the door. The flatware on the tray clanked together as her hands shook.

Roanna's heart squeezed for the girl. She was terrified.

"You do not have to tell me," she said. "I do not hold it against you. I know you have to obey your orders."

The girl met her gaze, though she quickly looked away. But Roanna had seen surprise there. And maybe curiosity.

The door opened and closed with another slight squeak. The sound of a lock clicking into place filled the air.

Roanna sighed. She closed her eyes and sat on the edge of the bed. She had to think of something and soon.

37

Gregory...

King Dawson did not permit Gregory or Ben to participate in the questioning of the guards on the south wing. Afterwards, he told them the guards revealed a contact whom they met at the farthest palace gate. The contact took Roanna away.

Gregory did not ask how the king had gotten this information out of the guards, nor did he ask what had become of the guards. They would likely share in Van Hoosier's fate if they hadn't already.

The contact had no name, nor a precise way to get in touch with whoever it was. The guards received a missive by post with instructions, and they followed the instructions.

Now Gregory and Ben sat in the safe house. Merry spoke softly with Wesley in the corner of the parlor. They spoke of Chester's Wake and options Merry might pursue when they returned. Wesley told Merry more about the Rejected homes, and the work Roanna used to do there.

Gregory watched them intermittently, watched the way Merry smiled. The way she moved, or the way the light caught her hair.

Ben was talking again. Now that the general and guards had been questioned, he felt ready to return home. "I have to return to Lox." Ben shook his head. "It is the only way."

Gregory doubted they would get anything out of Queen Frieda, but he agreed with Ben. What other choice did they have? They had run out of leads.

"The Dawsons will not understand," Gregory warned. "They'll see it as you deserting Roanna." They still had not revealed the letters they had found.

Ben snorted. "They see it that way regardless. I will tell them I'm seeking my parents' aide. Like I said, it's the only way."

"When will you leave?"

Ben stared at some invisible place on the wall. "Tonight. There is no reason to wait."

Gregory wanted to push for more information, but he held back. It was most likely that Ben didn't have an actual plan.

"Do you need anything from me?"

Ben's gaze returned to Gregory. "Don't let anyone find out what we've learned. Please. I want to see my parents first. To see their eyes."

Gregory understood. "You have my word."

Ben stood. "I should go."

Gregory stood as well. He wanted to send Gideon to take Ben back to the palace while he stayed on, but that would be foolish. There was no reason for him to stay any longer at the safe house.

He met Merry's gaze, and she smiled softly at him. His mind went to their time together at the Stern estate. They hadn't been alone together since that day. They hadn't spoken of it or anything else regarding their uncomfortable relationship. He still had no answers and nothing to offer her.

He should not stay. "Let's return, then."

Wesley hurried outside to alert Gideon. Ben nodded to Merry and made his way toward the door, leaving Gregory and Merry alone.

He stepped closer to her, wrestling with what to say. "Can you think of any other leads?"

Merry watched him, her eyes narrowed slightly and a line of worry creasing the space between her brows. She appeared troubled. "I have thought of someone, though I haven't decided if it's wise."

Gregory frowned. "Who?"

"No one has spoken to Bella de St. Paul. Her ambassador knew of the plans to attack Prince Benjamin. How did he know? Did Queen Frieda arrange that herself? Is he in contact with her?"

Gregory stared at her, his mind buzzing. Why had he never considered speaking to the princess? "She is Stefan's wife," he reasoned. "He may not wish us to speak to her. They do not seem on good terms, and he's been helping us. I don't wish to damage that."

Merry bit her lip, and he forced himself to stay focused. "I wish the prince had not seen me." She turned and paced, making lithe, quick steps.

How beautiful she was when putting her mind in motion.

"What are you thinking?"

"I could have spoken with Bella, and Stefan would have been none the wiser. Now, though, he knows I'm here. He will be suspicious of us because he does not know how you're using me here."

She seemed not to realize what she had said, but heat rose up Gregory's neck. Using her? Was that how she saw it? It sounded so unfavorable when spoken aloud. "Merry."

She spun to him, her eyes questioning.

"I am not using you anymore. I am working with you, and I am so grateful for the assistance you've provided."

Their gazes held for several long beats. An eternity of space seemed between them. He wanted nothing more than to close it.

A soft rap on the doorframe broke his concentration. "Your Highness," Wesley said, "the auto is ready."

Gregory swallowed, his throat tight. "Thank you, Wesley. I'll be right out."

Merry still watched him, but she did not make a move to come closer to him.

"I will consider ways to get you in touch with Bella de St. Paul."

She nodded slightly. The sun filtered through the window of the parlor, catching the golden strands of her hair.

He wanted to stay here with her. Make more plans.

"Good day, Merry." He spoke softly. Tenderly. Would she respond to his change of heart?

She did not waver. "Good day, Your Highness."

Gregory hurried outside for his return to the palace. He and Ben sat in the back while Gideon drove, and Wesley sat in the front seat beside him.

After a few minutes of driving, Ben raised his brows. "Are you nervous about something?"

"Why?"

"You haven't stopped tapping your knee since we left."

Gregory realized it was true. He forced himself

still. "I'm not nervous."

Ben watched him another moment, but he didn't press him further. Gregory almost returned to tapping. Instead, he clenched his fist.

He should have said more to Merry. If he didn't want her thinking he was using her then he needed to make of an effort to show her. She had obviously distanced herself from him.

Gregory pressed his eyes closed and refocused on their mission. They must find Roanna. Someone had taken her, but no one seemed to know who.

"Do you think it would be feasible for me to travel with you to Lox?" It was a foolish question. He couldn't leave Merry here, and he wouldn't very well take her with him.

Ben frowned. "No, not feasible. What if new information is gained here in Dawson's Edge? I do not trust that the Dawsons would share it with us immediately."

Gregory growled. "Of course not. I knew it was foolish. I'd just like to see your parents' faces to gauge their reactions. To know the intent behind their words."

Ben's face paled, and he looked out the window of the auto. "I have not trusted them for some time, though I had no idea it would lead to this. I will not be fooled by them. You needn't worry."

Gregory let the subject drop. They arrived back at the palace, and Ben agreed to message him as soon as he had any news. He left almost immediately for Lox, without fanfare.

Gregory poured himself into his search for Roanna. He sat in his room in the palace, scribbling bullet points to keep track of his thoughts.

The guards from the south wing took her and handed her off to someone at the north gate. She was taken to a waiting auto and driven away.

The north gate would suggest someone within Chester's Wake. But who would take her from Chester's Wake?

No one.

It was the Loxians who had a problem with Roanna's Dawsonian heritage. They had done away with her as a child.

Why?

"They didn't want their son to marry her." The spoken words rang true. They had made a marriage agreement but then realized they did not want their son marrying into that kingdom. So, rather than risk a disruption of peace, they got rid of the princess.

Only they didn't count on Dr. Presnell's conscience. He did not get rid of her. He only placed her in a different kingdom.

Now, eighteen years later, they find their son betrothed to the same woman. And they feel exactly the same way.

Had the Loxian rulers done it again?

His throat swelled with emotion, and he took several deep breaths. Ben felt that if they had taken her, they would not harm her. But what if he was wrong? If they had taken her a second time, they would want to be sure they never had to deal with the threat again. That put Roanna in more danger than ever.

Gregory closed his eyes and pressed his fingers into the bridge of his nose. "They wouldn't kill her. They love Roanna."

It was true, wasn't it? He could only pray so.

He finished making his notes. First things first, he needed to speak with Bella de St. Paul.

She would likely be at dinner tonight, but he mostly avoided her there. Or rather, she avoided her husband and her husband had spent ample time with Gregory of late.

Gregory readied quickly and left for the dining room, but he still had no plan. Speaking to Bella might be simple, but how would he then arrange a meeting with Merry?

The castle crawled with people as he descended the stairs. The dark walls and dim lighting worsened his anxiety as he moved. He straightened his shoulders and purposed to ignore the feelings.

Roanna had been missing for almost an entire week now. They had spoken with more rebels, uncovered more truth about her strange beginnings, and pinpointed the probable culprits. Yet the Dawsons were not aware of any of this. Was it time to clue them in? Perhaps given this new information they would be able to add more of their own.

The dining room was filled with diners as he approached. He scanned the room. Princess Bella sat across from her husband tonight. They each spoke with people on either side of them, never looking at each other.

A chair two seats to Bella's left was empty. Gregory slipped into it.

"Good evening, Princess. It's a pleasure seeing you again."

She smiled at him, her eyes bright but her expression guarded. Gregory hadn't realized it before, but she always wore that expression.

Gregory made idle chit chat as the meal

progressed. Being two seats down from her made private conversation impossible, but he was in a prime location for approaching her immediately after the meal.

"Any word on the princess?" The gentleman to his left leaned close. He had bushy white eyebrows, sharp green eyes, and a head full of fluffy white hair.

Gregory could not recall meeting him before. "Not anything particularly telling, no."

"Shame. The whole kingdom has been looking forward to her wedding with the Loxian prince. Romance, and all that." He nodded, his bushy eyebrows like two caterpillars bobbing in sync.

The whole kingdom. The thought brought a modicum of pleasure for his sister. "We have been anticipating it, as well," Gregory said. But the truth was that not everyone in Chester's Wake anticipated it. Many of the nobles staunchly opposed further ties with Roanna. He'd been hearing rumblings ever since her true heritage had been revealed.

Gregory frowned.

"Your parents must be using all resources to find her."

"Absolutely." But his mind was no longer in the conversation.

Chester's Wake.

The guards who took her from her rooms said they made the exchange at the north gate. The gate closest to Chester's Wake.

The man was asking more questions, but Gregory needed to move.

"Excuse me." He pushed away from the table and strode from the dining hall, leaving the man staring after him. If he were right, he had little reason to meet

Katie Clark

with Bella de St. Paul.

38

Merry…

Merry sat in the parlor reading. The front door opened, and a moment later, Wesley appeared. "Lady Merry, the prince is on his way. He says it's most urgent."

Relief poured through her. The last day had been torture, being stuck in the safe house with no one to talk to. Fraja always listened, was always kind, but she was not Gregory.

Merry had always had trouble connecting with other women. She had no close friends growing up, though when she considered it, she realized that was likely Papa's doing. Her anger toward him filled her, but she pushed it away. Anger toward Papa would do no good.

But Gregory? She understood him. And she knew, deep down, that he understood her as well. She had felt his silent invitation the day before. The invitation for reconciliation. Merry had held back. How could their relationship continue toward romance? No. It was doomed from the start.

Despite her resolve, she longed to be near him. She craved his friendship and respect.

At Wesley's announcement, she replaced her book on the shelf and paced to the door. Long minutes passed, and at last, he arrived.

Gregory stood with Wesley, firing off instructions for an auto, an airship, and a meeting.

"I'll take care of it." Wesley rushed away, leaving Gregory and Merry alone. He turned his attentions to her next.

It seemed all the air left her lungs in an instant. Why did being near him lately make it so difficult to think?

Gregory cleared his throat. "I have reason to believe Roanna has been taken to Chester's Wake. I need your help."

"Chester's Wake?" She worked through the clues they had uncovered, but what would lead him to believe such a thing?

"I will explain everything as we travel. I need you and your maid to pack as quickly as possible."

"Absolutely." Merry moved past him. Fraja was in the kitchen, and they could make fast work of readying their things.

As she stepped away, warm fingers grasped her upper arm. "Merry."

His fingers were like a welcome caress of warm air on a cool day. She pressed her eyes closed and took a deep breath. Then she turned toward him.

His gaze bore into her, his look nearing desperation. "I want to speak to you about other matters, as well. I—" he paused. His Adam's apple bobbed when he swallowed. "We must speak."

Warmth continued to spread through her. She nodded. "As you say." He held her arm another moment then released her.

She tore herself from his presence and hurried to fetch Fraja. She explained the situation briefly, and together they ascended the stairs and packed their meager belongings. In well under an hour, they were ready to leave.

Gideon drove the auto as he often did, and Fraja sat beside him. Wesley rode in the back with Merry and Gregory. The men sat beside each other discussing their plans, while Merry rode across from them.

Merry listened in, gleaning details as they drove.

"We've been focusing entirely on rebels within Dawson's Edge." Gregory shook his head. "It never occurred to us to look at Chester's Wake."

"There are so few nobles along the borders," Wesley said. "And the ones who reside there have strong ties with your family."

Gregory bent over a report and pointed at something. "We can still question them. The Dewalts will be first."

Merry frowned. "Dewalts?"

Both men glanced at her. "You know them?" Gregory asked.

"No. Duchess Higgins mentioned them one evening at supper when we dined in Chester's Wake. She said her family had acquired a manor from the Dewalts, and she looked forward to spending a holiday there. She said the estate was monstrous."

Gregory's eyes narrowed. He turned to Wesley. "When was the last time you saw Duchess Higgins and Lady Wendy in Dawson's Edge?"

"The day we visited the Van Hoosier estate. I remember noting they had left, but I thought little of it."

Gregory drew back. "I cannot reconcile a

kidnapping with what I know of that family."

Merry watched him, considering. Duchess Higgins had been congenial, and Wendy was certainly timid and naïve enough. But the best betrayals came from those closest to you. She should know.

"Message my father immediately." Gregory pulled out his own Messenger. "I'm going to find out more about this manor."

Wesley went to work, but Gregory turned to her. "Thank you."

Emotions swirled through her. She gave him a small nod but did not speak.

Soon, they reached the airship. The men gathered the luggage, and they boarded without fanfare. Merry's stomach twisted, and her shoulders tensed. She hadn't considered their means of travel before this moment. She could do this. She had done it before and would be safe.

Everyone moved ahead of her in their rush to board and lift off. She understood their hurry. They were close to finding Roanna. She could feel it.

Yet, her fears plagued her. Her racing heart made her feel faint.

"Lady Merry?" Wesley's kind voice pulled her out of her frozen inner turmoil.

She opened her eyes, not realizing she had even closed them. "I'm fine." The words came out strangled.

"I had forgotten you don't like to fly."

"I'm fine." As if repeating it would make it true.

Wesley took her elbow. "We will all be together on this flight. It's a small airship, and it won't be like our last flight."

That did sound slightly more tolerable. She took a deep, wobbly breath then nodded. "You're right. It will be fine."

He smiled. "I know you can do it."

They finished boarding, and Merry glanced at him. "Thank you, Wesley. You are always so kind."

He gave her a lopsided grin. "It comes naturally, I suppose."

She chuckled, and a moment, later they were seated. The inside of the ship was, indeed, small. Four rows of two seats each lined either side, with a center aisle in between them. At the front was the cockpit, and it looked like a small room beside it.

Merry spotted Fraja in the second row, next to the window. While her nerves still twisted, she was able to take a seat without too much panic. Gregory spoke with the captain in the cockpit, and Wesley and Gideon sat together in the front row.

Fraja patted her leg as they prepared for lift off. "It will be good, my lady. You will see."

Dear Fraja. "Yes, I believe you're right." She smiled at the woman, and Fraja returned the smile before looking back to the window to watch their ascent.

Merry leaned her head back and closed her eyes, willing the time to pass quickly. She felt the slight jolt as the ship lifted from the ground. Moments later they were gliding through the air.

Once they had been in the air for quite some time, Gregory approached. He sat in the seat across the aisle from her, so they were separated by only a couple of feet.

"Wesley has secured a small regimen of soldiers to meet us at the Dewalt manor at the Loxian border. We have permission from my father to speak with whoever we find there. Lady Wendy's father is currently at the capital, but Lady Wendy and her mother are at the manor."

"Do you think they have Princess Roanna at the manor?" And why would they take her? Merry had not asked Gregory about his relationship with Wendy, but it seemed things had not gone as Duchess Higgins had hoped.

He clenched his jaw and looked away. "I don't know. They don't seem like the type to do such a thing." He shook his head. "Then again, nothing about any of this has gone the way I expected."

"Our arrival is being kept secret from all," Gregory continued. "We don't want the manor to get wind of our suspicions. While they might be innocent, it's imperative we keep Roanna safe in case they are not."

"I understand." Merry paused. She bit her lip. "What do you need from me? It sounds as if your plan is a search and rescue." She didn't state what she was thinking, which was her strength was more along the lines of wining and dining people.

"I don't plan to return to Dawson's Edge, if this goes well, and besides that, I would very much like to have you with me."

Heat spread through her, and all she could manage was a nod.

"And as an aside, I believe your presence may rile Duchess Higgins."

"Rile her? I don't understand."

His pause was torturous. Finally, he went on. "Duchess Higgins will not be happy to see me with you. She was quite unhappy when I ended my relationship with her daughter."

"You believe getting her riled up will cause her to

what? Make foolish mistakes that will give away information?"

Gregory's eyes lit, and a small smile graced his lips. "That is exactly what I believe."

She frowned, not necessarily liking the sound of that—though she understood his thinking. "It is an easy enough role."

Wesley turned their way. "Not easy, my lady. You give yourself too little credit."

"How so?"

"It isn't easy to stand in the face of adversity. You do it over and over." He inclined his head toward her in a miniature bow. "I commend you."

Strange stinging burned her eyes. Why in all the kingdom should she be crying? She blinked away the moisture. "You're too kind, Wesley."

He did not argue with her, but his eyes told their own story. He believed her too modest.

"You know," she said. "It's too bad we hadn't brought Prince Stefan with us."

Now Gregory frowned. "Stefan? Why?"

She looked back to him, her mind working. "If Roanna can speak in her mind, it seems plausible that the prince can as well. They can likely speak to each other. He could help find her."

Gregory drew back, his eyes wide. "I should have thought of that." He looked to Wesley.

"I'll take care of it." Wesley turned back to the front.

Gregory met her gaze, and she wasn't prepared for what she saw there. Admiration, certainly. But something else. Something so opposite from the near hatred she had identified weeks ago.

"You're very good at these matters."

She knew she was skilled at what she did. It was why Papa had utilized her in his missions, and why Queen Charlotte had struck a deal with her in the first place.

He leaned toward her, the aisle still separating them. "When we finish here, Merry. When we find Roanna, we will speak in private." The soft words were for her ears alone.

She nodded, but her ever-practical mind kept her from answering. What would he say? That he regretted his earlier actions toward her? That he cared for her?

Then what? He could not marry her. And if he could not marry her, what did he want with her? She looked to her lap lest he see her thoughts written on her face.

Gregory shared a few more details of their plan, which included Gregory and Merry speaking with whomever they found at the manor while the regimen of guards who would be arriving searched the grounds.

Wesley spun back around and gave a sharp nod. "I've alerted Prince Stefan that we've gone to follow a lead, and we may require his immediate assistance if he finds he is interested. He has responded that he is, indeed, willing to help at a moment's notice."

A sudden burst of wind hit the airship. They swayed in the air, and Merry gasped. She clung to the arm rest.

"Are you all right?" Gregory asked.

She gulped and nodded. "Quite all right."

"Don't worry," he said. "We'll be there shortly." He looked to Wesley. "How far away are the guards?"

"They arrive within the half hour."

39

True to Gregory's prediction, they began their descent within fifteen minutes. The airship glided downward, touching grass shortly. Merry let out a relieved breath. She followed the men off the ship. Only Fraja remained, along with the captain.

They had landed in a green field. Rolling hills sloped in the distance, and in front of them stood a monstrous manor house. Duchess Higgins had not exaggerated when it came to the size of the Dewalt property.

"I did not know Chester's Wake had countryside like this." She had only seen cities and villages like the capital.

"We're very near the Loxian and Dawsonian borders. There is much countryside in the area." Gregory offered his arm.

Merry glanced at his arm, her stomach fluttering again. Drawn like a moth to flame, she relished taking it. For one brief moment, she imagined what it would be like if things hadn't gone so wrong—if she'd been properly courted by Gregory, and if Papa hadn't been a rebel. Would they be getting married soon?

"Do you believe this is the missing link?" She had

to think of something else, and she took a deep breath to calm herself. "What I mean to say is, do you believe we have finally found the missing link that will lead us to the princess?"

Gregory looked out at the distant hills. Then his gaze moved to the manor house. "I don't know. I don't feel any particular draw. I only know this is a solid move."

"Spoken like a military general." She appreciated his words.

Gregory used his opposite hand to cover her fingers that held his arm. The warmth of his skin seeped into her arm and straight to her soul. "Merry, I admire you deeply."

His words rumbled through her like distant thunder. A warning to her heart, yet a phenomenon so fascinating she could not abandon it.

They had almost reached the manor now. Two men stepped from the doorway onto the portico, awaiting their arrival. The men were servants, dressed in simple navy attire. Both men were well into their years, and where one was tall and thick like a tree, the other was small and lanky. They obviously recognized Gregory, as they bowed to him. "Your Highness," the tall one spoke. "How can we serve you?"

"I have come on important business from the capital. Who is the master of this house?" Gregory stood erect, his shoulders straight like pillars. His tone dripped authority.

"The Duke of Higgins. He is, unfortunately, not present currently."

"Who is here currently, outside of the house staff?" Gregory asked.

"The duchess is here presently, Your Highness."

"We will see her."

The man bowed again. "As you say. Please, follow me."

The men led them inside. The ceiling in the entryway rose three stories in the air. It was massive, as big as the palace entry at Chester's Wake. Doorways lined the space, leading to all areas of the manor.

The tall servant led them to a sitting room to their left. "I will alert the duchess." He bowed again before leaving them.

The shorter servant stepped forward. "Can I get you anything, Your Highness? Refreshments, perhaps?"

Gregory nodded once, and the servant was off. Gregory turned immediately to Wesley. "What's the status of the guards?"

Wesley looked again to his Messenger. "Minutes."

"Good."

Merry had a sudden thought. "Have you alerted Prince Benjamin?"

"No." A pained look crossed Gregory's face. "We will get in touch soon. He's dealing with enough today without worrying over us. We'll tell him as soon as we have something solid."

Long moments passed. The servant returned with tea and cakes. He assured them the duchess would be along soon.

Merry suspected the duchess was making them wait on purpose.

At last, she breezed into the room, followed by meek Lady Wendy. "Your Highness!" Pink colored the duchess's cheeks as she moved toward Gregory, but her gaze drifted to Merry. She stumbled slightly at the sight, recovering quickly.

"To what do we owe the pleasure?"

"Duchess," Gregory nodded toward them. "Lady Wendy."

Wendy curtsied slightly. Her gaze met Merry's before flittering to the hand holding Gregory's arm. She quickly looked away.

Merry's heart tightened. Poor Wendy. She had hoped. And now, here was Gregory dangling a false relationship before the girl in order to rile them.

Merry understood. All was fair in love and war, after all. Still, she felt sorry for the girl.

"I'm here on a rather unpleasant matter, I'm afraid." Gregory stepped forward, keeping Merry with him. "Our original mission in traveling to Dawson's Edge was not to attend the engagement ball as you were led to believe. It was our mission to seek out Dawsonian rebels."

He paused, letting the statement hang in the air.

The duchess's gaze moved between Gregory and Merry, as if she were putting together the pieces of what he was saying. Their mission—as in the mission of Gregory and Merry.

"Whatever does that have to do with Wendy and me, Your Highness?" The duchess held herself very well—royally, almost. If she were guilty, she hid it masterfully.

Gregory cleared his throat. "Our investigations have led us here, to this manor. Perhaps you have not heard that my sister, Princess Roanna, has been taken. You may have left Dawson's Edge before you could hear."

A small frown lined her lips. "We had heard. I am very sorry this has happened. Your poor family has been through quite enough."

Merry watched both women closely. While the duchess spoke, Wendy stood as still as stone. If she felt any sorrow for the royal family, she did not show it.

"As I said, our investigation led us here."

A low, steady rumbling sounded from outside. The airship of soldiers had arrived.

"I hope you'll forgive the intrusion, Duchess, but we need to search the premises." Gregory lifted his chin, authority oozing from him as if he commanded the world and no one could stop him.

The duchess paused just a moment too long. Her lack of surprise further implicated her guilt in Merry's mind.

"It is no intrusion, Your Highness. The princess's safety is of utmost importance to us."

Gregory gave a sharp nod. "Please stay in this room." He looked to Wesley, who departed quickly. Moments later, the pounding footsteps of soldiers sounded through the manor.

She and Gregory remained in the room with Duchess Higgins and Lady Wendy. No one spoke, and awkwardness filled the air.

After a few moments, warm fingers covered her hand. Merry looked to Gregory. He didn't meet her eye, but he did not remove his hand from hers. She wondered at his action, at the gentle move amidst the tension she felt standing at his side. Was Gregory worried?

He hoped to find his sister. He hoped he was making the right move. He hoped Roanna was safe. What would happen if Roanna wasn't here? Not only would they be out of leads. They would also have offended a noble family.

She could feel his emotional struggle as if it were

her own, yet on the outside he looked like nothing but the future king—composed and in control.

Merry swallowed the rush of emotions that flowed through her. A simple prayer filled her heart. *Please let it be so.*

~*~

Roanna...

Roanna reached out with her mind once again.

No one moved near her.

She had not received dinner, fresh water, or any visitors since the noon hour. It wasn't that she had need of these things, but it was odd. And disheartening. How was she to escape without the servant girl?

Roanna had determined that she must do whatever it took to escape. No good could come from her rotting in this room while no one knew her whereabouts. If that meant bending the servant girl's thoughts, so be it.

Only now the servant girl had vanished. She reached again and gasped. Someone came! Roanna waited, and a moment later the girl appeared at the door. She pushed her way inside, but she carried nothing. No water. No tray.

"Is something wrong?"

The girl had no reason to answer her, but she looked up at Roanna with wide eyes. Her hands trembled.

"I'm to move you, my lady."

"Move me?" This was exactly what she needed.

Getting out of this room would allow her to examine her surroundings and possibly escape.

The girl nodded once but did not speak.

"Where is the guard?"

The girl did not answer.

"Where are you taking me?"

"A secret place." She reached out her trembling hand.

Who would send such a child to care for the hostage? Roanna could overtake the poor thing without the use of her mind.

"Why?"

Again, the girl kept silent.

"Who told you to move me, then? I'm very confused, I admit." Perhaps if she pretended she understood the girl's plight, the child would open up.

But the girl shook her head and continued reaching for Roanna.

What on earth was she waiting for? This was her opportunity to escape and return to Ben.

She took the girl's hand, and they left the room. The girl led her to the right and down a long stone corridor. It was dim, lit only by the occasional small window at the top of the thick wall.

Wherever she was being kept, it was old. It didn't resemble the Loxian palace in any way.

Roanna's heart fluttered. How would she find her way home if she didn't even know her whereabouts?

At the end of the corridor, the girl turned left. A staircase lay ahead, heading downward, and a casing caught Roanna's attention. A window! It was low enough that she might be able to see out of it.

Roanna worked to keep herself from simply overpowering the servant girl, though she only did it out of the kindness of her heart. That and the fact that she did not know what was at the bottom of the stairwell, nor what was behind her.

They neared the window as a whirring reached her ears. The servant girl stopped at the window and her mouth fell open. Roanna swung her gaze to the outside world.

Hope bubbled inside her. An airship! Men unloaded, dressed in what looked to be Chester's Wake military uniforms.

The sight of the soldiers bolstered her confidence. She would not be led to the dungeon by this girl any longer. It was time to go into princess mode.

Roanna straightened her shoulders and gently spun the girl toward her. "What is going on?" she demanded.

The girl's wide eyes and pale face showed her fear. She only shook her head.

"Are you taking me to the dungeon?"

The girl nodded.

"Who told you to do this? Was it the queen?"

"No, my lady. I have never met your mother."

Roanna frowned, as did the girl.

"I will not go to the dungeon with you." Roanna changed her tactics. "Those men are soldiers of Chester's Wake, and they're here to rescue me. Unless you want them to put you into the dungeon, you need to help me. Do you understand?"

Tears pooled in the girl's eyes, quickly running down her cheeks. She nodded.

"How do I get out of here?"

The girl sniffed loudly and used her palms to wipe the moisture from her face. "This way, my lady."

40

Merry...

Long minutes passed. They spent the time pacing. Occasionally, Wesley returned to give an update to Gregory. The duchess and Lady Wendy sat silently, never speaking to one another or anyone else.

After more than an hour had passed, Wesley came in shaking his head. "We have found no hidden princesses," he said. He glanced at the duchess. "However, we did find a room where it appears someone was recently being kept. It is now empty."

"Show me." Gregory left the room.

Merry took a shuddering breath. She was now alone with the two women and Gideon, none of whom particularly cared for her. The men were only gone for a short while when a new rumble reached her ears. With interest, she moved to the window. A small airship landed nearby. A man and woman descended from the cabin.

Stefan and Bella.

Wesley had not said he'd confirmed their participation, at least not yet. Still, here they were.

Gideon had also noticed the newcomers, but he did not move from his post near the door. Another guard met them on the lawn, and after a few minutes, he entered the room. "We need to see the prince."

Gideon grunted. "Tell that Dawsonian he'll have to wait. The prince is busy."

The duchess glanced between Gideon and the soldier, obviously interested. She no longer held herself regally. Instead, her shoulders stooped, and her brows drew together.

Lady Wendy wiped a tear from her chin, and Merry's heart squeezed. She understood all too well how it felt to be caught up in a parent's ill plans.

A short time passed, and Gregory returned with Wesley in tow. The guard from before returned and alerted him to Prince Stefan's arrival.

"Bring him in at once."

Stefan and Bella stepped inside. The prince looked to Gregory, his eye blazing. "I know where Roanna is."

"You've heard from her?" Gregory looked as if he would pounce.

"She said a servant girl was taking her to the dungeon but agreed to help her escape instead. The girl led her to a different staircase, out a back door, and into a wooded area. Then, the girl ran. That was only moments ago."

Gregory nodded at Wesley, who sprung to action, barking orders at soldiers and guards.

Gregory turned to the duchess. "You will be taken to the capital where you'll be tried fairly." He glanced at Wendy. "Both of you."

Wendy's silent tears broke into a sob. She pressed a hand to her mouth. Guards moved forward and took both women.

"Can we gather our belongings?" The duchess's cheeks turned pink, her eyes wide and panicked.

Gregory opened his mouth, and Merry could see he would refuse. Yet, Merry's heart hurt for Wendy. She bolted forward and touched his arm. He looked to her; his brows lowered in—confusion? Irritation? She wasn't sure.

"The guards can accompany them, surely."

He watched her another moment then nodded. "Very well. You have ten minutes."

The guards led the women out of the room.

Gregory turned to Stefan. "How did you know to come?"

"We began preparing as soon as Wesley alerted us to the possibility a few hours ago. I knew that time would be of great importance if we were close to finding my sister."

Gregory held out his hand, and Stefan clasped it. "I'm glad you did." He looked to Bella. "I am surprised to see you here, princess. Thank you for aiding us."

Bella looked as beautiful as always, her dark hair flowing around her shoulders. She gave him a small, stately smile. "You're most welcome, Prince Gregory."

Stefan turned away, his eyes darting back and forth as if he were thinking.

Gregory frowned and stepped forward, but Bella stopped him. "He is speaking with the princess. I have learned the signs." She smiled again.

They all waited, watching Prince Stefan. At last, a grin broke across his face. "She is with Wesley."

Relief flooded Merry. They had found Roanna, and now they could return home.

Tendrils of fear and doubt worked through her at the thought. Return to what? Dawson's Edge? No, they had rooted out the rebels, and she had not found a way to save Papa. Rather, she had found proof of his condemnation.

Would she be taken back to Chester's Wake? They still had to deal with the Loxians as well as Ben and Roanna's engagement ball. And there was the matter of her sealed envelope she had yet to reveal to Gregory.

"I'll send for Ben." Gregory stepped away and began working on his Messenger. Only a few minutes passed before Roanna was brought into the room. She appeared dazed but unharmed. She ran for Gregory and wrapped her arms around him. A moment later, she and Stefan embraced as well. Even Bella hugged the princess.

Merry stayed back, feeling like an intruder.

Roanna's voice pulled her out of her thoughts. "Where is my maid?"

"Bette is in Dawson's Edge, unharmed." Stefan stepped forward, touching her arm. "She was not taken."

Tears pooled in Roanna's eyes, and she covered her mouth. "Thank the heavens. And where is Ben?"

Gregory paused. He looked to Stefan then back to Roanna. "There is much to explain. Let us do it on the way home."

"I suspect my father and mother will wish to see Roanna immediately." Stefan's clear voice held a warning, reminding everyone in the room that Roanna wasn't a princess of Chester's Wake any longer.

Merry watched Gregory, waiting for the telltale sign of his anger.

His face didn't turn angry red, however. His shoulders fell slightly, and he looked to Roanna. "Where would you like to go, Roanna?"

Her eyebrows drew together, and a small frown

pulled her lips down. She shook her head at Gregory. "I will return to Chester's Wake soon, I swear it. But I feel I should see my birth parents first."

Merry watched their interaction with tight shoulders. She wished to wipe away Gregory's disappointment. If only it were her place to do so.

"Let us speak now, then, privately." Gregory gestured to the sofa.

Stefan and Bella slipped from the room, but Wesley and Gideon remained. Merry kept her place on the far side of the room. No one bid her leave, and rather than draw more attention by striding past them, she attempted to remain out of sight and mind.

"Where is Ben?" Roanna repeated the question.

"He's in Lox. He had to return to speak with his parents."

Roanna gripped her hands together, twisting her thumbs. "Did they have something to do with this?"

"No." Gregory spoke firmly and with conviction. "This was the work of Lady Wendy and her mother."

Roanna's eyes widened. "Rebels within Chester's Wake?"

He nodded slowly, and Roanna looked away. She seemed to search out the window, thinking. "No one would have me. Not here, not in Dawson's Edge, and not even the Loxians. There is no place for me."

Merry raised her eyebrows in surprise. It was exactly how she felt.

"If Ben is speaking with his parents, what is the reason?"

Gregory hesitated and Merry held her breath, but he finally shook his head. "That isn't for me to say. Ben will explain all in due time. I suspect he will be back to Dawson's Edge by the morrow."

Roanna considered his words. "Very well. You will not return to Dawson's Edge with me?"

Emotions warred across Gregory's face. Merry did not wish to return to the safe house. She did not wish to return to Dawson's Edge. All the time she had been there, and she hadn't seen Papa once. Gregory had spoken to him, and he hadn't even asked to see her.

Perhaps she would never return.

"We should go to Chester's Wake to see Mother and Father in person. I need to give them a report and discuss what is to be done with the rebels here. There will also be details to work out as Dawson's Edge will be unhappy to learn this kidnapping came from within Chester's Wake."

Roanna smiled, but it didn't quite reach her eyes. "I will attempt to take care of that." She looked across the room and met Merry's gaze. Her brows raised. "Lady Merry."

Merry nodded a greeting. "Princess Roanna."

Roanna glanced between her and Gregory. "You've been helping my brother?"

"I have."

"Thank you." The simple words were short but heartfelt.

Merry's throat swelled with emotion. "You're most welcome, Princess Roanna."

Gregory had risen, and he joined Merry by the window. "We should go, then. Everyone is anxious for an update."

"Let's not keep them waiting." Roanna took Gregory's arm and they strode from the room. Merry trailed behind, followed by Wesley and Gideon.

Outside, Stefan and Gregory spoke briefly. They agreed to touch base the following day. Roanna hugged Gregory one last time. Then she left for the airship with Stefan and Bella.

Gregory turned to Wesley. "See that this manor is properly guarded by the men. We'll send instructions as soon as possible."

Wesley nodded and hurried to do Gregory's bidding, and Gregory held out his arm to Merry. "Will you sit with me?" He spoke softly, his eyes tired and his tone sad.

Merry's insides fluttered. "Of course, Your Highness."

"Merry, please stop calling me that."

Her flutters intensified, but she nodded. "Very well."

They boarded the airship. She expected to sit in the main hull the way they had on the way out of Dawson's Edge. Instead, Gregory led her inside the small room next to the cockpit. Inside she found four oversized seats.

Gregory spoke to Gideon, instructing that he wasn't to be disturbed. Then he closed the door. They took their seats, and he leaned back his head with a sigh and closed his eyes.

Merry waited for him to speak. To explain why he had wanted her here with him. To reveal whatever it was he'd said he needed to talk to her about.

He said nothing though, and a moment later, the airship rumbled to life.

Merry tensed. Gregory peeked at her with one eye. "Are you nervous?"

"Slightly." Was it ridiculous of her? She could speak with kings and dignitaries, dine with the rich, and pull information from a rock. Yet flying in an airship terrified her.

Gregory slipped his fingers into hers and squeezed. "All will be well."

Her pulse quickened, and she nodded.

He closed his eyes again but did not pull away his hand.

41

The air shifted as they descended for landing. Merry wiggled, eager to be on the ground.

Gregory straightened and pulled his hand from hers. He stretched. "That was entirely too quick."

So open. Vulnerable. Honest.

As it had been doing lately, Merry's heart quickened. Had he truly forgiven her?

She pushed down her hope and determined to be practical. "I'm happy to be getting back on the ground."

A moment later, they jolted slightly with the landing. They stood, and Gregory led her to the door. Now that their mission was over, there would be much to discuss. She and Fraja would need to speak of their future, and she would need to know what the Hamiltons intended to do with her.

Gregory stopped before opening the door. "Merry." He paused, his Adam's apple bobbing. "Do you forgive me for my beastly treatment of you?"

Looking into his eyes, how could she not? "Of course, I forgive you."

He smiled, but the sadness from before had not left his eyes. Gently, he cradled her face. He leaned toward her and kissed her.

Heat erupted inside her, and she returned the soft kiss. A moment later, it was over.

Confusion clouded her mind—confusion over the impossibility of their future and the uncertainty of her path.

She gulped as she pulled away from him, and a moment later, someone knocked on the door.

Gregory sighed. "I will have to report to my parents, and at some point, they will send for you. I do not plan to tell them what we found about Lox. Not yet, anyway."

She nodded, not trusting her voice to speak.

"But after that, we will talk. I have much to say."

She swallowed hard. "I will be ready." That would give her time to make a plan of escape.

He opened the door and Gideon stood on the other side. "Your father awaits you." His gaze flickered to Merry, but he quickly looked back to Gregory. It wasn't fast enough to hide his continuing distrust of her, but he did not speak it.

Gregory took her hand and led her from the airship. An auto awaited. Fraja was already seated inside along with Wesley. The city landscape sped past as they drove to the palace. Seeing the fountain in the square, the Rejected homes, and the palace in the distance brought to memory Merry's last arrival in Chester's Wake.

Her heart fluttered again. She needed to open the envelope Papa had entrusted to her. She needed to give it to Gregory and allow him to decide what to do with it.

Her eyes burned with tears at the thought of Papa, but she blinked away the moisture. Papa had chosen his path, and now she was choosing hers. She would be on the side of right.

They arrived at the palace and were greeted by Queen Charlotte. She hugged Gregory, and then Merry as if Merry were also royal and cherished. Again, tears clogged Merry's throat.

"Your father is in a council meeting." She held Gregory's hands as if she couldn't bear to let him go. "He will want to speak with you both as soon as he is finished."

Merry had intended to go to her room, to open the envelope to learn what leverage she held. That would have to wait.

"Are you hungry?"

"No, Mother. We're well. You've heard from Roanna?"

The queen gave them a shaky smile. "Yes, just. She arrived safely at the Dawsonian palace with Prince Stefan."

"I'm sorry I could not convince her to come home with us."

"Roanna is strong willed. She will do exactly as she wishes."

Gregory smiled at his mother. "I suppose you'll be going to Dawson's Edge soon?"

"Soon enough." She tugged Gregory's arm. "Come. Let us wait for the king."

Merry trailed behind them as they made their way toward the state offices in the center of the palace. Things had quieted substantially since she was last here. Had it only been two weeks? It felt much longer.

The queen deposited them in an office. "I'm going to have someone bring you something to eat."

"Mother, we're fine."

She *tsk'ed* at them and hurried out.

Gregory smiled at Merry and shrugged, but Merry's heart ached. She had not had a mother who fussed over her. Gregory was aware of this. They had discussed her mother when they had become acquainted months ago.

Now Gregory turned toward her. He placed his hands on her waist and pulled her close. "I will make up for my bad behavior, Merry."

Merry tried to push away her doubts. To simply enjoy the moment. The feel of his hands on her waist and the look of tenderness in his eyes. But her self-preservation instinct was too strong. She pulled away from him just as the door opened. A servant entered carrying a tray, and Queen Charlotte was close on his heels.

"The king is ready for you now." She smiled at both of them. "Bring the refreshments with us, please."

The servant nodded and followed behind them as they made their way to the king's office. Gregory met her gaze from the corner of his eye. His look would thaw even the iciest of hearts.

Merry quickly looked away before the queen caught her gawking at her son. How silly she felt entertaining the idea of a romance with the prince of Chester's Wake when she was little more than a commoner. Perhaps she had done enough to exonerate herself of her crimes, but she still held no title, and her family had an ill reputation.

The doors to the king's office opened, and they breezed through. The servant carried the tray and placed it on a low side table. Then, the servant exited, closing the massive doors behind him.

The king stood at his desk. He smiled when he

saw his son. "Roanna is safe?"

"She is well."

The king's expression did not change, but his relaxed shoulders bespoke his relief. "You have information for me."

Gregory stepped forward, and they began speaking immediately. Gregory used his Messenger to share notes with the king. They spoke of Dr. Presnell and the Van Hoosiers as well as Duchess Higgins. Gregory mentioned briefly their search of the Stern estate, but he glazed over it, saying only that they had found something that might be of interest in the future.

The king listened intently, not interrupting. When Gregory finished, he asked a few follow up questions, but he seemed to trust his son implicitly.

The tiniest sliver of hope erupted in her chest. Gregory was honorable. So honorable, in fact, that his own father the king had no doubt in his abilities to make wise decisions concerning his kingdom. Would such a man really toy with her heart? Would he pursue her without realizing the impossibility of success?

"Miss Stern, what can you add to this report?" The king's address took her breath away. Her heart thundered, and she wracked her brain for something suitable to say.

"I am of the mind we have rooted out the seat of the Dawsonian rebellion, Your Highness." She paused, taking a shaky breath. "When we left Chester's Wake, I was hopeful I would find information that would help free my papa. Instead, I found irrefutable evidence of his guilt. We found accomplices in high places, and I believe we can say we accomplished what we set out to do, though there are still unanswered questions regarding the involvement of Bella de St. Paul's country."

The king seemed pleased with her speech. "Thank you for your input, Miss Stern. You are dismissed."

Merry curtsied and moved toward the door.

"I will escort you, Miss Stern." Gregory moved toward her. He glanced between his parents. "Will you excuse me?"

Heat rose to Merry's cheeks. His behavior was all too telling. Surely, his parents would disapprove.

The king only nodded, though the queen stayed silent. She watched them closely.

Gregory opened the door and led her to the main lobby area. He offered his arm, and she took it as they made their way toward the grand staircase and the guest wing. A few guards nodded and smiled at the prince, welcoming him back to the palace.

Once they reached the stairs and had begun their climb, Gregory spoke. "You did well. I'm fairly certain my father has fallen under your spell."

A tingling spread through her stomach at his words. "What do you mean?"

He chuckled. "Everyone you meet falls under your spell. Haven't you noticed? My mother has long been in your favor. Now my father has joined her."

"I'm sure that's not true."

They had nearly reached her room. Gregory stopped her. "Merry, you could enrapture an entire kingdom if you put your mind to it."

She stared at him, breathless, her pulse quickening.

He squeezed her hand. "Supper will be served soon. I will see you then."

Merry nodded. That would give her plenty of time to retrieve the envelope from her bags and determine how to proceed. She could wait a few more hours.

42

Roanna...

Roanna settled into her seat in the airship. The seats were set in double rows, facing each other. She had always loved the airships. Loved the adventure of flying. But today, the adventure felt like too much.

Stefan sat at her side with Bella across.

"Will you tell me about Ben?" Gregory would not give her any information, but Stefan might. He had no loyalty toward Ben, and he had little reserve when it came to divulging information or following rules of etiquette.

I wasn't informed, but I have my suspicions. He spoke to her mind.

And?

Merry Stern has been in Dawson's Edge. Did you know this?

Roanna gulped. "I did not know, but I suspected." She spoke aloud. "She and Gregory are in love with each other, though I'm not sure they know it yet."

Stefan quirked an eyebrow but didn't comment on that. He continued in her mind. *I helped them gain permission to search the Stern estate. Prince Benjamin went along, and he left for Lox soon after. I suspect he did not like what they found.*

Shock slammed into Roanna. The Bellevues consorting with Dawsonian rebels?

Does our father know?

Stefan chuckled. *Are we yet at war? No, I have not told him. Though, after your kidnapping by rebels in Chester's Wake, I suspect things will not stay pleasant for long.*

Roanna clutched her hands, fear rippling through her. *We set out to make peace and instead have only stirred the pot.*

Stefan met her gaze, his look sad but in seeming agreeance.

"I will help however I can." He spoke aloud now, sparing a glance at Bella. "I want you to know your presence here has changed me."

How many surprises would this day bring? Her heart quickened, and she gave him a small smile. "Oh?"

"I have enjoyed my time getting to know Prince Benjamin as well as your brother Prince Gregory." He looked away a moment as if gathering his thoughts. "I see now how I've been isolated and have missed out. I am inspired to be better."

Roanna wanted to peek at Bella to see if this was a surprise to her as well, but she refrained.

"I am glad to hear this, Stefan. Thank you for telling me."

He nodded solemnly then began asking questions about her time away. Roanna explained how she knew nothing of her whereabouts and had been kept comfortably in a solitary room with no contact outside of the guard and the servant girl. She could offer no help on who had been involved, and she wouldn't tell him she'd feared she'd been in Lox. In light of this new information, it would only hinder their search for peace.

The airship landed in Dawson's Edge, and Roanna turned to Stefan. "You were able to pass easily into Chester's Wake?"

"I had clearance from Prince Gregory."

Roanna's heart warmed at the thought. If her families could learn to become friends surely anything was possible.

As they left the airship, her stomach rolled. She had been kidnapped and now rescued. Her hands shook. Bella gripped one of them and squeezed tightly. "All will be well, Roanna. You are home with us now."

Roanna smiled her thanks. Bella had spoken little to her these last few months. Her loyalties to the Dawson family were still in question as far as Roanna knew. Yet, she seemed in agreeance with her husband on being happy to find Roanna safe.

At the palace, Katherine met her with a tearful hug. King Dawson stood beside the queen, smiling. His nostrils flared, but he kept his emotions in check. Roanna's heart swelled with their care for her, but still, she longed to see her parents in Chester's Wake.

"My poor girl. What you have been through." Katherine stroked her face.

"I am thankful to be found safely. I wasn't harmed, but I cannot say what would have happened in the future."

"Someone will pay for this." The king's eyes flashed with anger. He looked to Stefan. "We will speak immediately in my office."

Roanna wanted to hear their briefing, but she knew how King Dawson ran his kingdom. He would not welcome her intrusion. He did not appreciate her input on matters of running the country.

Katherine led her away, chattering about baths and meals. Roanna wished Ben were here. When would he be back? Hopefully, soon.

"You weren't harmed, truly?"

Roanna shook her head. They ascended the mahogany staircase that led to the family wing. "Truly. I saw a guard three times a day, when he brought meals. And I saw the servant girl after each meal when she took away my tray and brought fresh water. My room was clean and comfortable."

Katherine's eyes filled with tears again. She gripped Roanna's hand. "It seems we cannot keep you safe here."

Roanna didn't like seeing her birth mother unhappy. "I fear I have brought about change that many do not like. We'll adapt, and precautions will be taken."

Katherine smiled. "So wise."

They neared the door to her room, and it burst open. Bette stood on the other side. She gasped and thrust herself toward Roanna. Tears poured from her eyes. "Oh! My lady!"

~*~

Three days passed. Roanna heard nothing from Ben, nothing from Gregory, and nothing from her Dawsonian family regarding plans to move on Chester's Wake. She sat at the breakfast table picking at her fruit but not eating it.

She could leave. Return to Chester's Wake amid her birth parents' stern disapproval. How could they stop her? She didn't think they would stop her, and she had promised to see her family there.

But what of Ben? What kept him?

"Excuse me, my lady."

Roanna dropped her fork and spun around. Ben stood behind her, smiling.

She gasped and jumped from her seat, throwing herself into his arms. He laughed and squeezed her, the air rushing from her lungs.

"I thought I'd never see you!" She laughed and pulled away. "You're like the beautiful sunshine after a dark night."

Ben shook his head. "No, it is I who thought I would never see you again. I shouldn't have doubted." He pulled her into another hug.

A moment passed and a small cough came from somewhere behind her. Roanna pulled away and glanced around the dining room. Every eye was on her and Ben.

She smiled sheepishly. "Please, sit."

Ben grinned, and the diners who had been beside Roanna shifted to make room. Roanna wanted to push him for answers, but now was not the time.

"I have heard your time away was not physically harmful."

"No, I was treated well."

"Good." He smiled again, and Roanna noticed for the first time his smile wasn't quite reaching his eyes. Something bothered Ben, deep down. It might be her kidnapping, but it was likely his family.

She would need to speak with him as soon as this meal ended.

Roanna's appetite returned, and she took advantage of the spread before them. Happiness and joy, yet fear, swirled through her.

She leaned close to Ben. "I feel we have proof now that most would be rid of me."

He lifted his eyebrows. "You shouldn't say that Roanna."

"But isn't it true?" The words were breathy. Whispered.

"Look around you. I am here. Your Dawsonian family is here. Back in Chester's Wake you have your parents and Gregory. You are surrounded by people who love you and are willing to fight for you. We're fighting for you every day."

Roanna stared at him, his words sinking into her heart. She hoped he was right.

A tinkling sound filled the air, and King Dawson stood. He held a butter knife and his crystal goblet, ringing them gently for everyone's attention. "Now that Prince Benjamin of Lox has returned to us, we are pleased to announce the engagement ball will move forward as planned. It is to be held tomorrow night."

Murmurs of excitement filled the room. "So soon?" She had thought it would be put off, for certain.

Ben offered another tight smile. "We should talk privately."

Her stomach clenched, but she forced her expression to remain joyful and glad. Congratulations were said all around as if it were the first announcement of their engagement. The meal came to an end at last. Roanna stood, and Ben took her arm. "Let's go to the garden."

They walked, and Roanna's three guards followed. Ben didn't comment on them. Of course not. He had likely suggested them himself.

Once outside, Ben stopped at the first bench they came to. It was situated at the base of a lemon tree, and the natural scent filled the air. Bees swarmed near one of the branches, but they didn't come near her or Ben.

"What has happened? Tell me what's the matter."

He watched her, his eyes drinking her in. He leaned forward and pressed his lips to hers.

Surprise washed over her but then happiness. She returned his kiss.

After a moment, he pulled his lips away, but he leaned his forehead against her. "I honestly feared I would never get to do that again. And I've only just recently become able to do it at all."

"I'm here, though. All is well."

Ben pulled away. He drew in a breath and blew it out slowly. "All is far from well."

"What do you mean?"

He searched her eyes again. "What did Gregory tell you?"

"Nothing. He said it was your story to tell."

Ben sighed. He took her hands in his. "My parents, after signing a marriage agreement at my birth, and while you were still unborn, learned of what would be your inherited abilities. They searched out rebels within Dawson's Edge and paid them to dispose of you however possible."

Roanna had considered this after Stefan's cryptic remarks on the airship. Hearing it confirmed, though, brought bile up her throat. Queen Frieda, her friend, had tried to have her murdered.

"They do not wish for us to marry." She knew this. Ben's long absences were not King Dawson's and Roland's doings. They were Queen Frieda's.

He shook his head. "It's so much worse than that, Roanna." He let go of her hand and leaned forward, propping his elbows on his knees. He covered his face with his hands. "They paid for your kidnapping and murder as a child. They are responsible for Dr. Presnell taking away the lost princess. They are wholly corrupt and unfit to rule."

He looked to her. Tears filled his eyes and his cheeks tinged pink. "If I do not reveal this corruption to the Dawsons, am I fit to rule? And if I do reveal it, what happens to my parents? To Lox?"

Dread filled her. She gripped his hands again and squeezed tightly. "Ben, Stefan suspects. He is waiting for you to come forward in your own time, but if you do not, he will speak up."

Ben's expression fell, and he shook his head. "I fear we're doomed already."

43

Merry...

Merry sat on the edge of her bed, the envelope from Papa in her hands. She would give it to Gregory this morning. It had been days since they had freed Roanna, and the princess would be arriving this afternoon to see her family. The prospect of freeing Papa had vanished, and there was no further reason to withhold whatever information the envelope contained.

She could always use it to bargain for something for herself—wealth, title, passage across the ocean—anything to get a fresh start. She had nothing, after all.

But she would not bargain with the envelope. It was time to wipe clean the dregs of the past. It was what Benjamin Bellevue of Lox was doing. She'd overheard Gregory discussing it with Wesley. The Queen and King of Lox would be retiring soon. Ben and Roanna would wed, and Ben would be coronated in short order.

Merry fingered the envelope, considering the situation. She suspected it was an agreement that had been reached to prevent all-out war between the kingdoms. Surely, King Dawson still knew nothing about it. Perhaps Prince Ben had spoken with Prince Stefan about the arrangement.

Taking a deep breath, she shoved the envelope into the folds of her skirt then left her room for the breakfast hall. Her soft footfalls barely made a pitter patter on the smooth, tiled, palace floors, and she quickly descended the stairs and turned left. It was good to be back in Chester's Wake and free of the confines of the safehouse.

The dining hall was abuzz with nobles, servants, and the royal family. They were excited to be welcoming Roanna this afternoon, no doubt, but what had the nobles in such a chipper mood? Perhaps it was because, with the kidnapping coming from local rebels, they'd had to choose which side they would root for— and those present had chosen Roanna's side.

Merry slipped into an empty chair unnoticed, but a moment later Gregory took the seat beside her. "Good morning, Merry."

She smiled a good morning greeting, her heart breaking into a flutter. She was growing used to the sensation.

"May we speak after breakfast?" He watched her face, his gaze intense. This was the talk he'd been hinting at for days. She could feel it. She would use it as her opportunity to give him the envelope.

Merry took a quick breath to calm herself and managed to keep her expression neutral. "Of course. I am at your service."

His hopeful look dimmed slightly at her cool and emotionless reply, but he didn't question her about it. They each fixed their breakfast plates and began their meal, making idle conversation as they ate.

The envelope in her skirt pocket filled her

thoughts. She would give it to him first before he had the chance to say whatever was on his heart. The contents of the envelope might change his feelings, after all. She wouldn't hold him to any promises made without full knowledge of the situation.

Gregory finished off his last piece of toast and glanced at her plate. She still had a heap of fruit and half a pastry.

He raised his eyebrows at her.

"I find I'm not very hungry this morning." She swallowed her nerves. "Shall we go?"

Again, he looked at her as if her behavior confused him, but rather than asking about it, he stood. He held out an elbow and she took it.

"The air is beginning to carry a chill. Fall is nearing." Gregory led her from the breakfast hall and toward the gardens. "We keep a full garden year-round, though, complete with winter foliage."

"Winter foliage?" She had never seen such a thing. It rarely grew very cold in Dawson's Edge.

He smiled. "You'll see. It isn't too cold yet. We can talk outside." They had reached the doors leading to the garden, and he held one to allow her to slip outside.

Merry looked at the large, colorful blossoms, sculpted bushes, and blooming trees. Her mind went back to months ago when she'd toured these gardens with Roanna when Prince Roland had visited as ambassador. Those were blissful, hopeful days.

She glanced at Gregory. He wore his usual dress attire, and his dark blond hair had been combed to perfection. He was the picture of a future king. Her heart squeezed, and she realized that in spite of the innocence from months ago, she preferred today's host.

He caught her looking and smiled at her. Heat crept up her neck. It was time to do what needed to be done.

Merry reached into her pocket and withdrew the envelope.

Gregory looked to her hands and frowned slightly. "What's this?"

"My papa gave it to me. I don't know what it says, but I have my suspicions. I believe it must belong to your family, and I'm sorry I withheld it for so long." She thrust it toward him.

Gregory pulled his brows low and took the envelope. In one swift motion, he tore one end and withdrew the paper. He unfolded the letter and scanned it.

His frown fell away, replaced with wide eyes and shock. He shook his head, looked to her, then back to the letter. "Merry, you'll excuse me." He bolted toward the door, barely getting it open a crack before he'd squeezed through and was gone.

Tears burned Merry's eyes. Did his reaction mean the letter contained what she'd suspected all along?

The tears spilled from her eyes, but she didn't bother wiping them away. Perhaps she should have let him declare some unfounded love for her first. She was unlikely to get the chance ever again. If she'd carried the knowledge of the whereabouts of the lost princess for all this time, how would they ever forgive her?

~*~

Gregory...

Gregory paced outside Father's office door. His parents had essentially kicked him out while they discussed details with their top aides. Rarely did Father do anything these days without consulting him, but he supposed this was more than a matter of national intelligence. This was a parental matter.

All these years, his birth sister had lived right in this city? In a Rejected Home, at that. And Baron Stern had held the information during all that time. He'd held the knowledge while visiting with Ambassador Dawson months ago, and when Gregory had visited him in the dungeon.

Gregory clenched his fists. If only he could be back in Dawson's Edge with the man. He would gladly relieve himself of this tension.

Wesley stood nearby, watching him pace. "You'll wear a path through the perfectly polished wood flooring if you don't stop soon. Why don't you sit?"

Gregory glanced at him, his look a warning.

Wesley nodded. "Right then." He grinned.

Gregory shook his head and went back to pacing. "You know the place?"

"It's the same one the princess frequented with her gifts." He frowned slightly. "I became acquainted with a few of the orphans there. I wonder who it is."

Merry's letter had only given details concerning an infant being taken to a Rejected Home near the Chester's Wake palace on the date of Roanna's presumed birth, along with notes of a stipend to be paid to the home. Nothing more, nothing less.

An odd record to keep locked away in an envelope all this time—odd, except it had to be the lost princess. At this moment, Father had his people looking into the named home, digging through their records to see which child had been deposited on that date.

Child.

He shook his head. It would not be a child now. She would be Roanna's age.

But why would Dr. Presnell take the true princess to a Rejected Home and leave the princess with an anomaly here in Chester's Wake? Why hadn't he taken Roanna to a Rejected Home in the first place? Or simply taken her to live with the village people they had met in the forest in Dawson's Edge?

It made no sense, yet it was what he'd done. Now Gregory would at last have the chance to meet his real sister, if she still lived.

He hoped that, for his parents' sake, she did.

The door to Father's office opened, and Father stepped out. His eyes were wide and his cheeks flushed, but he gripped Gregory's shoulders and smiled.

"We found her. You'll go retrieve her?"

Gregory froze. "You want me to go get her?"

For a moment, something like fear danced in Father's eyes, but he quickly hid it. "Bring her home, Gregory. Your mother and I will be preparing things here. Now go, quickly." He pressed a paper into Gregory's hand. "The home has already been notified."

Gregory nodded. He looked to Wesley, who already stood at attention. Together, they marched toward the doors.

In the palace garage, Wesley started an auto, and they climbed inside. He pulled from the garage and started away from the palace.

Gregory leaned forward in his seat. "You know where to go?"

"As I said, I've been there a few times."

Wesley maneuvered through the city streets as if he'd done it a thousand times. "What's the girl's name?"

Gregory hadn't thought to check. He still gripped the note Father had given, and now he unfolded it. His heart sped. "Gwendolyn."

Wesley didn't reply.

"Do you know her?"

"I do. We've spoken on occasion. She often helps Princess Roanna with the donations."

His nerves twisted at the thought. How many times had Roanna asked him to visit the Rejected with her, and he'd turned her down? Regret filled him.

They arrived a short time later, and they were greeted at the door of the home by an older woman named Hannah. She was the matron of the home, and she led them to a small, sparsely furnished office.

Hannah was short and round, but she had laugh lines around her mouth and eyes. She seemed kind, though she glanced at Gregory nervously.

"If you'll wait here, Your Highness. Gwen is at her treatment center, but she'll be back soon."

Gregory frowned. "Treatment center?" He looked to Wesley, who squirmed in his place by the door.

Hannah dipped in a slight curtsy. "That's right, Your Highness. She has a bone sickness. In fact, today is her last treatment. She was to leave the home by end of next month, as she's reached the age."

With that, Hannah slipped from the office.

Hot disgust settled in Gregory's stomach. His sister was sick, yet she had reached the age and would be kicked out of her home, no longer eligible to receive treatments.

Did Father know? He must, as his aides would have told him everything they knew.

Her situation here no longer mattered. He would bring her to the palace, and she would receive what she needed.

Loud laughing came from somewhere outside the confines of this office. Children's laughter. Rejected children.

These were someone's children, born with an anomaly then left here to be raised parentless. The reality of it hit him, turning his stomach. No wonder Roanna hated this system so fiercely. Why had he always turned away from forming an opinion on it?

He had just resolved to change that when the door opened, and Hannah returned. She brought with her the girl named Gwendolyn.

His sister had golden hair and green eyes with sharp cheekbones and a pretty face. She was of average height, but her frame was spindly. Sickly. He stared at her, speechless.

Wesley stepped forward. "Gwen, how do you fare?"

Gwen glanced from Gregory to Wesley. She smiled at him in recognition. "I'm well, thank you. And how are you, Wesley? I haven't seen you in quite some time."

"I'm quite well. We've come with important information for you. Rather, the prince has come. May I introduce Prince Gregory Hamilton?"

Gwen's eyes widened, and she gasped softly. She quickly bowed into a deep curtsey.

At last, Gregory spurred himself to action. He touched her shoulder. "Please don't bow to me."

She glanced at him, her gaze brimming with

confusion.

Gregory looked to Hannah. She must know what he'd come to say. "Will you gather Gwen's belongings, please?"

Hannah nodded and disappeared in seconds, seeming relieved to be out of the uncomfortable meeting.

"Gwen." Gregory paused, considering his sister's name. "May I call you that?" He hurried ahead without waiting for her reply. "You came here as a baby, yes?"

Gwen frowned but agreed.

"And you know of the situation that has arisen recently with Princess Roanna? That her true family is in Dawson's Edge?"

Again, Gwen nodded. How would she feel when she heard what he would say?

"My family has been searching desperately for our true princess." He gave her a moment to let his words sink in, but when she made no move of understanding, he went on. "Gwen, they believe you are the true princess."

Gwen continued to frown. "I'm sorry, I don't understand." She spoke quietly, glancing back to Wesley.

Now his guard and friend stepped forward. He touched Gwen's shoulder. "We've come to take you to the palace, Gwen. You'll take a genetic test to confirm your identity in the Hamilton family."

Gwen turned her green gaze back to Gregory. She stared a moment more. Then she collapsed.

~*~

Merry...

The next month passed in a blur for Merry. She remained in the palace, helping Queen Charlotte whenever she was called upon. Gwen's genetic testing revealed she was, indeed, the lost princess. Her medical condition needed immediate care, so healers, alchemists, and chemists were brought in from around the globe. They found sufficient treatments to help relieve her weakness and pain, though she would never be free of her ailment completely.

Merry often thought of the healer she had encountered in Dawson's Edge—Margie. Gregory had thought of the same thing, but when he broached the topic with his parents, they were not keen on the idea of enlisting one who used powers. Merry supposed some things would take more time to change.

Once Gwen's health was deemed stable, the palace jumped to action, arranging a party to celebrate. This, on top of the celebrations for Roanna's upcoming nuptials, kept them all busy.

Merry was currently being sent on errands around Chester's Wake. They were missions of good will, as Queen Charlotte called them. She was to sniff out those who seemed loyal to the crown despite the family's embracing of the Rejected, as well as those who seemed to resent the Hamilton's newfound acceptance.

She had used the time to adjust to her reality, including accepting that Papa wasn't who she'd always believed. She had burned his book of spells as she never wanted to set eyes on it again. She had also reached out to her sister via letter. Rachel had yet to write back.

Now it was the night before Princess Roanna's and

Prince Benjamin's wedding. In the morning, they would be travelling to the border of Chester's Wake and Dawson's Edge, along the Edge River, to take part in the royal wedding. The location was a compromise between Roanna's old family and her new.

Merry looked over her dress for the wedding one last time. It was a creamy silk dress that secured around her neck, leaving her shoulders bare. Jewels covered the skirt, along with a cream-colored lace. Her matching hat had been fitted with a silvery veil. It was stunning, and much too beautiful of a dress to befit her station here at the palace.

Merry had seen little of Gregory during the last month. He'd been busy on his own missions—interrogating Lady Wendy and her family, visiting Prince Ben in Lox, and getting acquainted with his new sister. Merry had spent minimal time with the family during this time, but she'd been around enough to notice the sweetest acts of kindness toward the new princess from Gregory's guard, Wesley.

Merry smiled slightly at the thought. She hoped Wesley would find his own love someday. He deserved it.

Regarding the matters taking place in Lox, to date, no one had revealed to the monarchs in Chester's Wake or Dawson's Edge exactly what had transpired with the King and Queen to their west. None of the princes were interested in going to war, and they kept the intelligence from their parents. The official story was that the queen had fallen into bad health, and she and the king would be retiring to the country so their son could take the throne.

A knock sounded at the door, pulling Merry from her thoughts. She strode to the door and opened it.

A guard stood on the other side. He held out an envelope, and a large rectangular package lay against his uniformed leg.

"I am to take a reply," he said.

Merry took the envelope and broke the seal. She pulled out a small card and read the neat script.

Dear Merry,

Please accept this gift as a thank you for your help these last few months. I hope it brings you a modicum of joy in the years to come. I also write to request permission to escort you to the royal wedding on the morrow. This would bring me great pleasure.

My deepest thanks,

Gregory

Merry glanced at the waiting guard. Her gown for the wedding was still there, across her bed, sparkling with jewels. What would Gregory think of the dress? The thought caused her heart to speed.

"Wait right here, please," she said. Then she stepped to the small desk in her room and penned her reply.

Dear Gregory,

I would be pleased to attend Princess Roanna's wedding as your guest.

Sincerely,

Merry

Her heart continued to flutter as she sealed the envelope and returned to the guard. He took the missive and reached for the package at his leg. Merry took it, and he retreated down the hallway.

Back inside her room, she hefted the large, flat

package onto her bed. She tore away the brown paper, and tears sprung to her eyes.

It was a painting of her home. The artist had rendered the estate at dusk, with soft light and the setting sun in the background. The colors blended beautifully — greens, blues, purples, and oranges.

It was breathtaking. Gregory had done this for her? Emotions swelled her throat. She touched the painting. His note had said he hoped it would bring joy in the years to come.

"I'm sure it will," she whispered to no one but herself.

44

Roanna's Wedding...

Bells tolled in the distance, ringing the happy news for miles on end. Roanna smoothed her fingers over the silky red dress she would wear in just a few hours. The material had been embroidered with tiny red roses, and it hugged her waist before falling in an A-line to the floor. Thin black lace lined the sleeves, and a black sash would be tied around her waist to finish off the look.

Excitement rushed through her at the thought of the wedding, of being married to Ben, her best friend.

Her heart sped, and she picked up the note that lay on her bed. She'd read it a hundred times since she'd received it a week ago.

At last, all my dreams come true.

Yours, Ben

She smiled, the excitement threatening to burst from her veins. She would be Ben's wife!

The day would be happier, certainly, if Ben's parents weren't on the side of wrong. She hadn't seen them, but Ben had told her pieces of conversations that had transpired. When they'd learned Roanna was, indeed, the princess they'd thought long dead, they had been filled with immeasurable guilt and shame. If King Dawson learned of their treachery, war would be inevitable, and they had known they must retire the throne rather than risk the lives of their people in that way.

Still, they had not reached out to her. Not apologized. They would not be present today.

The sting threatened to dampen her high spirits, but she straightened her shoulders and clutched the note tighter. They had made their choices, and she and Ben would make theirs.

Bette breezed into the room, her smile bright and cheerful. "Queen Katherine says we leave in half an hour. I should pack up your dress."

Roanna stepped out of her maid's way and instead, moved to the vanity mirror. They had already dressed her hair—long ringlets that surrounded her face and shoulders. She admired them as if she'd never seen curls before. She had seen curls, but never on herself. Her hair had never been so long.

Once the dress was packed, Bette led her through the palace to the auto that would take them to the airship. They would meet Ben at the Edge River.

Katherine waited in the auto, her smile wide but tears brimming in her eyes. "Are you nervous?"

"No." She shrugged, smiling slightly. Most girls were nervous on their wedding days, weren't they? But she knew without a doubt this was exactly what she was supposed to be doing.

King Dawson would not join them until they reached the airship, so once Bette had climbed in, they began their journey to the air station. Stefan and Bella would be joining them for the wedding, as well, while Roland would stay behind to keep the Dawsonian palace.

A tinge of sadness wormed through her that she wasn't sharing these moments with her mother, the queen of Chester's Wake. Mother would be at the river, certainly, but she would be with Gwen. The reality of their situation was almost too spectacular to believe, yet it was their truth.

Gwen was shy and uncomfortable in her new role, but the people of Chester's Wake were being gentle with her. Roanna had spoken with her on multiple occasions, and she had promised to be there for her in whatever way the girl needed.

Mother would no doubt make time for Roanna today. She would dote on her, smoothing her dress and patting her hair. But at the end of the day, she would go home with Gwen.

Roanna smiled slightly as they drove. Mother would not have to miss her too much. This was good. Gwen's presence was a blessing, then.

She understood that Chester's Wake had been thrown into even more of a whirlwind when they'd learned both princesses of Chester's Wake were Rejected. But the people were starting to see the virtues of those they'd once feared. Gregory had vowed to work on those relations.

The drive to the air station passed in a blur, and soon they were boarded onto the ship and flying toward the Edge River. Once they landed, Bette and Katherine whisked her to a makeshift tent that had been erected near the ceremony site. Inside, they began the tedious work of changing her into her silky wedding gown.

"May I come in?" Mother's voice filled the tent, and Roanna spun toward her.

She rushed to her and threw her arms around her.

Mother hugged her tightly. "You look stunning, my darling."

Roanna held her for long moments before relinquishing and returning to Bette and Katherine for more dressing. Katherine didn't meet her eyes, and Roanna's heart tightened. She hoped one day she would have a close relationship with both women.

Once they finished, Roanna took in her appearance in front of a full-length mirror. Her red, silky gown, curled hair, and sparkling tiara took her breath away.

Soft musical strains drifted on the air from outside the tent.

"The guests are arriving." Mother peeked out. "It's almost time."

Roanna took a deep breath to keep from barreling out of the tent. She knew how to keep her emotions close, but today she was finding it hard to practice. She gave the other three women a self-conscious smile.

Bette stepped forward. "You are beautiful, my lady."

The women took turns hugging her, and then, it was time to go. Katherine and Mother went first, so they could find their seats. Then, Bette helped Roanna leave the tent and make her way toward the ceremony.

Gregory sat beside Merry near the front of the crowd, and Stefan sat with Bella on the other side. They all smiled at her, and her excitement built.

Ben stood at the front of the crowd beside a priest. Their eyes met, and the others around them faded away. She reached him and took his hands, and together they recited their vows to always remain faithful—in both good times and bad, as life would surely give them both. The priest announced their marriage official and binding. Then Ben placed the sweetest of kisses on her lips.

The crowd cheered happily, and Roanna couldn't stop her smile. She did not know what the future held for their small kingdoms, but with Ben by her side she was willing to face whatever came their way. Life had not and would not be a fairy tale, but they could still make their very own happily ever after.

45

Merry…

A marriage festival had been set up along both sides of the river, a bridge erected to allow free range. Guests danced and ate merrily, the sweet strains of laughter filling the air.

Gregory and Merry danced twice before he bowed away to claim a dance from first his mother and then Roanna. Merry danced with Wesley once before seeking out solace at the edge of the crowd. The Dawsons had seemed wary of her throughout the day, though they had not been unkind. She understood the family's hesitancy, and she did not wish to cause hard feelings today.

As she sipped her drink, Gregory approached. He wore a pale gray waistcoat and pants with a gray top hat, and he looked as dashing as always. He smiled at her, though his eyes were guarded. "Would you care to walk with me?"

Merry looked to the open space behind them. Fewer guests mingled this far from the crowd. She nodded her consent and they started away.

"It has been quite the whirlwind this last half a year, hasn't it?" He said it as if it tired him out just thinking of it.

The truth of his words squeezed her heart in pain. Papa had betrayed her and everyone else. Now she lived in a new kingdom.

She steeled herself against the pain. "A whirlwind is an accurate portrayal." She glanced at him. "Thank you for the painting, by the way. It is beautiful, and it means so much."

"Did you like it? I was afraid it would bring you pain, but in the end, I hoped it would bring you joy."

"I love it." And she meant it, wholly.

They walked along the river, the rushing water giving them a sense of privacy. "I've never thanked you for what you gave us by handing over that envelope."

Merry stared straight ahead. She couldn't help but frown, her brows pulled low. "I thought you would be angry."

He stopped her and put his hands on her shoulders. "Angry?"

"I kept it from you for so long. Weeks and weeks." She shook her head.

He dropped his hands, but his gaze didn't leave hers. "I'm not angry about that. I understand now what I didn't then. You had to discover truth for yourself, and when you did you chose to side with right."

Merry hadn't thought of it that way, but she supposed it was true.

They had left behind the carefully decorated festival area, and now they found themselves surrounded by nature. They were completely alone, though Merry suspected guards must be somewhere nearby.

A slight breeze rustled the tall grasses around them, but it wasn't enough to cause her to shiver.

"Merry." Once again, Gregory stopped her. He took her hands in his. "I've apologized for my treatment of you when you first arrived."

Merry waited for him to go on. Her heart sped at the prospect. Would he still declare love for her after all? She hardly dared to hope.

"You've been a tremendous help to my family. Mother can't sing your praises enough."

Merry's stomach clenched. This sounded a bit like the opening lines of a farewell. She held her breath.

Gregory watched her closely. "Are you happy here?"

"Happy?" Surprise rippled through her. "I hardly know. I'm not unhappy."

"Would you like to return to Dawson's Edge? To the Stern estate? If that's what you long for, we can probably arrange it."

His words bespoke truth. Relations between the kingdoms were better than they'd ever been. As far as she knew, her family estate had not been given to a new family within the kingdom. It could be that the Dawsons would name her the heir and allow her to continue with the nobility in her father's place.

Merry looked away from his probing gaze. She watched the rushing river. It flowed over rocks both smooth and rough, molding to whichever shape was necessary to keep going. Much as she had tried to do.

She bit her lip, considering his words. "I have no desire to return to Dawson's Edge."

Gregory squeezed her hands. "What do you desire, Merry?"

Her gaze found his once again, but the words

stuck in her throat. She would not speak what was in her heart, not unless she was sure he wouldn't scoff at her or reveal he'd chosen a queen from some noble family. She hadn't heard rumors of his courting anyone as she traveled the kingdom, but that didn't mean negotiations hadn't been underway.

Instead, she only stared.

Gregory's gaze saddened, but he didn't drop her hands. "I badly damaged things, didn't I?"

"No worse than I did." The words came out as barely a whisper.

He drew her closer. "Can we start again, then? Put all that behind us? Merry, would you allow me to court you?"

Her chest tightened at his words, yet she didn't want to hope. "How would the people ever accept it?" The truth still stood between them.

At last, a grin broke across his face. "You have spent the last four weeks traversing the kingdom, causing everyone to fall in love with you. I have no worries on that front."

Merry searched his eyes. Did he jest? But she knew it was truth. She was good at making friends, and she had done just that as she travelled all over Chester's Wake endearing herself to lords and ladies.

Was it possible, then? Taking a slow, steadying breath, she nodded. "I would like to start again, Gregory."

Deep satisfaction shone on his face. "Very well. Would you allow me to escort you to Gwen's homecoming celebration?"

She hoped she would see him before then, but she suspected this was only a formality. She squeezed his hands. "Yes, I would like nothing more."

Gregory's eyes practically twinkled. He bent toward her and placed a gentle kiss on her lips. After a moment, he pulled away and rested his forehead against hers. "Nor would I," he whispered. "Nor would I."

Thank you…

for purchasing this Watershed Books title. For other inspirational stories, please visit our on-line bookstore at www.pelicanbookgroup.com.

For questions or more information, contact us at customer@pelicanbookgroup.com.

Watershed Books
Make a Splash!™
an imprint of Pelican Book Group
www.PelicanBookGroup.com

Connect with Us
www.facebook.com/Pelicanbookgroup
www.twitter.com/pelicanbookgrp

To receive news and specials, subscribe to our bulletin
http://pelink.us/bulletin

May God's glory shine through
this inspirational work of fiction.

AMDG

You Can Help!

At Pelican Book Group it is our mission to entertain readers with fiction that uplifts the Gospel. It is our privilege to spend time with you awhile as you read our stories.

We believe you can help us to bring Christ into the lives of people across the globe. And you don't have to open your wallet or even leave your house!

Here are 3 simple things you can do to help us bring illuminating fiction™ to people everywhere.

1) If you enjoyed this book, write a positive review. Post it at online retailers and websites where readers gather. And share your review with us at reviews@pelicanbookgroup.com (this does give us permission to reprint your review in whole or in part.)

2) If you enjoyed this book, recommend it to a friend in person, at a book club or on social media.

3) If you have suggestions on how we can improve or expand our selection, let us know. We value your opinion. Use the contact form on our web site or e-mail us at customer@pelicanbookgroup.com

God Can Help!

Are you in need? The Almighty can do great things for you. Holy is His Name! He has mercy in every generation. He can lift up the lowly and accomplish all things. Reach out today.

Do not fear: I am with you; do not be anxious: I am your God. I will strengthen you, I will help you, I will uphold you with my victorious right hand.

~Isaiah 41:10 (NAB)

We pray daily, and we especially pray for everyone connected to Pelican Book Group—that includes you! If you have a specific need, we welcome the opportunity to pray for you. Share your needs or praise reports at http://pelink.us/pray4us

Free eBook Offer

We're looking for booklovers like you to partner with us! Join our team of influencers today and periodically receive free eBooks!

For more information
Visit http://pelicanbookgroup.com/booklovers

How About Free Audiobooks?

We're looking for audiobook lovers, too! Partner with us as an audiobook lover and periodically receive free audiobooks!

For more information
Visit
http://pelicanbookgroup.com/booklovers/freeaudio.html

or e-mail
booklovers@pelicanbookgroup.com